DON CAMILLO'S DILEMMA

Giovanni Guareschi
has also written
THE LITTLE WORLD OF DON CAMILLO
DON CAMILLO AND HIS FLOCK

DON CAMILLO'S DILEMMA

By GIOVANNI GUARESCHI · Translated
from the Italian by FRANCES FRENAYE

GROSSET & DUNLAP · PUBLISHERS · NEW YORK

CONTENTS

CONTENTS

INTRODUCTION

*How Don Camillo and Peppone were born and how
they go on living*

I am perpetually irritated by the virtue of the punctilious pen-pushers who have penetrated the most unsuspected places and lie in ambush wherever I go. They favor me with a bored and pitying glance when I rush in at the last minute before the dead-line with my typewritten pages and India-ink drawings.

"Poor Guareschi! Just under the rope, as usual!" they are obviously thinking.

At such times I am full of coffee, nicotine, bicarbonate of soda and fatigue. My clothes are sticking to me because I haven't taken them off for three days; I have dirty hands and stubble on my chin. My mouth is furry and my head, stomach, heart and liver are all aching. A lock of unkempt hair is hanging down over my nose and black dots dance before my eyes.

"Why do you always wait until the very last minute?" they ask me. "Why don't you do your work little by little, while there is still plenty of time?"

But if I had paid attention to the punctilious penpushers, I wouldn't have got even as far as I am today.

I remember distinctly the day of December 23, 1946. Because of Christmas, the work had to be in "ahead of time," as the penpushers put it. At that time, beside editing the magazine *Candido,* I wrote stories for *Oggi,* another weekly put out by the same publisher. On December 23, then, I was up to my ears in trouble. When evening came I had done my piece for *Oggi* and it had been set up by the printer, but the last page of *Candido* was still unfinished.

"Closing up *Candido!*" shouted the copy boy.

What was I to do? I lifted the piece out of *Oggi,* had it reset in larger type and put it into my own paper.

"God's will be done!" I exclaimed.

And then, since there was another half hour before the deadline of *Oggi,* I wrote a hasty story to fill the gap.

"God's will be done!" I said again.

And God must have willed exactly what proceeded to happen. For God is no punctilious penpusher. Because, if I had heeded all the good advice poured into my ear, Don Camillo, Peppone and all the other characters in this book would have perished on the day they were born, that December 23, 1946. For the very first story of the series was written for *Oggi,* and if it had appeared there, it would have gone the way of its predecessors, and no one would have heard of it again.

But after it came out in *Candido,* I received so many letters from my two dozen subscribers that I wrote a second story about the big priest and the big Red mayor of a village in the Po River valley. Now, what with one joke following after another, I turned in three hours ago—late, as usual, to the disgust of the punctilious penpushers—the two hundredth installment of the adventures of Don Camillo. And an hour later a letter arrived from France to announce the sale of eight hundred thousand copies of my first published volume, *The Little World of Don Camillo*.

And so I am not in the least bit sorry to have put off until the morrow that which I could perfectly well have done the day or the month before. At times it saddens me to look over the things I have written, but I don't suffer too awfully much because I can honestly say that I did my best not to write them. And I outdid myself in putting them off from day to day.

There, my friends, is the story of how the priest and the mayor of a village in the Po River valley were born. Two hundred times I have pulled the strings and made them do the most extravagant things that anyone can imagine. So extravagant that often they are literally true. Over and over I complain: "Now that I've brought them into the world, what shall I do about them? Kill them off and call it a day?"

It is not that I claim to be their "creator"; all I did was put words into their mouths. The river country of *The Little World* created them; I crossed their path, linked their arms with mine and made them run through the alphabet, from one end to another. In the last weeks of 1951, when the mighty river overran its banks and flooded the fields of the happy valley, readers from other countries sent me blankets and parcels of clothing marked "For the people of Don Camillo and Peppone." Then, briefly, I imagined that instead of being an unimportant fool I was an important one.

I gave all due explanation of the river valley and its little world in the preface to the first volume, and today I can subscribe to every word I said there. I don't know what will be the fate of this third book of stories and I refuse to worry about it. I know that when I was a little boy I used to sit on the bank of the mighty river and say to myself: "Who knows? Perhaps when I'm grown up I'll manage to get to the other side." My greatest dream was to own a bicycle. Now I am forty-six years old and the bicycle is mine. Often I go to sit on the river bank where I sat as a boy. And as I chew a blade of grass I can't help thinking: "After all, this side is the better." I listen to the stories borne down the mighty river, and people say:

"He grows more absurd every year!"

Which isn't true, because I was absurd from the very beginning. Thanks be to God.

G. G.

DON CAMILLO'S DILEMMA

ELECTIONEERING IN THE HOME

PEPPONE HAD HARDLY GOB-
bled down the last mouthful of his supper when, as usual, he
started to jump up from the table and go out for the rest of the
evening. But this time his wife didn't let him get away.

"I want to have a talk with you."

"I haven't time," said Peppone. "They're waiting for me at
headquarters."

"Let them wait! After all, you're not married to them. For months we haven't been able to exchange a word."

"Don't harass me," said Peppone, breathing hard. "You know I'm not going out for fun. Elections are coming. Just a few days more, and then here's hoping we've seen the last of them for another five years."

"Good. But if we don't discuss it now, when election day does come around, I'll find myself with a ballot in my hand and not a thought in my head. What am I supposed to do? For whom should I vote?"

"That's the limit!" exclaimed Peppone. "You want me to tell you how to vote!"

"Where should I go to ask? To the priest? You're supposed to tell me what's what."

"But things are exactly the way they were before."

"Then I vote again for you?"

"No, when you voted for me, it was a local election. This is a nation-wide affair, the way it was in 1948."

"I see. Then I should vote for the Garibaldi ticket."

"No, silly! The Garibaldi ticket's a thing of the past. Every party has a symbol of its own. Do you at least know the symbols?"

"Yes, I do."

"Then all you have to do is make an X over the symbol of the party you have chosen. I don't see what else there is to explain. Nothing has changed."

She shook her head in perplexity.

"Even now that he's dead, is the Party just the same?"

"Just the same, only more so!" shouted Peppone, bringing a fist down on the table. "Men may pass, but ideas are eternal!"

"But this Malenkov doesn't seem to me powerful as Stalin. He looks more like a compromiser."

"Don't listen to foolish gossip! Just give Malenkov a chance and you'll see! He employs different tactics, but the goal is still the same."

"Then you think we're still moving toward the proletarian revolution?"

"It's closer than ever!" Peppone declared. "Present tactics are designed to allay the enemy's suspicions. Then, when the time comes, we'll put one over."

She did not appear to be altogether convinced.

"You say the situation's the same as it was in 1948 . . ."

"Where Communism's concerned, it's a hundred percent better. In 1948 Communism was terrific, and now it's tremendous. Stalin may be dead, but his spirit marches on, at the head of the victorious armies of liberation."

"So it isn't true that the Russians want peace, the way they say they do, is that it?"

"Of course it's true! They want peace, but as long as there are warmongers, peace is impossible. In order to obtain peace, the western warmongers must be eliminated. And that means America, the Vatican, big businessmen, priests, landowners, reactionaries, fascists, royalists, liberals, social-democrats, imperialists, nationalists, militarists and intellectuals. It will take an enormous blood-bath to cleanse the world of this medieval residue. We must destroy a rotten old world in order to build up one that's healthy and new. Don't listen to gossip, I tell you. The Garibaldi ticket has been replaced by one that bears our own symbol, but the situation is just what it was before. You can go right ahead, without any misgivings, and vote as you did in 1948."

"All right, Chief," she said, not mentioning the fact that in 1948 she voted for the Christian Democrats.

"Anyhow," Peppone said as he got up, "I'm not imposing my choice upon you. You're free to do as you please, and I shan't even ask what is your decision. Even as a husband, I'm genuinely democratic."

"Oh, I'm not changing my mind," she protested. "I chose, once and for all, last time."

"Good," said Peppone, starting toward the door. "And would you get my gun out of the drawer this evening so I can clean it when I come home? If we win, then we're to start shooting. That's orders."

After Peppone had gone, his wife stared for a long time at the door. Then she raised her eyes to heaven and prayed:

"Lord, make them lose!"

Meanwhile, as Peppone passed by the church on his way to the People's Palace, he mumbled to himself:

"Lord, please let us win. But without my wife's vote, if you don't mind!"

BACK TO 1922

IN THE VILLAGE AND ITS
surrounding there were quite a lot of people who started as
early as February to lay aside money for the pre-Lenten Carnival. There were twelve rival clubs, five in the village and seven
in the countryside, and every Saturday the members contributed
part of their pay to the decoration of the floats which each one

: [17] :

entered in the parade. In short, the brief Carnival season was a very important affair.

The floats came into being bit by bit in farmyards scattered over the plain. Each club chose the farmyard most suitable for the purpose and with poles, sticks, reed mats and blinds, strips of canvas and tarred paper built a shed which housed the construction. Only members of the club were allowed to look in until the great day came. Then the shed was joyfully torn down and the float emerged, for all the world like a chick newly hatched from the shell. There were sizable prizes to be won, and individual floats and costumed figures came from nearby townships and even from the city. For three whole days the village was crowded.

The Carnival was a serious affair, not only because it drew so many people in a spending mood to the village, but also because it brought with it a complete truce to all political activity. For this reason Don Camillo never made it the butt of any of his sermons.

"Lord," he explained to Christ over the main altar, "we've come to a point where men behave themselves only when they're silly. Let's allow them their fun: *Semel in anno licet insanire.*"

As for Mayor Peppone, he frowned upon the Carnival because it irritated him to see that men couldn't pull together for any cause other than a frivolous one.

"They'll all come across with the money to decorate one of those stupid floats," he protested. "But just try to put over something worthwhile, such as the People's Revolution, and every last one of them is a pinchpenny."

Peppone spoke against the Carnival for six months of the year. For the other six months he worked overtime organizing the parade and helping to build his own club's float. Incidentally, he put up considerable money. And if a local float failed to win the first prize, he took it as a personal insult.

That year everything smiled upon the Carnival, because it came in a period of exceptionally fine weather and people came from far and wide to see it. Competing floats and wearers of fancy dress arrived from a widespread area, and no one had ever witnessed so long a parade, which as usual wound its way around the village three times. From his post in the grandstand Peppone looked down at the first round with general satisfaction, finding it worthy of the population gathered in such large numbers to acclaim it. As a result his deportment seemed to be modeled upon that of the Lord Mayor of London.

When the parade came around for the second time, he began to look more closely at the various entries in order to determine whether those of the village were likely to carry away the first prize, or at least the second, third, fourth and fifth prizes. In other words, he was transformed from Lord Mayor of London into mayor of his own town. And among the single competitors for a fancy-dress prize his eyes fell upon a Red Indian riding a motorcycle. After the fellow had gone by, he wondered exactly what had drawn his attention, for the costume had nothing extraordinary about it, being composed chiefly of a big cardboard nose and a band of chicken feathers around the head. He concluded that it must have reminded him of something from times gone by, and sure enough, it came to him in a flash that it was the billboard figure that used to advertise "Indian Motorcycles."

During the third round Peppone ascertained that there was indeed a basis for his conclusion. This was the "Indian Motorcycle" figure, and no mistake about it. Only the figure wasn't riding an "Indian" at all; he was astride an old BSA model. Where motorcycles and their motors were concerned, Peppone was like one of those musical quiz experts, who no sooner hear a few notes from a piece than they can tell you its title and composer. And there was a further reason why he could make no mistake: this particular motorcycle had been in his hands for repairs at least a hundred times. Only one question remained in Peppone's mind: Who was riding in Indian costume on Dario Camoni's old BSA?

He left the grandstand, having momentarily lost all interest in the parade. This was a matter that had nothing to do with the mayoralty; it was of a strictly private character. He made his way with difficulty through the crowd, trying to keep up with the Indian, and during a brief pause, the latter turned his head and looked at him. Peppone's doubts vanished. The rider of Dario Camoni's old BSA was Dario Camoni. Even behind a cardboard mask, those were unmistakably his eyes.

Peppone continued to follow the parade, step by step, and nothing in the world could have stopped his implacable *Panzer* pursuit. When the parade had gone around for the third time it drew up in the open space between the village and the river and disbanded. There was such an array of floats, trucks and farm wagons that the Indian could not possibly escape. The only opening in the crowd was onto the street that had led them away from the central square. He was aware that Peppone had been following him and did not hesitate to turn around in this direction, even at the risk of running down a pedestrian. But after he had gone a few yards an enormous float blocked the street and he had to dart into an alley on the right, with Peppone practically panting down his neck from behind.

The smaller square in front of the church was deserted, and the redskin sped up the alley with this destination in view. A few seconds later, he braked his machine abruptly in order not to run down Don Camillo, who was smoking a cigar butt in front of the rectory. Once upon a time this alley had made a right-angle turn just in front of the rectory and gone into the road leading to the river, but for the last ten years it had been blocked off.

Don Camillo was stunned by the abruptness of the motorcycle's arrival. His impulse was to grab the fellow by the chest and knock his head against the wall for his reckless folly. But he was too late. The motorcyclist had dropped his machine on the street and dashed through the rectory's open door. A second later Peppone rushed upon the scene, and without so much as a glance at the priest, followed the fugitive's example. But Don Camillo's powerful body stood in the way.

"What the devil?" Don Camillo shouted. "What in the world are you doing? First an Indian nearly runs me down with a motorcycle and then a mayor bumps into me on foot. Is it all part of some symbolical charade?"

"Look, you've got to let me in," panted Peppone, reluctantly drawing back. "I have a score to settle with Dario Camoni."

"Camoni? How does he come into the picture?"

"That Indian is Camoni!" said Peppone between clenched teeth.

Don Camillo pushed Peppone back, went into the rectory and fastened the door behind him with a chain. The Indian was sitting in the study, and the first thing Don Camillo did was to pull off his cardboard nose.

"Well, it's me, all right," said the Indian, rising from his chair. "What are you going to do about it?"

Don Camillo sat down at his desk and relighted his cigar.

"Nothing at all," he answered, after he had blown several puffs of smoke into the air. "But you'd be better off if you really were an Indian."

Back in 1922 the river country of the little world was still in a state of political ferment, even although elsewhere the Fascists had consolidated their governmental position. The land had something to do with it, and so did the boiling-point of its people. Dario Camoni was seventeen years old, and he wanted to make up for the time when he was too young to take part in the Black-versus-Red battle. In 1919, when he was a mere fourteen years old, some Reds had beaten up his father for refusing to take part in a farm labor strike, right in front of his eyes. This explains, among other things, why three years later Dario was still in a combative mood, and ready to beat up any stray Red he could find for revenge.

Dario Camoni was a husky boy, and above all a hotheaded one. When he went into action his eyes blazed in a way that was more convincing than any amount of words. Peppone was several years older and stood head and shoulders above him, but those cursed eyes caused him to steer clear. One evening when Peppone was talking to his girl on the bridge in front of her house, Dario Camoni rode up on a motorcycle.

"Sorry to intrude," he said, "but I've been given a job to do."

He took a glass and a bottle out of his pocket and proceeded to empty the contents of the bottle into the glass.

"The doctor says you have indigestion and a little laxative will do you good," he continued, advancing with the full glass in one hand and his other hand grasping a hard object in his pocket. "My advice to you is to take your medicine, because some of this castor oil dripped onto my revolver and I don't want the trigger to slip in my fingers. If the dose is too strong for you, you can share it with your girl. I'm going to count to three. One two . . ."

Peppone took the glass and drained it to the last drop.

"Good for you!" said Dario Camoni, mounting his motorcycle. "Be careful not to step on certain people's toes, or you may get something worse next time."

Although Peppone had managed to drink the castor oil, a form of punishment which the Fascists had brought into style, he could not swallow the insult, which was all the more grave because Dario had humiliated him in front of his girl. As it happened, he married the girl later on, but that made it worse rather than better. Every time that he raised his voice at home his wife taunted him:

"If the fellow who gave you the dose of castor oil that night were here, you wouldn't be up on such a high horse, would you?"

No, Peppone had never forgotten this dirty trick, and neither, for that matter, had Don Camillo. In that far-away 1922, Don Camillo was a greenhorn priest, just out of the seminary, but he was nobody's fool and preached a sermon against violence in general, and in particular against the bullies who were going around forcing unsavory drinks upon other people. For this reason, one night he was called downstairs because someone was fatally ill and needed Extreme Unction. When he came down, there was Dario Camoni, with a Mauser in one hand and a glass of castor oil in the other.

"You're the one that needs the oil, Father, even if it's unholy. This will make your motor hum. And because I owe you particular respect as a member of the clergy, I'll count to four instead of to three."

And Don Camillo drank his ration down.

"There, Father," said Dario Camoni, "you'll see how much more clearly your brain will function tomorrow. And if you really want to be reduced to a condition where you'll need holy oil rather than unholy, just go on sticking your nose into our business."

"The Church's business extends to everything that concerns good Christian people," objected Don Camillo.

"If we'd used Christian behavior toward the Reds, your church would be a Red headquarters and seat of the Consumers' Co-operative today! Anyhow, whenever you need to change the oil in your motor, just whistle!"

Like Peppone, Don Camillo had found it easier to swallow the oil than the insult.

"Lord," he said several times to Christ over the altar. "If he'd beaten me up, it would be different. But castor oil is too much. You can kill a priest, but you have no right to make him ridiculous with a dose of castor oil!"

Years went by, and Dario Camoni remained an active Fascist as long as there was strong-arm work to be done. Then he retired from politics altogether. But he had oiled and beaten up too many people in his time to be forgotten. When the regime was overturned, in 1945, he found things too hot for him and went away. And Peppone sent word after him to say that if he showed his face in the village it would be at the risk of his skin. More years passed, without news of Dario Camoni. And now he had returned, in the disguise of a Red Indian.

"I'd like to know what got into your head to think up something like this," Don Camillo said to Dario Camoni.

"I've been away from home for six years," murmured the Indian, "and I wanted like anything to come back. The only way I could do it was in disguise. Seems to me it wasn't such a bad idea."

"Poor Camoni!" Don Camillo said with a sigh. "You're so comical in your Indian dress that I'm inclined to be sorry for you. An Indian on a motorcycle, who takes refuge in the priest's house from a mayor who is chasing him on foot. It's almost as melo-dramatic as the comics. Well, you may as well take it easy. You're almost a hundred percent safe. If there weren't that glass of

castor oil between us, I'd say a hundred percent with no reserva-
tions."

"Is that silly business still on your mind?" asked the Indian,
who was still panting from the chase. "That was thirty years ago
and childish."

Don Camillo was about to embark upon a long harangue when
the study door swung open and Peppone appeared on the scene.

"Excuse me, Father, for coming through the window," he said,
"but I had no other choice, since I couldn't come through the
door."

The Indian had leaped to his feet, for the expression on Peppone's face wasn't exactly pretty. Moreover, Peppone had an iron
bar in his hand and looked as if he intended to put it to use. Don
Camillo stepped between them.

"Don't let's have a tragedy in the middle of the Carnival," he
interposed. "We must all be calm."

"I'm perfectly calm," said Peppone, "and I have no intention
of causing a tragedy. I have a job to do, that's all."

He took two glasses out of one pocket, then without taking his
eyes off the Indian, a bottle out of the other and divided its
contents between them.

"There," he said, standing back against the door. "The doctor
says you have indigestion and a little laxative will do you good.
Hurry up, because the oil has greased my iron bar and I'm afraid
it may slip and fall onto your head. Drink down both glassfuls,
one to my health and the other to the health of Don Camillo.
I'm happy to pay my respects to him in this way."

The Indian turned paleface as he backed up against the wall,
and Peppone was truly fear-inspiring.

"Drink them down, I tell you!" he shouted, raising the iron bar.

"No, I won't," answered the Indian.

Peppone rushed forward and grabbed him by the neck.

"I'll make you drink!" he shouted.

But the Indian's neck and face were covered with greasepaint
and he managed to free himself. He leaped behind the table, and
as Peppone and Don Camillo noticed too late for their own good

he took down the shotgun hanging on the wall and pointed it straight at Peppone.

"Don't do anything crazy," shouted Don Camillo, drawing over to one side, "that thing is loaded."

The Indian advanced on his enemy.

"Throw down that bar," he said sternly, and his eyes were as blazing as they had been thirty years before. Peppone and Don Camillo both remembered them distinctly, and knew that Dario Camoni was quite capable of shooting. Peppone let the bar fall to the floor.

"Now *you* drink," the Indian said between clenched teeth to Peppone. "I'll count to three. One ... two ..."

Yes, he had the same wild eyes and the same voice as long ago. Peppone gulped down the contents of one of the glasses.

"And now go back where you came from," the Indian commanded.

Peppone went away, and the Indian barred the study door.

"He can send his police if he wants to," he said, "but if I'm killed, I won't go to Hell alone."

Don Camillo relit his cigar.

"That's enough of your horseplay," he said quietly. "Put down that gun and go away."

"Go away yourself," said the Indian coldly. "I'm waiting for them here."

"Very unwise, Redskin," said the priest. "I don't believe the palefaces will come, but if they do, how can you defend yourself with an empty gun?"

"That's an old joke and poor one," laughed the Indian. "I wasn't born yesterday, for your information!"

Don Camillo went to sit down on the other side of the room.

"Just look and see," he suggested.

The suspicious Camoni peered into the gun and his face whitened. The gun was not loaded.

"Put the gun down," said Don Camillo quietly; "take off your costume, leave the rectory on the garden side and cut through the fields. If you hurry, you'll make the bus at Fontanile. I'll put your motorcycle in safekeeping, an` you can either let me know where to send it or else come fetch it in person."

The Indian laid the gun on the desk.

"No use looking for the cartridges," Don Camillo told him. He had put on his glasses and was reading the paper. "The cartridges are in the cupboard and the key to the cupboard is in my pocket. I warn you that unless you get out of here in double-quick time, I'll be reminded of that drink you pressed upon me long ago."

The Indian tore off the remains of his costume and wiped the grease-paint off his face. He took a cap out of his pocket and jammed it down over his head. Dario Camoni started to leave the room, but he lingered at the door and turned hesitantly around.

"Let's even the score," he said, and picking up the second glass of castor oil, he drained it.

"Quits?" he said interrogatively.

"Quits," answered Don Camillo, without even rasing his head. And the Indian disappeared.

Peppone came back later, looking green around the gills.

"I hope you won't sink so low as to go around telling what happened to me," he said gloomily.

"I should say not," Don Camillo answered with a sigh. "You had one glass, but that wretch made me drink the other."

"Has he gone away?" asked Peppone, sitting down.

"Gone with the wind."

Peppone stared at the floor and said nothing.

"Well, what can I say?" he finally mumbled. "It was a little like going back to the time when we were young, thirty years ago . . ."

"True enough," said Don Camillo. "That Indian brought back a bit of our youth."

Peppone started to relapse into anger.

"Easy there, Peppone," Don Camillo advised him. "You don't want to endanger the dignity of your office."

Peppone went cautiously home, and Don Camillo made a report to the crucified Christ over the altar.

"Lord," he explained, "what else could I do? If I'd told Peppone the gun wasn't loaded he'd have killed the other fellow for sure. Those Camonis are too pig-headed to ever give in. As things are, there was no violence, and the Indian had a dose of oil, which You must chalk up to his credit. And by sacrificing my personal pride, I managed not to humiliate Peppone."

"Don Camillo," Christ answered, "when the Indian told Peppone to drink the oil, you knew the gun wasn't loaded and you could perfectly well have stepped in."

"Lord," said Don Camillo, throwing out his arms in resignation, "what if Peppone had found out that the gun wasn't loaded and failed to get that healthful drink?"

"Don Camillo," Christ said severely, "I ought to prescribe a drink of the same kind for you!"

It seems that as Don Camillo left the church he was muttering something to the effect that only Fascists could order any such prescription. But this is not altogether certain. In any case, when he hung the shotgun up on the wall, he placed the Indian bonnet as a trophy beside it, and every time he looked at it he reflected that there is perfectly good hunting to be found without benefit of a gun.

A SOUL FOR SALE

NERI, THE MASON, HAD BEEN
hammering away for three hours without accomplishing much
of anything. The wall seemed to be an unbreakable solid mass,
and he had to smash every brick before he could get it out. He
stopped for a minute to wipe the sweat off his forehead, and
cursed when he saw how small a hole he had made with so much
effort.

"It's going to take patience," said the voice of old Molotti, who had engaged him to do the work, behind him.

"Patience, my eye!" Neri exclaimed ill-humoredly. "This is no wall, it's a block of steel. It'll take something more than patience to pierce a door."

He started pounding again, but a few minutes later he dropped his hammer and chisel and let out another oath. He had given his left thumb a tremendous crack and it was bleeding.

"I told you to take it easy," said Molotti. "If you'd had a bit more patience you wouldn't have lost your temper and banged your own thumb."

Neri's only answer was another outburst of profanity.

Old Molotti shook his head.

"God Almighty has nothing to do with it," he said. "You can only blame the fellow who was wielding the hammer. And remember, you'll never get to Heaven without a lot of pain."

"It's painful enough to make a living," Neri retorted angrily. "I don't give a damn for your Heaven."

Neri was as Red as they make them, and one of Peppone's most excitable followers, but although Molotti was over ninety years old, he wasn't going to let that upset him.

"I'd forgotten that you don't give a damn for our Heaven," he said. "You're one of the Reds, aren't you, and they promise some sort of heaven on earth."

"That's a lot more honest than promising it somewhere up in the sky," countered Neri. "We promise things you can see and touch with your own hands."

"Never fear!" said Molotti, raising an admonitory finger. "Some day you'll see and touch things that are now hidden from you."

Neri burst into loud laughter.

"When I'm dead, I'm dead, and that's the end of everything for me. Anything else is just priests' chatter."

"May God save your soul!" sighed old Molotti.

Neri resumed his hammering.

"Who could have believed that people would still go around preaching all that stuff and nonsense!" he muttered. "My soul, eh? A soul flapping through the air with a brand-new pair of wings, and receiving a prize for its good behavior! You must take me for a complete idiot!"

"If I didn't think you were talking tough just to enjoy the sound of your own voice, when all the time you know better deep down inside, then I'd say you were crazy."

"You priests and landowners are crazy, to imagine you can still hand us out all that nonsense!"

Old Molotti shook his head. "Do you really think the soul dies with the body?" he asked.

"Just as sure as I am to be alive. There isn't such a thing as a soul!"

"And what have you got inside you?"

"Lungs, liver, spleen, brains, heart, stomach and intestines. We're flesh-and-blood machines, which run just as long as these organs are working. When one of them breaks down, the machine stops, and if the doctor can't repair it, then it's goodbye, machine."

Old Molotti threw out his arms in indignation.

"But you've forgotten the soul!" he shouted. "The soul is the breath of life!"

"Bunk!" said Neri. "Try taking out a man's lungs and you'll see what happens. If the soul were the breath of life, he ought to be able to get along without them."

"That's blasphemy!"

"No, I'm just using my reason. Anyone can see that life is linked to the internal organs. I've never seen a man die because they've taken his soul away. And if you say the soul's the breath of life, then chickens must have souls just like the rest of us, and go to the same Heaven, Purgatory and Hell."

Old Molotti saw that it was no use to argue further and so he walked away. But he hadn't given up the struggle and at noon, when Neri had stopped to eat his lunch, he came over to the shady spot where he was sitting.

"Look here," said Neri, "if you want to fight some more, you're wasting your time, I can tell you."

"I have no intention of fighting," said the old man. "I want to make you a strictly business proposition. You're perfectly sure, are you, that you have no soul?"

Neri's face clouded over, but Molotti did not give him time to protest.

"In that case, you may as well sell it to me," he continued. "I'm offering you five hundred liras."

Neri looked at the banknote in the old man's hand and burst out laughing.

"That's a good one! How can I sell you something I haven't got?"

"That's not your worry," Molotti insisted. "You're selling me your soul. If you actually don't possess such a thing, then I lose my money. But if you do have it, then it's mine."

Neri began to enjoy himself thoroughly. He thought the old man must have softening of the brain.

"Five hundred liras isn't much," he said gaily, "you might at least offer me a thousand."

"No," said Molotti, "A soul like yours isn't worth it."

"But I won't take less!"

"Very well, then, a thousand. Before you go home we'll put it in writing."

Neri hammered away, more cheerfully, until evening. When it was time to knock off, the old man brought him a fountain pen and a sheet of legal paper.

"Are you still willing?" he asked.

"Of course."

"Then sit down and write: 'I, Francesco Neri, hereby legally bind myself, in return for the sum of one thousand liras, to sell my soul to Giuseppe Molotti. Having paid me this sum, Molotti enters from this day forth into possession and can dispose of my soul as he sees fit. Signed: Francesco Neri.'"

Molotti handed Neri a thousand-lira note, and Neri made his signature with an appropriate flourish.

"Good!" said the old man. "The business is done, and that's all there is to it."

Neri laughed as he went away. Yes, Molotti was in his dotage, that was the only explanation. He only wished he'd asked for more money. But this thousand-lira note was so much gravy.

As he pedaled off on his broken-down bicycle, he couldn't get the strange contract off his mind. "If Molotti isn't in his dotage, as he seems to be, why would he give me a thousand liras?" he wondered. The rich old man was notoriously stingy, and he wouldn't part with his money for no purpose. All of a sudden Neri saw the whole thing clearly. He let out a volley of oaths and pedaled back as fast he could in order to make up for his stupidity. He found old Molotti in the yard and came out immediately with what was on his mind.

"Look here," he said gloomily. "I was a fool not to think of it before. But better late than never. I know your reactionary methods. You got that contract out of me for propaganda purposes. You're going to publish it in order to ridicule my Party. 'Here are the Communists,' you'll say, 'people that go around selling their souls for a thousand liras!'"

The old man shook his head.

"This is a strictly private affair," he answered. "But if you like, I'll add a guarantee to the contract: 'I swear never to show this document to anyone whatsoever.' Does that suit you?"

Molotti was an honorable man, and his solemn oath was to be respected. He went into his study, wrote down the codicil and signed it.

"You've nothing to worry about," he said. "But as far as that goes, you needn't have worried before. I didn't buy your soul for political purposes. I bought it for my own private use."

"That is, if you can lay your hands on it!" said Neri, who was restored to his good humor.

"Naturally," said Molotti. "And as far as I'm concerned it's good business. I'm quite sure you have a soul, and besides, this would be the first time in my life I'd failed to strike a good bargain."

Neri went home feeling completely reassured. Molotti had softening of the brain. At his age, that wasn't surprising. He wanted to tell his cronies the story, but he was afraid that if i got around, the reactionaries would use it to shock their public of churchgoing old ladies.

The alterations of Molotti's house lasted for over a week and Neri met the old man every day. But Molotti made no mention of the contract and entered into no political discussion. It seemed as if he had forgotten the whole thing. After the job was done, Neri had no further occasion to see him, and a whole year went by before the matter returned to his mind.

One evening Peppone called him to lend a hand in the workshop. He had forged the parts of a wrought-iron gate, and now it was a question of putting them together.

"It's an order from old man Molotti," Peppone told him, "and he wants it finished by tomorrow morning. The gate's for his family tomb. He says he wants to have it made before he dies, because none of the rest of them has enough sense to do the proper thing."

"Is he sick?" Neri asked.

"He's been in bed for a week with a bad cold that's gone down into his lungs. And at ninety-three years of age, that's no joke."

Neri began to work the bellows.

"Then there's one more reactionary swine gone," he muttered. "Even the family ought to be glad, because he's in his dotage."

"I wouldn't say that," put in Peppone. "Only a month ago he made a deal with the Trespiano farm which netted him at least fifteen million liras."

"Just disgusting good luck," said Neri. "I happen to know that he's been dotty for some time. Chief, shall I tell you a story?"

And he proceeded to tell how he had sold his soul to Molotti. Peppone listened attentively.

"Don't you think a man must be soft in the head to buy another man's soul for a thousand liras?" Neri concluded.

"Yes, I do, but the man that sells it is even softer."

"Well, of course I should have got much more money than that out of him," said Neri, shrugging his shoulders.

"I'm not speaking of the price," said Peppone.

Neri took his hand off the bellows.

"Chief, are you joining the Children of Mary? What in the

world do you mean? Never mind the attitude of the Party and the policy of not making a frontal attack upon organized religion, but just between ourselves, don't you agree that the soul, Heaven, Hell and all the rest of that stuff are just priestly inventions?"

Peppone continued to hammer out the red-hot iron.

"Neri," he said, after a long pause, "that's irrelevant. I say that for a man to sell his soul for a thousand liras is non-productive and counter-revolutionary."

"Now, I understand, Chief," said Neri with relief. "But you needn't worry. In order to prevent him from turning the thing to political use, I had a codicil added, which stipulates that Molotti will never speak about it to anyone."

"Well, with that codicil, it's different," said Peppone. "That makes it your own private business, which is of no concern to the Party. As far as the Party goes, you're in perfectly good standing."

Peppone proceeded to talk of other matters, and Neri went home at midnight in an excellent humor.

"The main thing is to be in good standing with the Party," he said to himself before falling asleep. "Then everything else is in line, too."

Molotti got worse and worse every day. One evening, when Don Camillo was coming back from his bedside, he ran into Neri.

"Good evening," said Neri, and Don Camillo was so bowled over that he was moved to get off his bicycle and go look him in the face.

"Extraordinary!" he exclaimed. "You're Neri, sure enough, and you said good evening to me. Are you sure you weren't making a mistake? Did you take me for a tax collector instead of the parish priest?"

Neri shrugged his shoulders.

"With you, it's hard to know how to behave. If we don't speak to you, you say we're godless Reds, and if we do, then you think we're crazy."

"You've got something there," said Don Camillo, throwing out his arms. "But that's not the whole story. Anyhow, good evening to you."

Neri stared for a minute at the handlebars of Don Camillo's bicycle. Finally he asked:

"How's old man Molotti?"

"He's dying by slow degrees."

"Has he lost consciousness?"

"No, he's perfectly clear-headed and has been all along."

"Has he said anything to you?" asked Neri aggressively.

Don Camillo opened his eyes wide in astonishment.

"I don't understand. What should he say?"

"Hasn't he said anything about me and about a contract between us?"

"No," said Don Camillo, convincingly. "We've talked about practically everything, but not about you. And besides, I don't go to talk to a dying man about business matters. My concern is with souls."

This last word caused Neri to start, and Don Camillo nodded and smiled.

"Neri, I have no intention of preaching at you. I told you what it was my duty to tell when you were a little boy and came to hear. Now all I do is answer your questions. I've had no talk about any business contract with Molotti and I have no intention of bringing up any such subject. If you need help of that kind, consult a lawyer. But hurry, because Molotti has one foot in the next world, already."

"If I stopped you, it's because I needed a priest's help, not a lawyer's," Neri insisted. "It's just a small matter but you must give Molotti a thousand liras and ask him to return a certain legal paper."

"A legal paper? A thousand liras? That sounds to me very much like a lawyer's affair."

By this time they had come to the rectory, and after casting a suspicious eye about him, Neri followed Don Camillo in. The priest sat down at his desk and motioned Neri to a chair.

"If you think I can really help you, go ahead and tell me what it's all about."

Neri twisted his hat in hands and finally said:

"Father, the fact is this. A year ago, in return for a thousand liras, I sold Molotti my soul."

Don Camillo started. Then he said threateningly:

"Listen, if you think that's a good joke, you've come to the wrong place. Get out of here!"

"It's no joke," Neri protested. "I was working in his house and we had a discussion about the soul. I said there was no such thing and he said: 'If you don't believe the soul exists, then you may as well sell yours to me for a thousand liras.' I accepted his offer and signed a contract."

"A contract?"

"Yes, an agreement written and signed by my hand, on legal paper."

He knew the terms of the contract by heart and recited them to Don Camillo. The priest could not help being persuaded of his sincerity.

"I see," he said, "but why do you want the paper? If you don't believe you have a soul, then why do you care whether or not you sold it?"

"It's not on account of the soul," Neri explained. "I don't want his heirs to find that paper and make political capital out of it. That might damage the Party."

Don Camillo got up and stood in front of Neri with his hands on his hips and his legs far apart.

"Listen to me," he said between clenched teeth. "Am I supposed to help you for the sake of your party? You must take me for the stupidest priest that ever was! Get along with you!"

Neri went slowly toward the door. But after a few steps he turned back.

"Never mind about the Party!" he exclaimed. "I want my paper!"

Don Camillo was standing with his hands on his hips, defiantly.

"I want my paper!" Neri repeated. "For six months I haven't had a decent night's sleep."

Don Camillo looked at the man's distraught face and eyes and the perspiration on his forehead.

"My paper!" he panted. "If the swine insists upon makin

money, even on his deathbed, then I'll pay something extra, whatever he asks. But I can't go to his house. They wouldn't let me in, and besides, I wouldn't know how to put it."

"Take it easy!" interrupted Don Camillo. "If it's not for the Party, what does it matter? The soul and the next world and all that sort of thing are priestly inventions—"

"The reason's not your affair," Neri shouted. "I want my paper, I tell you!"

"Very well, then," said Don Camillo resignedly, "I'll try to get it for you tomorrow morning."

"No, right now!" Neri insisted. "Tomorrow morning he may be dead. Take the thousand liras and go to him right away, while he's still alive. I'll wait for you outside. Hurry, Father, hurry!"

Don Camillo understood, but he still couldn't tolerate the miscreant's peremptory way of speaking. And so he continued to stand there with his hands on his hips, looking into Neri's distraught face.

"Father, go ahead and do your duty!" Neri shouted in exasperation.

All of a sudden Don Camillo was overtaken by the same impatience. He ran out, minus his hat, jumped onto his bicycle and rode away in the darkness.

An hour later Don Camillo returned and Neri once more followed him into the rectory.

"Here you are," said the priest, handing him a large sealed envelope. Inside were another envelope, closed with sealing-wax, and a short letter. The letter ran as follows: "The undersigned, Giuseppe Molotti, hereby declares null and void the contract he made with Francesco Neri and restores it to him." And there, in the smaller envelope, was the famous piece of legal paper.

"He didn't want the thousand liras," said Don Camillo. "Take them. He said to do with them whatever you liked."

Neri did not say a word, but went out with all his belongings in his hands. He thought of tearing up the contract, but on further reflection decided to burn it. The side door of the church was still open and he could see candles blazing. He went in and paused in front of the big candle behind the altar rail. Holding the paper in the flame, he watched it crumple, then squeezed it in his hand until it was reduced to ashes. Finally he opened his fingers and blew the ashes away. Just as he was about to leave, he remembered the thousand liras, took them out of the envelope and stuffed them in the poor-box. Then, quite unexpectedly, he took another thousand-lira note out of his pocket and put it in the same place. "For a blessing received," he thought to himself as he went home. His eyes were drowsy and he knew that this night he would sleep.

Shortly after this, Don Camillo went to lock up the church and bid good-night to the Christ over the altar.

"Lord," he asked, "who can possibly understand these people?"

"I can," the Crucified Christ answered, smiling.

BEAUTY AND THE BEAST

THEY HAD MET DOZENS OF times in the People's Palace, marched side by side in parade, gone out as a team to collect signatures for the Peace Crusade and other deviltries of the same kind, and so it was natural enough that things should come spontaneously to a head one summer evening.

"It seems to me we two work pretty smoothly together," Marco said to the girl as they came out of the People's Palace.

"I think so too," Giulietta admitted.

They didn't say anything more, but the next evening Marco went over to Brusco's house to call for Giulietta. Then they went to sit together on the bridge that spanned the Po River. That was how it all began, and everyone found it the most logical thing in the world. Marco and Brusco's daughter did indeed seem to be made for one another. They were of the same age and had the same wild ideas, and if Giulietta was the prettiest girl in the village, Marco was certainly an up-and-coming young man. Both of them were so bitten by the political bug that they thought of practically nothing else.

"Marco," said Giulietta, "I like you because you're different from other boys. You talk to me as if I weren't just a mere woman."

"Giulietta," he answered, "what difference does it make if we're of opposite sexes, as long as our ideals are the same?"

They continued way into the autumn to meet four evenings a week on the bridge. Finally, one time when it was pouring rain, Giulietta's mother met Marco at the door and said he and Giulietta might as well come onto the porch for shelter. And when winter came, she suggested that they'd better come into the house. Brusco's wife was a truly old-fashioned woman. She was completely absorbed in her home and thought of everything beyond the bridge as a foreign land, whose goings-on were of no interest to her. As far as she knew, this foreign land was just the same as it had been twenty or thirty years before. And so, when Marco came into the kitchen she pointed to a chair near the cupboard and said:

"Sit down."

After that she motioned her daughter into a matching chair on the other side of the cupboard and returned to the seat where she had been knitting, in front of the fire. Giulietta and Marco went quietly on with the conversation they had begun on the porch. Two hours later Marco went away and Giulietta took herself off to bed. Her mother didn't say a word, but she thought plenty, and when Brusco came home, she let off steam.

"That young man came to the house," she told him.

"Did he?" asked Brusco. "And what do you think of him?"

"He's a poor wretch, that's what I think."

"He's a good boy, a boy with his head on his shoulders," said Brusco. "I know him well."

"I say he's a wretched creature," his wife repeated. "For two whole hours they talked of nothing but politics: political parties, party papers, Russia, America and other such ridiculous things. And she lapped it up! Poor wretches, both of them, that's what I say."

"What do you expect them to talk about?" said Brusco. "That's what interests the youth of today."

"Chattering about politics doesn't lead anyone to get married. Marriage means starting a family, not a political party. No, I don't like the fellow at all."

"Well, you don't have to marry him," said Brusco, starting upstairs. "The main thing is that he's a thoroughly good boy."

"No one that belongs to your godless party can be a good boy!"

"Well, your daughter belongs to my godless party, too," Brusco countered. "And isn't she a good girl?"

"She's not my daughter, she's yours!" answered his wife, throwing out her arms in despair.

As she thrashed about in her bed, trying vainly to sleep, a suspicion came into her mind. Perhaps they had talked about those ridiculous things simply because she was there. When they were alone, they might talk of something completely different.

She decided to put this suspicion to the test, and when Marco came to call she said she was dead tired and supposedly went up to bed. Once upstairs, she lifted up a board which she had previously loosened from the floor, and was able to hear everything they were saying below. Marco and Giulietta talked quietly for some ten minutes or so, and then Marco raised his voice to say:

"Now that your mother's gone to bed, we can talk more freely. I say that if we go on with the halfway methods of Peppone and your father, we'll never get anywhere. We've got to get tough with the landowners if we want results."

: [41] :

"I agree with you a hundred percent," said Giulietta gravely. "Next time there's a meeting, we'll have to let Peppone know what's what. As for my father, I've been trying to put it over for some time, but it's no use. They're getting old, and you can't expect them to have any flexibility in their thinking."

Upstairs, the woman held her breath. This was even looser talk than that of the night before. But it was so boring that she couldn't keep her eyes open, and when Brusco came up he found her asleep, with her ear glued to the floor.

"Fine ideas they have, those two!" she exclaimed, pulling herself together. "If you want to know, your daughter told that wretched boy that you and Peppone are old fuddy-duddies and the landowners twist you around their fingers."

"These young people are full of enthusiasm," said Brusco, shaking his head, "but of course they carry everything to extremes. And as far as Peppone and myself are concerned, we're in perfect harmony with the Party."

Things went on in very much the same way, but Brusco's wife had lost all interest in Giulietta and her young man. Whenever he appeared upon the scene, she simply said:

"Here comes the committee!"

Finally something different did happen, and it was brought about by Giulietta. One evening she came late to supper, waving a magazine in her hand.

"Look at this!" she shouted, opening it up before them, "I'm in the finals!"

Brusco looked at the magazine and passed it over to his wife.

"Do you know who this is?" he asked, pointing to a photograph.

"It looks like her," his wife answered.

"It looks like me so much that it *is* me," said the girl, laughing. "And there's my name underneath to prove it."

Still her mother didn't understand.

"What's it all about?"

"It's the contest for 'Miss New Life.' I'm in the final round."

Her mother looked again at the magazine and shook her head uncomprehendingly.

"Anyone can see," said Giulietta. *New Life* is our Party magazine and it runs a contest every year. Girls from all over the country send in their pictures and a jury decides among them. Those that last as far as the finals are called to Rome to be looked over in person, and then the winner is proclaimed 'Miss New Life.' Now I'm one of the eight called to Rome for the final selection."

There was still something her mother didn't understand.

"But what's the basis of the selection? What sort of a contest is it?"

"A beauty contest, of course!" Giulietta exclaimed. "The prettiest girl wins the title and a whole lot of prizes. It's a serious business, I tell you. The jury is made up of artists, moving-picture directors, newspapermen, and so on. And you can be sure it's conducted the way it should be, since it's sponsored by the Party."

The woman turned to her husband. "Are you letting your daughter get her picture into print and then show herself off in Rome?"

"Don't turn it into a tragedy," said Brusco, shrugging his shoulders. "There are plenty of contests of this kind, and I don't see anything the matter with them. Haven't there been beauty queens as long as we can remember?"

"There've been no-good girls as long as we can remember, too," she said, "but that doesn't mean we have to encourage ours to be one."

"Don't be stupid, Mother!" cried Giulietta angrily.

The woman looked at her husband, but he went right on eating. Finally she got up and went over to the stair. Brusco wolfed down the rest of his supper and hurried out, mumbling something about a meeting. Giulietta cleared the table, washed the dishes and sat down to wait for Marco. This was his regular evening, and he arrived promptly.

"Have you seen this?" she said at once, showing him the magazine.

"Yes, I have," he answered. "Your picture came out very well. I didn't know you'd sent it in."

Giulietta was still in a state of excitement. She leafed through the magazine pages.

"Look at the other girls in the finals," she said, "and tell me what you think."

"It's hard to judge from a print on cheap paper," he said, after a thorough examination.

"That's why they call us to Rome," said Giulietta. "There they'll look us over from head to toe. And all modesty aside, it seems to me I have a chance."

"When do you go to Rome?" he asked.

"On the twentieth, it says here. That's just four days away."

"It's a long trip," Marco observed.

"Four hundred miles! And all expenses paid. It's the opportunity of a lifetime to see the city."

Marco agreed that it was an opportunity.

"But this whole idea of a beauty contest has something terribly bourgeois about it," he added.

"Beauty isn't a bourgeois monopoly," laughed Giulietta. "Beauty's universal."

"Right," Marco admitted, "but you don't catch them holding beauty contests in Russia."

"Russia's different," she protested. "They don't have strikes or seizures of factories there, either. In Russia everything's done for the People. There's not a beastly bourgeoisie whose propaganda paints all Communists as monsters, as creatures with three nostrils and the like. *New Life*'s contest will prove there are plenty of pretty girls in the Party, much prettier than your bourgeois young ladies. If the contest didn't have a serious purpose, the Party wouldn't permit it. The Party knows its business, after all."

Marco agreed that the Party was always right.

"But, personally, I'm a little sorry that you sent in your picture."

"Marco," she said severely, "what sort of silly talk is this? Are you giving into ordinary masculine conventions?"

"You misunderstood me," answered Marco. "I've always admired you because you weren't like other women. You didn't

: [44] :

seem to have their vanity and petty ambition . . . now . . . your idea of going into this contest makes me wonder . . ."

Giulietta drew herself up proudly.

"If the Party's sponsoring it, that means it's beneficial to the Party. And if I can benefit a cause that benefits the Party, it's my obligation to do so."

"Forgive me, Giulietta," Marco said, blushing. "To tell the truth, I have feelings I've never had before. It bothers me to see your picture on display and it bothers me to think of your going to Rome."

Giulietta gave a sarcastic laugh.

"Control yourself, Comrade, or you'll turn into one of those idiots that lose their head every time they see a pretty girl. And I don't want you to disappoint me. After you've led me to believe you were different from other men and capable of a platonic friendship, please don't show yourself up as the kind that thinks only of putting over a fast one."

"Giulietta!" cried Marco, turning very pale. "Now you've hurt my feelings."

"No, Marco, you've hurt mine. And beside that, you've insulted my father. Because, remember, my father hasn't breathed a word of opposition."

"Don't take it so hard, Giulietta," said Marco throwing out his arms in despair. "I don't want to hurt or insult a soul. I'm only asking whether, for my sake, you're not willing to give up the trip to Rome. Why do you care about being the *New Life* beauty queen, when you're the queen of my heart?"

He spoke in a most unusually gentle voice, which caused Giulietta to stare at him in disgust.

"You fool!" she shouted.

Marco turned even more pale, and came toward her, attempting to grasp her hand.

"Go away, and don't hurry back!" shouted Giulietta, pushing him back roughly and pointing to the door.

Marco lowered his head and started to go. But he wasn't really such a fool; in fact, he was a young man of considerable character. So it was that he wheeled around and said sternly:

"Giulietta, I forbid you to go to Rome. I won't have you take part in a beauty contest or anything of the kind. Your father may be an idiot, but I'm not."

Giulietta planted herself in front of him with her hands on her hips.

"Forbid me?" she shouted. "What right have you to do that? Who do you think you are?"

"I'm somebody that loves you," said Marco, losing his usual self-possession. "I'm not the kind that puts his wife on public display."

Giulietta giggled, and after a minute or so Marco clenched his fists and said:

"You're not going to Rome, I tell you!"

Giulietta stopped giggling and looked him straight in the eye.

"Instead of waiting four days, I'm going tomorrow," she said defiantly, "and I'll appear before the jury in a bathing-suit. I have a new one right here in the drawer, if you want to see it, in two pieces . . ."

She could not finish because Marco tore the package out of her hands, threw the contents on the floor and stepped on them.

"There are plenty more where that came from," said Giulietta angrily. "You'll see my picture in a bathing-suit in all the papers. And now get out of my house! I'll send you a postcard from Rome."

Marco was beside himself with rage and despair, but there was nothing he could do. He looked around without knowing exactly what for, and saw a shotgun, with a hunting bag and cartridge belt hanging up on the wall beside it. And on the mantelpiece another sinister object was gleaming. Giulietta didn't have time to escape because Marco had reached out with one hand while with the other he grabbed Giulietta by the neck. His fingers were like iron bands, and Giulietta could barely breathe. Marco raised the weapon and brought it down on her head. The girl couldn't even cry out, because fright had caused her to faint away.

When Giulietta came to, she was sitting on the floor and

Marco was watching over her. She didn't yet know what had happened, because her head felt quite empty. No wonder, for the object that Marco had taken from the mantelpiece was a pair of shears and with it he had shorn all the long, silky hair from her head. Now he threw the scissors at her feet and Giulietta began to realize what he had done.

"Go to Rome, if you like," said Marco fiercely. And he disappeared through the door.

Lying on the floor of their upstairs room, Brusco's wife had through the aperture left by the removed board followed every detail of the scene.

"I told you he was a good boy, didn't I?" murmured Brusco, who had sneaked home through the garden and in the back door and was now on watch beside his wife.

The next day the whole village had heard about the shearing. There was no way of knowing who told the tale but in the river country of the little world everyone knows everyone else's business. And, of course, a girl friend came to see Giulietta in the afternoon and told her that the whole village was buzzing.

"Listen, Giulietta," her friend said through a crack in the door; "nobody's actually seen you. If I were you, I'd clear out and go to your uncle's up in the mountains for a couple of months. While you're there you can wear a little wig and tie a scarf around it. And meanwhile your hair will grow back."

"Thanks for the good advice," said Giulietta coldly.

She stayed at home all day, but after supper she went to sit on the side of the bridge. It was a magnificent August evening, with an enormous moon in the sky, and the first passer-by could see Giulietta's condition quite clearly. He ran to spread the news, and soon a whole procession of people came by. And at the end of the crowd came Marco. He stood there hesitatingly until Giulietta said:

"Well, aren't you coming to see the show?"

Marco swallowed hard and then said: "Giulietta, if you want your revenge, take it right away. But don't throw vitriol in my face. I'd rather you shot me."

"Shoot you?" said Giulietta in amazement. "If I shoot you while

I'm in this condition, where can I find another fool ready to marry me right away?"

Giulietta wore a Party-approved gray tailored suit and a shirt-waist with a black bow to the wedding, and when Don Camillo found this strange pair standing before him he looked in perplexity from the one to the other, with his eyes coming to a pause on Giulietta's shorn head.

"Which one of you is the groom?" he asked.

"He is," sighed Giulietta, covering her baldness with a veil.

BRUSCO LOOKED AT THE wall and shrugged his shoulders.

"Well, what do you say?" asked Don Camillo.

"I don't know," Brusco answered.

"If a mason doesn't know whether or not he can make a door through a wall, then he'd better change trades!" exclaimed Don Camillo. "Perhaps I should call Neri."

"This wall is as old as the hills," Brusco explained, "and an old wall can be very tricky. Unless you let me knock off a bit of plaster and explore underneath, I can't give you any definite reply."

And so Don Camillo authorized him to make an exploration.

"Just remember you're in a sacristy," he admonished him; "try to do a neat job and not cover the place with litter."

Brusco took a hammer and chisel out of his bag and began to knock plaster off the wall.

"It looks bad," he said after two or three strokes of the hammer. "The wall's filled with clay and stones. If it were made of bricks, we could put a re-enforced cement architrave in just at the point of the first break-through and then carry the break down to the floor. But this way, it looks like trouble."

Don Camillo borrowed the hammer and knocked some plaster off another part of the wall. But here, too, he came upon a conglomeration of stones and clay.

"Queer," he observed. "The outside walls of the church are all brick. Why should they have put stones inside?"

Brusco threw out his arms with a baffled air.

"They may have made the supporting columns and an outer layer of bricks," he said, "and then stuffed the rest with stones. But let's take it easy and explore a little deeper."

By means of a big nail he loosened the clay around an uncovered stone and pulled it out. Then he hammered at the clay behind it and came to another stone. While he was trying to dig this out too, it disappeared.

"There must be an empty space behind the stones, and I don't understand it. You'd expect the stones to go all the way to the brick outer wall."

Don Camillo widened the hole and soon they found an enormous wardrobe which the secondary wall had been built to conceal. Of course the priest was feverishly anxious to open it, and when they had come back down into the sacristy he said to Brusco:

"Thanks. I don't need you any more."

"I'm afraid you do," said Brusco calmly. "A wall fifteen feet long, nine feet high and eighteen inches thick makes a consid erable mass of stones and clay. And if you want to open the wardrobe, the whole thing will have to come down."

"And what makes you think I'll tackle that wall?" Don Camillo asked. "I'm not totally mad."

"You're worse than that; you're Don Camillo!" Brusco retorted.

But when Don Camillo had thought twice about the dimensions of the wall he had to acknowledge that it was too much for him.

"Very well," he said. "Go get enough men to tear it down and wagons to carry the debris away. But once the work is done, I want it understood that you will all go home. I want to open the wardrobe myself."

Ten minutes later most of the people of the village were on the church square and all of them for this reason:

"Don Camillo has discovered a hidden treasure in the sacristy."

They imagined pots and pans filled with gold ducats, paintings and all sorts of other objects of art, and so great was the excitement that everyone wanted to see. Brusco's eight helpers soon turned into eighty, and a long line of volunteers passed buckets full of debris from one hand to another. The wall came down very fast and the majestic wardrobe began to stand out in all its mystery. Darkness fell, but no one thought of going away, and soon after the last bucketful of clay and stones was carried away. Don Camillo took up his stand right in front of the wardrobe and said to the crowd in the sacristy.

"Thanks for your help, and good night to you!"

"Open it up! Open it up! We want to see!" they shouted at him.

"It's not your personal property," said an angry woman. "A hidden treasure belongs to all of us together."

"You're not out in the public square," Don Camillo replied. "You're in the church. And I'm responsible for everything in the church to the ecclesiastical authorities."

The carabinieri and their sergeant lined up beside Don Camillo, but the people were so frenzied that no one could keep them from pushing forward.

"Very well," said Don Camillo; "step back and I'll open it up."

They stepped back, and Don Camillo opened the first door. The compartment was filled with books, every one of which bore a number. And there were more and more books in all the other compartments. Don Camillo pulled out a book at random and leafed it through.

"It *is* a treasure," he explained, "but not of the kind you imagined. These are birth, death and marriage registers of the two hundred and fifty years ending in 1753. I don't know what happened in that year, but apparently the priest was afraid they might be destroyed and walled them up here for safekeeping."

Things had to be arranged in such a way that everyone could see with their own eyes the truth of what Don Camillo was saying, and only when they had all marched by the wardrobe could Don Camillo call it a day.

"Lord," he said when he was left alone in the church, "forgive me if through my fault Your house was turned into an encampment of sacrilegious gold-diggers. I repeat that the blame is not theirs but mine; I was the first one to be in an indecent hurry. When the shepherd acts like a madman, what can you expect of his flock?"

In the course of the following days Don Camillo was stricken with another madness; his impatience to examine all the registers at once. He looked at them quite at random, one after another and this turned out to be a good idea, for along with the registers of 1650 he found a notebook in which the priest had written up all the events worthy of remark every day.

He threw himself eagerly upon this diary and discovered all sorts of curious things. But among the notes of May 6, 1650 he found two really remarkable items, the first one of which was concerned with Giosue Scozza, whose marble statue stood in the main square of the neighboring village of Torricella on a pedestal marked with the following inscription:

> Giosue Scozza
> Creator of Divine harmonies
> Beloved son of Torricella
> Who wrote its name and his
> own on the rolls of Glory
> 1650–1746

Torricella had dedicated to this favorite son not only this monument but also its main square, the theater, the widest street, the primary school, the public orphan asylum and the local band. His name inevitably came out in every piece of writing or speechmaking in these parts and even big-city newspapers and magazines always referred to Giosue Scozza as "the swan of Torricella."

For centuries there had been a feud between the two villages, and the compatriots of Don Camillo and Peppone could not bear to see or hear this name. Now, in the old diary, Don Camillo found a passage which, translated into contemporary language, ran:

"Today Geremia Scozza, blacksmith, moved away to enter the service of Count Sanvito of Torricella. With him went his wife, Geltrude, and his son, Giosue, born in this parish on June 8, 1647."

The records of 1647 confirmed the fact that the great man had indeed been born in this parish, and those of preceding years made it clear that the same was true of his family. In short, Torricella had acquired its "swan" when he was three years old.

This item in the diary was preceded by another equally extraordinary:

"Today, May 6, 1647, Giuseppe Bottazzi, blacksmith, 18 years old, was decapitated in the public square, having on April 8 made an armed attack and inflicted wounds upon Don Pathil, rector of Vigoenzo for the purpose of stealing a bag of gold. Giuseppe Bottazzi, a skilled worker but a man of sacrilegious ideas, was not born here but came twenty years ago and married a local girl, Maria Gambazzi, who bore him a son baptized Antonio, now fifteen years old. Giuseppe Bottazzi has turned out to be the chief of a band of brigands who have committed thefts and murders in the land of Count Sanvito. Last December they surprised and murdered the men-at-arms of the Castello della Piana where Count Sanvito himself was in residence and managed to save his life only by fleeing through the secret underground passage."

Don Camillo took a look at the records of later years and clearly established the fact that the present-day Giuseppe Bottazzi, known as Peppone, mayor and Red leader, was a direct descendant of this blacksmith of the same name.

"When elections come around, I'll cook his goose," muttered Don Camillo. "I'll have this page of the diary photographed and plaster it up at every street corner, and under it the phrase: 'Blood will tell.' History repeats itself!"

This project was one that could not be carried out until the time was ripe, but its appeal was tremendous, for it meant killing two birds with one stone. Don Camillo planned to stake an indisputable claim to "the swan of Torricella" and strike a fatal blow at Peppone.

But the news about Giosue Scozza was so exciting that Don Camillo couldn't help dropping hints about it, and one day Peppone came to the rectory to see him.

"Father," he said, "there's a lot of talk about some of the things you've discovered in the famous books. Since it's no political matter, but one concerning the honor of the village, may I ask you to tell me the whole story?"

"What's this?" muttered Don Camillo, throwing out his arms. "It's just a bit of history, that's all."

"What do you mean by history?"

"I mean something in the nature of geography—geography is what makes history, you know."

"I don't get it," said Peppone, scratching his head. "Will you kindly explain?"

"I don't know whether it's really proper."

"I see. You're cooking up some of your usual reactionary propaganda and planning to destroy somebody's reputation."

Don Camillo turned bright red.

"If I go in for propaganda, there's nothing false about it. I have documents to show that "the swan of Torricella" was born not in Torricella, but right here, three years earlier than it's always been stated."

Peppone leaned forward.

"Either you're telling tall tales or else you're a man completely without honor. Because if you can demonstrate in private that Scozza came from here rather than from Torricella and refuse t do so openly, then you're depriving the village of a God-given right."

Don Camillo pulled out the diary and shoved it in front of Peppone's nose.

"Here's the whole truth for you; and there's other proof, besides."

"Then why don't you release it?"

Don Camillo lit his cigar butt and blew several mouthfuls of smoke up to the ceiling.

"The only way to release the news is to print a photograph of a whole page of the diary, or at least to be ready to show it to anyone who asks to see."

"Well, what's the matter with that?"

"I can't make up my mind to do anything so drastic. The note about Scozza is preceded by another one corroborating the date, which happens to bear *your* family name. So, in the last analysis, it's up to you."

"*My* family?" exclaimed Peppone, dumbfounded.

"Yes, the Giuseppe Bottazzi who fills the entry for May 6, 1647 is the unfortunate ancestor of the tribe of Peppone. I've checked the whole thing, and it's indubitably correct."

Don Camillo pointed out the entry to Peppone and the latter proceeded to read it.

"Well," he said afterwards, "what have I got to do with a Bottazzi of 1647?"

"You know how people are. The original Giuseppe Bottazzi revealed to be a blacksmith, a priest-baiter and gang-leader, just like you! Your enemies would be able to put that to good use in their campaign. Just think it over."

Peppone read the two items several times and then gave the diary back to Don Camillo.

"I don't care what the reactionary swine may say. The important thing is to add Giosue Scozza to our village's glory. I put the village's reputation before my own. So go ahead and make the whole thing public."

Peppone started to go, then wheeled about and went over to the desk where Don Camillo was sitting.

"And do you know what?" he added. "I'm proud to have that Bottazzi for an ancestor. It means that Bottazzis had the right idea even in 1647; they knew that they must get rid of priests and land-owners, even at the cost of their own lives. And it's no use your smiling, Father. Your turn is coming!"

"Remember that my name's Don Camillo, not Don Patini!" said the priest in reply.

"Politics may divide us, but for the good of the village, we are as one," Peppone shot over his shoulder. "We'll talk of that later; meanwhile, let's get after Giosue Scozza!"

Don Camillo threw himself like a lion into the chase for "the swan of Torricella." Without dragging Peppone's ancestor into the picture, he placed devastating articles in the provincial paper. Eventually the big-city papers chimed in. The romantic discovery of the archives sealed into the church wall made a good story, and they spread it so widely that Torricella had to surrender. And when people of Torricella were convinced that Giosue Scozza belonged to their enemies, they turned against him. A "public safety committee" was formed, for the purpose of wiping out all traces of the interloper, beginning with the statue in the public square, which was to be replaced by a fountain. Thus the blot would be washed away.

At this point Peppone appealed to the Reds on the other side. He proposed to give Torricella a marble fountain in exchange for the marble statue of the great man. It was settled that the exchange of gifts should be made into a solemn occasion. A wagon drawn by white oxen would carry the fountain to the boundary-line of the village, and meet there a similar wagon, bearing the statue. The money for the fountain was quickly raised, and a month later the wagons set forth. Giosue Scozza arrived in the village nailed to his pedestal and tied with ropes to the sides of the wagon, but looking very proud indeed. And Peppone, who was waiting to receive him, with the rest of the persons in authority and the local band, pronounced a speech written for the occasion, which began:

"Greetings, illustrious brother, upon your return, after centuries of absence, to your native place. . . ."

It was all very moving. When the wagon from Torricella had taken over the fountain and gone away, Peppone took a hammer and chisel out of his pocket and knocked off the tablet which described Giosue Scozza as the "beloved son of Torricella." The smashed tablet was thrown outside the boundary line, and the little procession wound its way happily into the central square. There everything was ready: masons, marble-workers, a crane and a stone for the base. Soon the statue stood erect on its new foundation and a new tablet was fastened to the pedestal. A canvas had been thrown around it, and this was removed at just the right moment. Don Camillo pronounced a blessing and made a short speech on the theme of the return of the prodigal son. The welcoming committee, which was non-political in nature, had done things up brown, and the festivities did not end until evening, when Peppone rose to explain the significance of the occasion.

"We have seen your face, dear long-lost brother," he said, "but we have not heard your voice, that divine voice which you raised to the heights of immortal glory. And so a string orchestra is to play a program which will acquaint all of us with the greatest melodies of our own celebrated Giosue Scozza."

The square was crowded with people, and after Peppone had finished speaking there was a burst of applause, followed by a religious silence. The string orchestra, which had been brought from the city, was really first-class, and the first of the twelve pieces on the program *The Andantino Number Six*, turned out to be a musical jewel. After this came the *Air in C sharp Minor* and the *Sonata in D*, which met with equal success. But when the fourth piece, *Ballet in F*, began, there was a chorus of voices shouting:

"Verdi, Verdi!"

Peppone and Don Camillo were sitting in the front seats, and the conductor looked beseechingly at Peppone. Peppone looked at Don Camillo and Don Camillo nodded. Then Peppone called peremptorily:

"Verdi!"

Everyone was wild with joy. The conductor held a whispered consultation with his musicians, tapped the music stand with his baton, and the crowd was silent. At the first notes of the prelude to *La Traviata*, people had difficulty restraining their applause and after it was finished it was almost overpowering.

"This is real music!" shouted Peppone.

"You can't beat Verdi," answered Don Camillo.

Verdi supplied all the rest of the program, and at the end the orchestra conductor was carried in triumph. As Smilzo passed in front of the statue of Giosue Scozza, "creator of divine harmonies," he observed:

"The climate of Torricella didn't do him any good."

"Exactly," said Bigio. "If he'd stayed here, he'd have written much better music."

"Historical things are beautiful even when they're ugly," put in Peppone severely. "Giosue Scozza belongs to history, and he'll go down as a very great man, don't you agree, Don Camillo?"

"Of course," Don Camillo answered. "You must always look at an artist against the background of his times."

"But Verdi . . ." objected Smilzo.

"What's Verdi got to do with it?" Peppone interrupted. "Verdi's no artist; he's just a man with a heart as big as this—"

And he threw out his arms so eloquently that they cut a wide swathe all around him. Don Camillo wasn't agile enough to get out of the way, and received a blow in the stomach. But out of respect for Verdi he said nothing.

REVENGE IS SWEET

THE PEOPLE OF TORRICELLA
were furious over having lost their musical supremacy and dead
set on winning a championship in some other field. So one fine
morning our villagers found posters stuck up all over the place,
which read as follows:

If you have eleven young men
who know the difference
between a soccer ball
and a can of tomato sauce,
Send them to the sports field at
Torricella
to see what's going on.

As soon as Peppone had read this challenge he turned to his lieutenant, Smilzo, and said:

"Tell the Dynamo team to start training immediately and then go to Torricella to decide on a day for the match."

Smilzo got on his bicycle, rode off at full speed and came back an hour later. Peppone was waiting impatiently in his office, and before him were proofs of the poster to be plastered, by way of a reply, on the walls of Torricella.

"Well, is it all set?" he shot at Smilzo.

"Set, my eye!" Smilzo growled. "We came in on the caboose."

"What do you mean?"

"I mean that the priest's team got there ahead of us."

Without hesitation Peppone pulled his cap down over his eyes and marched on the rectory. He found Don Camillo in the square in front of the church and plunged right into the subject which was on his mind.

"If there's any team that has a right to defend the village honor, it's the Dynamos," he stated emphatically.

"Ditto for the Diehards," answered Don Camillo.

"The Diehards aren't a team, they're a deformation."

"The Dynamos aren't a team, they're a collection of chickens."

On these premises, there seemed to be no likely agreement, and the argument continued in such an excited key that it attracted nearly a hundred listeners. Finally, after Peppone and Don Camillo had reached so high a pitch that it seemed as if they could never climb down from it, the voice of reason intervened. The voice was that of the local druggist.

"There can be no real discussion here," he said. "The teams are neck and neck, and we must choose between two solutions. Either we flip a coin to see which one is to represent the village, or else we take the best men of both and weld them together."

"The Diehards have eleven best men," maintained Don Camillo.

"And the Dynamos twelve," retorted Peppone, "because I'm including the masseur, who may be lame but rates as high as any Diehard you care to mention."

But the idea of welding the best men of both teams into one was obviously sensible and eventually both Peppone and Don Camillo had to admit it.

"We'll talk about it another day," said Don Camillo, retiring to the rectory.

"Yes, another day," echoed Peppone, withdrawing to the People's Palace.

The next day the two men met on neutral ground, each of them accompanied by a group of backers.

"I don't want to be mixed up in this business," said Don Camillo. "My job is to be a priest, and so I've turned it over to this committee of experts."

"My job is to be mayor," echoed Peppone, "and so I've put it up to a committee too."

"Then let the two committees get together," concluded Don Camillo.

"Exactly," said Peppone, "I shall stay on merely as an observer, and whatever the committees decide suits me. It should be easy enough to reach a decision, because after having made a dispassionate analysis of the Diehards, it's obvious that we should take their center man and leave the rest of the places to the Dynamos."

"That's just what we thought after we had taken the Dynamos under careful consideration. Give us Smilzo, and we'll supply the other ten."

Peppone gritted his teeth.

"I don't want to influence the committees' decision, but one thing is sure: if you like it, then it's just as I say, and if you don't, then it's just as I say too. And you can thank God for the honor of having one of your men play with a team like ours."

"Smilzo will be a decided handicap to the Diehards," said Don

Camillo, "but we want to show that on our side there's a real spirit of conciliation."

"Then you and your dummies can go to hell," Peppone shouted.

"If the committees have no more to say," said Don Camillo, "we may as well adjourn."

The head of the committee chosen by Don Camillo threw out his arms in despair. And so did the head of Peppone's committee. Then both parties went home.

Three days later a new challenge arrived from Torricella.

NOTICE

In order to give a chance to the two teams
which we have challenged
Instead of beating them one after the other,
Our Torricella team has decided to take
them both on together.
Hence the Torricella Eleven will play the
Diehard-Dynamo twenty-two.

The necessity of forming a single team was now more urgent than ever, and the druggist, together with the doctor, managed to form a committee to effect a liason between the two already existing committees. This was a very complicated affair, but finally the two committees met for the purpose of making a final decision.

"I bow to the will of the joint committee," said Don Camillo, who was the first to take the floor. "But since it's inevitable that the committee make up a half-and-half team, I say that the Diehards will furnish six players and the Dynamos five."

"I agree," said Peppone, "Diehards five and Dynamos six."

For a moment Don Camillo respected the silence which followed upon this declaration. Then he said:

"Since this point is bound to hold up the committee's deliberations, why don't we settle it by drawing cards?"

A pack of cards was produced, and Don Camillo and Peppone drew a card each. Peppone won by a single point, and it was decided that the Dynamos should contribute six men to the team and the Diehards five.

"In this case," said Don Camillo, "it's only fair that a Diehard be the captain."

"Democracy has very definite regulations," retorted Peppone. "You may not know it, Father, but there you are. In a democratic system the majority rules. So we shall choose our own captain."

Don Camillo shook his head.

"That's Communism for you!" he exclaimed. "Once they've seized power, they install a dictatorship under a democratic label."

"Sport has nothing to do with politics," Peppone protested. "But in order to give the lie to your reactionary slander, let's settle it with another draw."

This time Don Camillo won, and the Diehards chose a team captain. The next day the mixed team met for a first practice. The game lasted exactly eight minutes, after which the two factions had a free-for-all fight. The next day brought considerable improvement, because the Dynamos and Diehards began roughing it up in the dressing-room long before the game. On the third day the players didn't fight either in the dressing-room or on the field. They fought outside the field, before they ever got there. On the fourth day, after they had exhausted all other possible dodges, they actually played a game, but with the saddest results imaginable. And the following day things went even worse. They couldn't operate with any teamwork whatsoever, but seemed to be eleven savages who were making their first acquaintance with a ball and kicking it around at random.

Meanwhile, time was going by. The day of the match was drawing near, and still no progress had been made. Finally the last day came. After the final, eminently unsuccessful practice game, Don Camillo and Peppone found themselves going back to the village together.

"So," said Peppone, "we're going to reap the result of your stubbornness tomorrow. If you'd given in to me and let the Dynamos defend the honor of the village, we shouldn't be having any of this trouble."

"Peppone," said Don Camillo, "I know my boys, and I say that all our trouble is your fault. You used your usual obstructionist tactics to make us hand you over the controls. I said 'make us' because anyone with fine feelings and conscience will always yield a point, and that is exactly what we are going to do. Your bullying has met with success. The Diehards are withdrawing and your Dynamos will play. Don't pretend to make a fuss, because I know that the Dynamos have been holding a practice of their own every day, on the sly, and your pretense of training with us hasn't hurt your form."

Peppone did not bother to make a denial. He slipped away, and two hours later the village was plastered with big red posters.

> The Diehards have withdrawn their men
> because of admitted technical failings
> and so tomorrow's match will be
> played by an all-Dynamo team,
> sole defender of the village's honor.

Before going to bed Don Camillo went to kneel before the Crucified Christ.

"Lord," he prayed, "don't let them lose the match tomorrow. Not for their sake, because they don't deserve to win, but for mine. Don't let them lose, that is, unless you want to lead me into the temptation of rejoicing over their defeat."

"Don Camillo," Christ answered, "you know that I have no dealings with sport!"

Peppone's men made a miserable showing and Torricella scored a large number of goals against them. Don Camillo was unable to resist temptation and inwardly rejoiced over their discomfiture. He rejoiced outwardly as well, and with the devil hot upon his trail challenged the Torricella team to a match with the Diehards the following Sunday. The Diehards won. This victory seemed to call for a celebration and he called the Diehards together.

"Boys," he said, "I have three magnificent capons in my chicken coop. Sunday evening we'll eat them and drink to the health of the Dynamos. This isn't top secret, so if you happen to say something about it, no harm is done."

Obviously several people did, quite accidentally, spread the good word, because almost immediately the whole village knew that on Sunday evening the rectory would be the scene of what was dubbed "the revenge supper."

In order to make the occasion more festive, the Diehards needed a song, and Don Camillo sat up most of one night in order to write the words and most of the next in order to set them to music on the church organ. On Thursday night, he emerged from the sacristy with words and music complete and plenty of time to teach his boys the song so that they could come out with it at the supper. The tune was simple, and if necessary they could always read the words. He was quite pleased with himself as he returned to the rectory for the night, and before going to bed, he decided to take a look at the three capons in his chicken coop. Alas, the capons were gone, and so were three hens. All that was left were one bedraggled chick and a scrawny rooster. To take the place of the missing capons, a sign was hung on the wall which said in dog-Latin: *Crescete et moltiplicorum.*

Increase and multiply, indeed! Don Camillo was breathless with indignation, and seizing the sign, he went to tell his troubles to the Christ over the main altar.

"Lord," he panted, "they've stolen my chickens!"

"I'm sorry to hear it," Christ answered with a smile. "But before making any such categorical statement you'd better make sure they didn't just run away."

Don Camillo held up the sign.

"I know what I'm talking about, Lord," he said. "Look what the thieves left behind! Isn't it disgusting?"

"You don't expect a petty thief to write good Latin, do you, Don Camillo?"

"I'm not talking about the Latin. I'm concerned with the impudence of his adding insult to injury. Lord, who in the world could it be?"

These words reminded Don Camillo of the real delinquent, his dog Thunder. Why hadn't Thunder barked and given the alarm? He went to look for the dog and found him lying peacefully in his kennel.

"You traitor!" the priest shouted. "You're in enemy pay!"

What angered him even more than the loss of the chickens were the disturbances of the festive supper. He was pacing up and down the church square, when a voice roused him from his ire.

"Have you insomnia, Father? What keeps you up so late?"

The speaker was the carabinieri sergeant, who was coming back from his evening rounds, together with one of his men.

"I've been robbed of my chickens! Don Camillo exclaimed. "At ten o'clock, when I went into the sacristy, they were there, and when I came out at eleven, they had disappeared. I was playing the organ, and someone crept up, under cover of the music . . ."

"Didn't your dog bark?"

"That's just what I mean. Perhaps he did bark, but I couldn't hear him."

"And do you suspect any one in particular?"

Don Camillo threw out his arms.

Don Camillo shut himself up in the rectory and refused to see a soul. The whole village knew what had happened, and the Reds were rubbing their hands and laughing.

"It seems that the Sunday-night supper will be a paltry affair. Well, if they haven't the capons they can feed on their new song!"

The supper was canceled, and that evening Don Camillo was in the depths of despair. At eight o'clock he whistled for Thunder to come get a bowl of soup, but Thunder failed to respond. Don Camillo resolved to find him, and went out on the road leading away from the village. Ten minutes later he walked through Peppone's vegetable garden and into the dark hall of his house. From the kitchen there came echoes of loud laughter, and Don Camillo turned the doorknob and went in. Peppone was sitting at the table, together with Smilzo, Brusco, Bigio and the rest of the gang, over a dish of roast chicken, and at the sight of Don Camillo they were positively petrified in their chairs.

"Excuse me, Peppone," said Don Camillo, "but I'm looking for my dog. Do you happen to have seen him?"

Peppone shook his head, but Don Camillo had keen eyes and knew better. He lifted up the edge of the table-cloth and saw

Thunder crouching under the table with a heaping dish of chicken bones before him.

"He just dropped in," Peppone exclaimed lamely.

"I see," said Don Camillo.

Thunder flattened himself out on the floor in shame.

"If you'd care to join us, Father, please sit down," said Peppone.

"I've had my supper, thank you. Good evening."

Don Camillo walked out, and Thunder, after a questioning look at Peppone, followed the priest at a distance, dragging his tail. When they reached the rectory, the priest turned on him and said indignantly:

"You thief!"

And since this word seemed to make very little impression the priest added with utter scorn:

"You've sold out to the Russians!"

The next day the carabinieri sergeant received several anonymous letters, and the affair assumed a sudden importance. Six chickens don't amount to much, but when there is reason to think that the theft has been committed by the mayor, then there is a political angle to it. Peppone received an unexpected visit from the law.

"Sorry, Mr. Mayor, but I must do my duty. Can you tell me where you were between ten and eleven o'clock of last Thursday evening? You weren't at home, we know that. At five minutes past ten you were seen climbing over the fence around the rectory garden. There are three witnesses to that. And others saw you climb over your own fence three quarters of an hour later."

Peppone was as confused as a child.

"That's my business," he finally sputtered.

"And where did you get the five chickens you ate at your house Sunday night?"

"That's my business, too."

The sergeant received equally unsatisfactory replies to his other questions, and finally went away saying:

"You'll have to tell the court."

Now the affair took on really colossal proportions. Mayor Giuseppe Bottazzi was accused of being a vulgar chicken thief and summoned to appear before the magistrates' court in the nearest city. How had the mighty fallen, when the tamer of lions was laid low by a church mouse.

Don Camillo found himself in court, without knowing exactly why. But there he was, and there in the dock, was Peppone. It looked very much like the end of his career.

"The accused has steadily refused to say where he spent the hour between ten and eleven o'clock, that is between the time when he was seen climbing the rectory fence and the time when he was seen sneaking back over his own. Has he, even at this late date, anything to say?"

The magistrate looked at Peppone and everyone in the courtroom turned their eyes in his direction. But Peppone helplessly threw out his arms.

"I can't say where I was," he answered in a low voice.

"Do you refuse, absolutely?"

"It isn't that I refuse, Judge. I simply can't do it."

At this point Don Camillo asked if he might be allowed to say a word.

"From ten to eleven o'clock, Mayor Bottazzi was with me in the sacristy," he stated.

"Why didn't you say so before?"

"Nobody asked me. And besides, before testifying, I had to secure my superiors' permission."

The magistrate shot him a questioning look.

"Excuse me, Father, but what brought him to the church at that hour, when you were playing the organ. Was it for a singing lesson?"

"The sound of the organ doesn't prevent one of the faithful from saying his prayers."

"I don't deny that, Father, but I don't see why the accused didn't give the law this explanation. No one need hesitate to use church-going as an alibi. If I'd spent my time in church I'd be glad to say so."

"But you're not a Communist Party leader and mayor of a village in a region where the Party is so strong," Don Camillo re plied. "He comes to church at an hour when his Party comrades can't see him. If your Honor requires any further explanation . . ."

"No, nothing more," the magistrate interrupted, smiling broadly.

"Then just let me say this: Giuseppe Bottazzi is a good-hearted, hard-working, God-fearing fellow," concluded Don Camillo.

Don Camillo made the trip home on Peppone's motorcycle, but Peppone did not open his mouth the whole way. When they came to the rectory he gave a deep sigh.

"You made a laughing stock of me," he said plaintively. "The reactionary press will have a heyday with this story."

"They'd have treated you a good deal more roughly if you'd been convicted of being a chicken thief," said Don Camillo.

"But you've got me in hot water with the Party. If I tell the truth they'll bawl me out for being so stupid as to steal chickens. And if I stick to your version of events, then they'll brand me as even more of a fool."

"Never mind about the Party," grumbled Don Camillo. "I'm in hot water with Almighty God. Here I am, a priest, and I've given false testimony before a court of law! How shall I ever get up my nerve to go into church?"

Peppone jumped off his motorcycle and marched into the church and straight up to the main altar. He remained standing there for several minutes and then went back outside.

"You can go in now," he said. "I've fixed things up for you. I'd like to see you straighten things out for me with the Party in the same way!"

Don Camillo threw out his arms.

"Of course it's easier to deal with God than one of your Party bosses. They never forgive anything."

Exactly in what terms Peppone had "fixed things" up no one ever knew. But when, late that night, Don Camillo summoned up the nerve to go into church and kneel in front of the main altar, the Crucified Christ said:

"What in the world have you been up to now, Don Camillo?"

"I had the Bishop's permission," said Don Camillo in justification of his perjury.

"He's quite a fellow, too!" Christ sighed, half smiling.

: [69] :

THE MAN WITHOUT A HEAD

DON CAMILLO LEAPED TO HIS feet and very nearly shouted, because the discovery was so sensational. Just then the sound of the clock in the church tower ringing three o'clock in the morning brought him around to the thought that the only sensible thing to do at that hour was to go to sleep. But before dozing off he read over the extraordinary bit of news he had just found in his predecessor's diary. "On November 8, 1752," the passage began, "something quite terrible happened . . ."

The eighteenth-century parish priest had explained the mystery of the black stone and at the same time provided Don Camillo with an excellent subject for his Sunday sermon. Now he closed the book and hurried to bed, because three hours of Sunday morning had already gone by.

"Brethren," Don Camillo began his sermon, "today I want to talk to you about the black stone, the one you have all seen in one corner of the cemetery with the mysterious inscription: *November 8, 1752. Here lies a man without face or name.* For years this stone has been the subject of research and discussion. Now at last the mystery has been made clear."

A murmur of amazement greeted these words. And Don Camillo continued:

"Every evening for the last few months I've been looking over the old books and registers which were turned up in a forgotten wardrobe some time ago, and as you know I've found all sorts of interesting information. But just last night I came across the most extraordinary item of all, which I shall now translate into contemporary language for your benefit.

"'On November 8, 1752, something quite terrible happened. For a whole year some marauders known as the 'hole-in-the-wall' gang" because of the method they used to break into respectable houses, had been wreaking havoc all over the countryside. None of them had ever been caught red-handed. But on the night of November 8, Giuseppe Folini, from Crocilone, a merchant by profession, was awakened by a suspicious noise and after he had got out of bed to go down to his cellar storeroom, he realized that the noise came from that part of the wall which bordered on the open fields and had no door or window of any kind. Obviously someone was boring his way into the cellar and such an enterprise could only be conducted by the "hole-in-the-wall" gang.

"'A few minutes later, while Folini was still standing there, indecisively, a piece of plaster fell from a spot about six inches above the floor and the moonlight streaming in from a window across the way allowed him to see a brick moving. Soon the brick was lifted out and a gaunt white hand came through the hole and removed another brick beside it. Now that the hole was sufficiently widened, an arm came through, all the way up to the elbow, and began feeling the surface of the surrounding wall in order to ascertain whether anything hung there which might fall and spread the alarm.

" 'Folini, who is a big, strapping fellow, took hold of the wrist, determined not to let it go, and at the same time he shouted for help. Various members of the family arrived upon the scene and one of his sons tied a rope around the intruder's arm, thus making him a prisoner.

" 'Because Folini's house is in a lonely and isolated spot, they could not hope to arouse the village by giving the alarm. And for fear of falling into a trap set by the prisoner's accomplices, they did not dare set foot outside until morning. They had captured one member of the gang and when he was turned over to the police he would probably supply the names of the others.

" 'They ventured out at dawn and made their way cautiously toward the back of the house. But all they found was a headless body. The bandits had feared that the captured man might be compelled by torture to reveal their names, or that the knowledge of his name might lead to the discovery of the rest. And so, in order to cheat the law of any clue whatsoever, they had chopped off his head and carried it away.

" 'Since nothing on the body permitted identification, I buried it by night in one corner of the cemetery and raised a stone over the grave with the inscription: *November 8, 1752. Here lies a man without face or name.*' "

Don Camillo closed the old diary, looked down for a moment at the confusion written upon his hearers' faces and concluded:

"And so, brethren, this terrible tale has cleared up a mystery. Under the black stone there sleeps a man without face or name. A terrible tale, indeed. But there is something far more terrible rampant among us at this very hour: the presence of a hundred headless men in this village of ours who are working night and day to bore a hole through the unguarded wall of our houses, steal the householders' brains away and leave in their place the propagandistic stuffing of an extreme left-wing party, which for obvious reasons I shall not call by name. . . ."

The story of the headless man made a great impression upon the village, and everyone felt an urge to go look at the black stone. The old Folini house at Crocilone was still standing, but it served only as a barn and the foot of the wall on the side of the open fields was overgrown with weeds. Now these weeds were cut down and the hole mentioned in the story was exposed to view. All those who passed this way after dark pedaled their bicycles extra fast or accelerated their motorcycles because of the shiver that ran up and down their spines.

Then came the November mists, and the river took on a dark and mysterious air. One evening, as she walked along the embankment road, on her way back from Castellina, old Signora Gabini met a man without a head. She ran all the rest of the way home and arrived in such a state of collapse that she had to be put to bed. She asked for the priest, and the fellow who went to the village after Don Camillo stopped for a drink in the arcade cafe and told the whole story. It spread like wildfire through the village, and when Don Camillo returned from his visit to Signora Gabini he found a small crowd of people waiting in the church square to hear what sort of deviltry was in the air.

"Sheer nonsense!" said Don Camillo. "If the old woman weren't in such a bad way, it would be laughable."

As a matter of fact, she had told a tale that made very little sense.

"Father! I saw him!"

"Saw whom?"

"The headless man, the one buried under the black stone. I came face to face with him, all of a sudden."

"Face to face? But if he didn't have any head? . . ."

"He didn't have any head, that's just it. He was riding slowly along on a bicycle . . ."

Here Don Camillo couldn't help smiling.

"That's a good one! How could he ride a bicycle if he died in 1752, before bicycles were invented?"

"I don't know," she stuttered. "He must have learned how in the meantime. But I know it was him for sure, the man without a head."

Don Camillo's retelling of this account proved to be highly amusing and the notion of the headless man's having learned to ride a bicycle after his death was repeated from one house to another. For a couple of weeks, nothing out of the way happened, and then suddenly the man without a head reappeared. Giacomone, the boatman, met him shortly after dusk, on the path leading through the acacia grove. This time he was not on a bicycle, but on foot, a means of locomotion much more suitable to an eighteenth-century ghost. Giacomone himself told the story to Don Camillo.

"You've been drinking too much, Giacomone," was the priest's comment.

"I've sworn off for the last three years," Giacomone replied. "And I'm not the sort to be easily scared. I'm just telling you what I saw with my own eyes: a man minus a head."

"Don't you think he might have been a man with his jacket pulled up over his head in order to protect himself from the rain?"

"I saw the stump of his neck, I tell you."

"You didn't really see any such thing; you just fancy you did. Go back tomorrow to the exact place where you thought you saw him and you'll find the branch or bush that gave you the illusion."

The next day Giacomone did go back, and some twenty other villagers with him. They located the exact spot of the encounter, but they saw no feature of the landscape which might have seemed to be a man without a head. But the headless man appeared a week later to a young man, and at this point people stopped wondering whether or not the apparitions were genuine. They asked, rather: "Why is the headless man among us? What is he after?" And they did not have to look far for an answer. The headless man was looking for his head. He wanted it to lie with the rest of his body, in consecrated ground. Only Don Camillo refused to offer any guess as to the motive which caused the headless man to wander about the river roads and embankment. "I don't want to hear such foolishness," he said to anyone who questioned him. But one day he was deeply disturbed and confided his trouble to the Christ above the altar.

"Lord, since I've had this parish, I've never seen so many people come to church. Except for Peppone and his henchmen, the whole village has turned up, old and young, infirm and healthy."

"Well, aren't you glad, Don Camillo?"

"No, because they're driven only by fear. And I don't mean the fear of God, either. And it bothers me to see them in distress. I wish the nightmare could have an end."

Christ sighed.

"Don Camillo, aren't you one of these fear-stricken people yourself?"

Don Camillo threw out his arms in protest.

"Don Camillo doesn't know what fear is!" he said proudly.

"That's very important, Don Camillo. Your fearlessness is sufficient to liberate the others from their fear."

Don Camillo felt better, but the apparitions of the headless man continued, and they were further complicated by the intervention of Peppone, who came up to him one day in the square and said in a voice loud enough to be heard on the other side of the river:

"Father, I hear strange talk of a man without a head. Do you know anything about him?"

"Not I," said Don Camillo, feigning astonishment. "What's it all about?"

"It seems that a man without a head has been seen at night around the village."

"A man without a head? It must be someone looking for the People's Palace in order to sign up with your party."

Peppone did not bat an eyelash.

"Perhaps it's a ghost cooked up in the rectory and sent out to scare people into hiding behind the skirts of the priest."

"No ghosts are cooked up in the rectory, either with or without a head," retorted Don Camillo.

"Oh, do you import them from America?"

"Why should we import them, when your party manufactures the best headless ghosts to be found?"

Peppone gave a mocking laugh.

"It's a known fact that the ghost is of your fabrication."

"It's fabricated by diseased minds. It's true that I told the story of the headless man, but that's history. Anyone can see the document for himself."

Don Camillo led the way to the rectory, with Peppone, Smilzo, Brusco, Bigio and the other Red big shots following after. The book was still on the priest's desk, and now he pointed it out to Peppone.

"Look up November 8, 1752, and read what you find there."

Peppone leafed through the diary until he came to the passage in question. He read it twice through and then handed the book to the others.

"If you have any doubts as to the authenticity of the document, you're free to submit it to any expert you please for study. My only fault is not to have foreseen that a two-hundred year old story would work so dangerously upon people's imaginations."

Bigio nodded.

"So there's some truth to the story of the headless man, after all," he mumbled.

"The truth is just what's set down in that diary," said Don Camillo. "All the rest is reckless imagination."

Peppone and his henchmen went thoughtfully away. That same evening two more villagers ran into the headless man, and the next day a delegation of mothers came to Don Camillo.

"Father, you must do something," they told him. "You must bless the grave marked by the black stone or say a Mass for the repose of the occupant's tormented soul."

"There's no tormented soul," said Don Camillo firmly. "There are only your benighted imaginings, and I don't want to bolster them by appearing to take them seriously."

"We'll go to the bishop!" the women shouted.

"Go where you please. But no one can compel me to believe in ghosts!"

The nightmare became more and more of a menace. Dozens of people had seen the headless man and even the most hard-headed of the villagers were tainted with the contagion of fear. Don Camillo finally resolved to do something about it. Late one night, after everyone had gone to bed he knocked at Peppone's door.

"I've been called to the bedside of a dying man. It's too far for me to go by bicycle. Will you take me in your car?"

It was pouring rain, and this request seemed logical enough. Peppone took out the car which served by day as a public bus.

"Just drive me by the rectory first," said Don Camillo.

Once they were there he got out and insisted that Peppone come inside.

"I've got to talk with you," he explained once they were in his study.

"And was it necessary to put up such a show?"

"Yes, and this isn't the end of it, either. The whole village is going mad and those of us with our wits still about us must do something to dissipate this terror. What I am about to propose isn't honest, but I assume full responsibility for it before God and man. We must pretend to have found a skull. We'll decide together on the most appropriate place, and I'll bury it there, together with half of an eighteenth century coin. The other half, of course, will go under the black stone. Then you, as mayor, will order some digging in the place where we have left the skull. Is that clear?"

"It seems rather gruesome to me," Peppone stammered, with perspiration breaking out on his forehead.

"It's more terrible to see the growth of a collective frenzy among our people. We must drive out one fear with another. Now, let's get down to details."

It was two o'clock in the morning when Peppone went out to his car. Almost immediately he began cursing.

"What's the matter?" called Don Camillo from the door.

"The battery must be on the blink; it won't start."

"Leave it here and come back tomorrow morning," said Don

Camillo. "I'll walk home with you. Getting wet doesn't bother me."

They had walked some distance along the road skirting the village when all of a sudden Peppone halted and gripped Don Camillo's arm. There walking ahead of them was the headless man. A flash of lightning allowed them to make him out quite clearly. He walked slowly on, and Peppone and Don Camillo followed. At a certain point he took a narrow road leading toward the river, and stopped under an old oak tree. Don Camillo and Peppone stopped too, and once more they saw his figure in a flash of lightning. A third flash followed, and almost simultaneously a blast of thunder. The lightning had struck the hollow oak and leveled it to the ground. And the headless man had disappeared.

Don Camillo found himself curled up in bed without the slightest idea of how he had got there. They awakened him early the next morning and dragged him outside. Half the village was gathered around the fallen oak and amid the uptorn roots there shone a white skull. No one had any doubt whatsoever. The skull belonged to the man without a head, and the way it had appeared proved it. That same morning they buried it under the black stone, and everyone knew for certain that the nightmare was over. Don Camillo went home in a daze and stopped to kneel before the altar.

"Lord," he stammered, "thank you for having punished my presumption. Now I know what it is to be afraid."

"Have you taken up a belief in headless ghosts, Don Camillo?"

"No," the priest replied. "But for a brief moment last night, my mind was invaded by the collective fear."

"That's practically a scientific explanation," Christ murmured.

"It's just a way of covering up my shame," Don Camillo said humbly.

Anyhow, the headless man acquired a head. Was it rightly his, or no? The main thing is that it pacified him and he no longer inflamed the popular imagination. And the great rolling river quietly carried one more story, like a dead leaf, down to the sea.

THE STRANGER

THE DILAPIDATED LITTLE CAR
drove slowly around the village square, skirting the arcades, and
came to a stop in front of the draper's. A thin, almost distin-
guished looking man about forty-five years old, got out. His left
arm seemed to be glued to his side, all the way down to the
elbow, and this detail contributed to the definite picture his ap-

pearance left in the mind of an onlooker. He took a big leather case out of the car and strode decisively into the draper's shop. The draper didn't need to look at the calling-card held out by the visitor to know what he was after.

"I'm overstocked," he explained. "Business has been slow for some time, and the floods gave it a knockout blow."

The stranger opened his case and showed his samples. The material was very fine, and the draper couldn't help eyeing it with interest.

"I can't buy a thing just now," he said finally. "Try coming back in the spring. I can't make any promises, but I hope we can do some business together."

The salesman thanked him politely, asked if he might jot down the name and address, put his samples back in the case and returned to the car, which sputtered some twenty yards down the street and then stopped, obviously because there was something drastically wrong with the motor. Luckily for the stranger, Peppone's workshop was only fifty yards farther on, and he was able to cover this distance fairly fast in spite of the fact that he had to get out and push the car. When Peppone heard the blast of a horn, he came promptly to the door.

"Hello there," said the stranger. "I'm having a little trouble. Can you see what it's all about?"

Peppone had shuddered when he heard the stranger's voice and now he said rudely:

"Not now. I'm too busy."

"Well, I can't get it started, so I'll just leave it here. Give it a look as soon as you can, will you?" And he walked away, while Peppone stared after him from the door.

"As soon as I can, eh? No, as soon as I feel like it!"

He went back to his lathe in the workshop, but try as he would to put the matter behind him, he couldn't get the stranger off his mind. No matter how often he told himself that the similarity was a matter of pure coincidence, the more he was persuaded that it wasn't coincidence at all. Finally he interrupted his work, threw open the wide glass-paned door of the workshop and pushed in the car. Shutting the door behind him, he searched the car's dashboard compartment for its registration paper. He took a quick look at this and quickly put it back where he had found it. No, it wasn't a coincidence at all. He had a wild impulse to kick the car to pieces, but on second thought he decided to repair it. The roar that burst from the motor when he pulled out the self-starter caused him to chortle with joy.

"I'd like to see his face when he finds out what a mess it's in!" he said to himself. He lifted off the hood and started to work. When he had taken out the cylinder block, he called his boy and sent him to find Smilzo. A few minutes later he was giving Smilzo some very definite instructions.

"I'm your man, Chief," said Smilzo. "I'll stand out there under the arcade and as soon as I see the fellow coming, I'll run to call the police. Then, when a policeman arrives, I'll follow."

Ten minutes later the stranger returned and immediately scrutinized the motor of the car.

"I thought so," he said after a while.

"It's a serious business," Peppone explained, enumerating all the minor bits of business connected with it. But he was interrupted by the arrival of the village policeman, in full uniform.

"Good morning, Mr. Mayor," said the policeman, lifting his fingers to his cap in a salute. "There's a paper here which you must sign."

Peppone looked at him with annoyance.

"Tell the clerk that this isn't my time for signing papers. I'll sign it when I come to the Town Hall this afternoon."

The policeman saluted again and made an about-face. Peppone continued to list the deficiencies he had found in the motor until for the second time he was interrupted. Smilzo drew himself to attention before him, raising his left arm and a clenched fist.

"Chief," he said, "the proofs of our poster are here. We've got to decide whether the speech will be at nine o'clock or ten."

"Ten," Peppone answered decisively.

"Very good, Chief," said Smilzo, raising his fist again and swinging about on his heels.

This time Peppone managed to finish his description of the motor's woes. And at the end the stranger said:

"Now tell me whether you can make the repairs, and if so how long you will take and what you will charge me."

Peppone shrugged his shoulders.

"If we telephone to the bus station in the city, we may be able to get the necessary parts out by the evening bus. The work will take two and a half days and the cost will be, in round figures, between twenty and twenty-five thousand liras."

The stranger did not blench.

"I'll put in a telephone call to Milan and an hour from now I can give you an answer."

Peppone went back to his lathe.

"Nuts to you!" he whispered to himself as the door closed behind the stranger.

Early in 1943, when Peppone had received his draft call, he went to the nearest recruiting station to say:

"I'm forty-four years old and I went all through the last war. Why do you have to pick on me?"

"If you hadn't been called up and were left at home, what would you do?"

"I'd keep up my usual trade, which is that of a mechanic."

"Then just pretend you're still at home. It's because you're a mechanic that the army needs you."

Peppone was sent to some old barracks, which had been turned into a repair depot for army vehicles, and there, in the uniform of a corporal, he went on with his old trade. For a month this job was quite a soft one, because in spite of the gray-green uniform and insignia, Peppone and his fellows enjoyed considerable liberty. Until one day a cursed captain came into the picture, and then their troubles began.

The cursed captain had been in active combat all over the map. On his chest he wore a complete assortment of decorations and in his buttonhole a German ribbon. During the retreat from Russia a shell fragment had put his left arm out of commission, and because he didn't want to be invalided home, they had sent him to create some order in the depot where Corporal Giuseppe Bottazzi was working. At first the boys thought that within a week they could make mincemeat of the captain with the withered arm. But instead, after a week had gone by, they found that their soft job had turned into a very tough one, for the captain was a martinet who had army regulations on the brain.

Corporal Peppone, the top mechanic, simply couldn't believe it when he was confined to the guardhouse for ten consecutive days. One morning, in the courtyard, when the captain with the withered arm passed by, he presented arms with a shaft of cement which the strength of three ordinary men would not have have sufficed to lift off the ground. But the captain was not impressed. He looked at Peppone and said coldly:

"An ordinary crane, without even the rank of corporal, can lift heavier weights than that with less waste of energy. Perhaps that's because the crane is more intelligent than you are. Ten more days of confinement will give you time to think it over."

Two days later Peppone's wife and child came to the nearby town for a visit, but Peppone wasn't allowed to see them. When the captain looked in at his cell he found him a raging tiger.

"Take it easy, Corporal," he said, "or you may get into really hot water."

"I want to see my wife and son!" howled Peppone.

"Thousands of better men than you would like to see their mothers and wives and children, but they've given their lives for their country. You're a very poor soldier and you're only getting what you deserve."

Peppone could have knocked the captain down with a single blow, but all he did was grit his teeth and protest:

"I went all through the last war and brought home a silver medal!"

"The fact that you were of age when the last war came

around isn't any particular virtue. And it isn't enough to win a medal; you've got to live up to it."

Every last man at the depot had it in for the captain with the withered arm. He stood over them from reveille to taps, and because he knew a thing or two about motors, he wouldn't let them get away with any work that wasn't absolutely first class.

On the evening of July 26, 1943, Mussolini suffered his well-known eclipse from the political scene. The next morning the captain was in the sleeping quarters when the men got up. Before they could go to breakfast he addressed them as follows:

"There's to be no change here. The same repair jobs are waiting for us, and it's still our duty to carry them out as best we can."

During the heavy air raids of that August, the captain arrived at the men's quarters along with the first signal of alarm and stayed until the all-clear had sounded. On September 8, the Germans' liberation of Mussolini complicated the political situation further. There were panic and disorganization everywhere. The captain gave each of his men a gun and a round of ammunition and said simply:

"You'll sleep fully dressed, in order to be prepared for any emergency."

He slept on a table in the quartermaster's office and the next morning, after passing his men in review, he told them:

"The colonel has assigned us to the defense of the west side of the barracks and the vehicle entrance. Our orders are to let nobody in."

The west side of the barracks, including the repair depot, was located in the former stables, adjacent to the open fields, and when Peppone and the others heard the word "defense," they thought of the single round of ammunition each one of them had upon him, and stared nervously at one another. At ten o'clock the place was surrounded by German tanks and a German officer came to ask the colonel to surrender. Upon the colonel's refusal the heavy *Panzer* in front of the main gate shattered it with a single shot and rolled in. Meanwhile, the *Panzer* at the vehicle entrance didn't even bother to fire. It just bumped the rusty gate and with the first bit of pressure put upon the hinges, the whole thing collapsed, as if it had been attached to the walls with thread.

Some of the mechanics were drawn up along the wall, while Peppone and four others were stationed in the sentry-box which guarded the gate. Now, where the gate had been, there stood the cursed captain with the withered arm, his legs spread far apart and a pistol in his hand, pointing at the *Panzer*. It was a ridiculous thing, if you like, but the captain wore a German ribbon in his buttonhole and this brought the German tank to a stop. These professional military types have a special way of looking at things and you can't take it away from them. Out of the tank turret popped a German officer, who proceeded to give a salute. The captain put his pistol into its holster and answered in kind. The German jumped down from the *Panzer*, drew himself up with puppet-like stiffness in front of the Italian and saluted him again, receiving the same salute in return.

"I'm sorry to say, I must ask you to surrender," said the German type in hesitant Italian.

The Italian type took the decoration out of his buttonhole and handed it to the German. Then he stepped out of the way. The German made a slight bow, climbed back into the tank, stood up to his waist in the turret and shouted an order, which caused the vehicle to move forward. As he passed before the Italian, the German raised his hand to his cap in a salute, which the Italian duly returned. After that, the Italian calmly lit a cigarette and when two German soldiers approached, he preceded them to the center of the courtyard, where the colonel, along with the other officers and men who had been made prisoners, had been standing waiting.

The mechanics made for the open fields. Peppone was the last of them to run for freedom, because he wanted to see the business of those two military types through to the end. Two hours later he was in civilian clothes, and the next day, from the attic in which he was hiding, he saw a little group of Italian soldiers marched off under German Tommy guns to the train that was to take them to a prison camp far away. At the end of the group were the officers, and among them the cursed captain with the withered arm.

"I hope you don't come back until I call for you in person," Peppone mumbled to himself.

But he did not forget the captain. The final insult still rankled in his mind. When the *Panzer* was still outside the gate and the captain was on his way to meet it, he had called out to Peppone, who was trembling in the sentry box with his four companions:

"Now we'll see if Corporal Bottazzi is a real weight lifter!"

Peppone had sworn that one day he would make the captain with the withered arm eat these words, and now by some miracle he had the fellow at his mercy. It gave him no little satisfaction to see that cocky "active combat" officer reduced to the status of traveling salesman.

The stranger didn't go to make a telephone call. He went to sit down in the church, where he could quietly count his resources. Turning his pockets inside out and squeezing the last penny from them, he figured that he had twenty-two thousand three hundred liras. And he would have to spend two or three days in the village.

"If it comes to the worst, I can always pawn my watch," he concluded, and he went back to Peppone's workshop.

"All right, you can go ahead with the work," he said. "And when you've finished, send word to me at the tavern, where I expect to rent a room. Try to get it done as fast as you can."

Without looking up Peppone muttered:

"*As fast as I can,* eh? We're not in the army now, good-looking! Here I work as I please."

That evening, before he laid off, he cast a scornful glance at the dilapidated car.

"His good times are over, all right!" he sneered.

At the tavern he saw the stranger sitting in a corner over a plate of bread and sausage, with a bottle of water in front of him.

"If all your customers are so lavish, you'll soon be a rich man!" he whispered to the proprietor.

The proprietor grimaced.

"They're just as proud as they're poor," he grumbled.

Peppone went home early. Sleepy as he was, he went into the workshop first. The bus had brought the parts necessary for the repair of the car. Peppone looked at the package and then swung it against his bench.

"*As fast as you can,* eh?" he exclaimed angrily. "Half starving, and he thinks he can still give out orders in the old way! I'll take three or four days, or a whole week, if I want to! And if that doesn't suit you, push your jalopy straight to hell. If you start kicking, I'll give you a couple of punches to go with it!" And as he passed in front of the midget car, he spit into the motor. "There's for you and your driver, you little fool!" he exclaimed.

After he had gone to bed he thought with irritation of the stranger, sitting there in the tavern.

"Stony broke, and yet he eats his salame with a fork!" he said disgustedly.

"Who's that?" asked his wife, waking up with a start.

"A pretty rascal, I can tell you! If he has the nerve to open his mouth, I'll murder him!"

"Don't get yourself in trouble, Peppone," murmured his wife, going back to sleep.

His anger at the rascal with the withered arm so upset Peppone's stomach that he got up after half an hour and went down to the kitchen after some bicarbonate of soda. He fancied he heard a noise from the workshop and took a look inside. Everything was in good order, and the dilapidated midget car was waiting peacefully, with its guts exposed to the air.

"*As fast as you can,* eh?" he exclaimed ironically. "Go give orders in your own house, jackass! The days of the puppets in uniform are over, you beastly reactionary warmonger!"

A moment later he turned back from the door.

"I want to look at those parts that came down by bus," he said to himself. "Here's hoping there are a few mistakes, such as to cause further delay. And you'll have to grin and bear it, that is unless you want to push your jalopy away."

The parts seemed to be quite satisfactory. In order to be quite sure, Peppone took the worn parts out of the motor and compared them. One piece had to be fitted more closely and he started to adjust it.

At six o'clock in the morning, Peppone was still working frantically, sweating and swearing all the while.

"I want to get this thing out of the way," he shouted between clenched teeth. "Otherwise I'll find myself in trouble."

At noon Peppone got into the car, slammed the door and tested the motor.

"It moves, and that ought to be enough to suit you," he grumbled. "If once you're out on the highway it breaks down, that's just too bad."

The important thing was to be sure it really would reach the highway. With this end in view, it was natural enough for Peppone to regulate the motor again, change the oil, test the clutch, brakes, points, carburetor and tires, tighten some screws on the chassis, fill the battery with distilled water, grease all the points that needed greasing and finally take a hose and wash the body. There is a limit to everything, and logically enough Peppone did not feel like doing any more. So Peppone's wife was the one to brush the upholstery, and not knowing anything about the rascal of an owner she did the job with impartiality and care.

When everything was done, Peppone sent his boy to tell the proprietor of the tavern to pass on the word that the jalopy was ready. Meanwhile Peppone went upstairs. He wanted to impress the stranger with his physical appearance as well as his accomplishment, and so he washed, shaved and put on a clean shirt.

"Now is time for the real fun!" he said, inwardly rejoicing. From the living-room he took a big sheet of paper with the heading: *Giuseppe Bottazzi. Repairs. Welding. Brakes. Ignition. Grease and oil.* He had always been proud of this paper, and now if ever was the time to use it. *"Bill no. . ."* And he proceeded to add the date and the debtor. He knew the stranger's first and last name perfectly well, but it seemed to him more impressive to leave them out. Let him appear to be someone totally unknown. Then he began to itemize the charges.

New Parts (detailed)......................	11,000	liras
3 quarts of oil	1,200	
Greasing and washing	800	
Telephone call and bus delivery	500	
Total expenses	13,500	
Labor	7,000	
Overtime	4,500	
Grand total	25,000	

Twenty-five thousand liras, and he could cough up every last one of them, if he wanted his car back. *"As fast as you can,* eh? But it costs more to get something in a hurry. It used to be different, but that was in the army!

Peppone came downstairs upon the stranger's arrival.

"Your car's ready," he said coldly.

"All fixed?"

"All fixed."

"And how much do I owe you?"

Peppone was inwardly jeering. This was the big moment. He took the bill out of his pocket, looked at it and then put it back.

"Everything included, parts and labor, 13,100 liras."

The stranger took three five-thousand lira notes from his wallet.

"Keep the difference," he said, getting into the car.

At the door he leaned out to ask:

"Do I make a left turn for the highway?"

"Yessir!" said Peppone, clicking his heels.

"Goodbye, Sergeant Bottazzi," said the stranger.

A quarter of a mile along the road, the stranger wondered why the devil he had dubbed the fellow a sergeant when he knew perfectly well that he was only the most pestiferous of corporals? Then he listened to the hum of the motor, which was acting as if it had only three instead of thirty thousand miles behind it.

Peppone stood at the door to the workshop, looking after the car.

"Devil take you and whoever brought you this way!" he exclaimed angrily as he went back inside. But he felt as puffed up as if he really were a sergeant.

THE GOLD RUSH

THE BOMBSHELL EXPLODED around Monday noon, when the newspapers arrived from the city. Someone from the village had won ten million liras in the National Lottery. The papers gave the names as Pepito Sbezzeguti, but there was no one in the village by either of these names. The local ticket-seller was besieged by questioners, but he could only throw out his arms discouragingly and say:

"Saturday was a market day and I sold tickets to any number of strangers. Probably one of them bought it. It's bound to come out, sooner or later."

But nothing came out at all, and curiosity remained at a high pitch, because people were convinced that Pepito Sbezzeguti was a false name. Sbezzeguti alone was plausible enough. Among the country people who came to the market there might be a Sbezzeguti. But a Pepito was out of the question. No exotic Pepito could possibly have come to a village market, where the trading was in corn, wheat, hay, livestock and cheese.

"I say it's an assumed name," said the keeper of the Molinetto tavern. "And if somebody goes under an assumed name, it means he's not a stranger, but a local man who wants to remain under cover."

This was a debatable point, but it was received as a piece of perfect logic, and people transferred their attention from the idea of a stranger to that of someone right among them. They conducted the search as ferociously as if they were looking for a criminal rather than a lottery winner. Even Don Camillo, with less ferocity, but almost equal curiosity, took an interest in the search. And because he had an idea that Christ didn't altogether approve his bloodhound activities, he went to justify himself before the altar.

"Lord, I'm not merely curious. I have a duty to perform. Anyone who has received such a favor from Divine Providence and not told his neighbors about it, deserves to be branded as an ingrate."

"Don Camillo," Christ replied, "even if Divine Providence takes an interest in lotteries (a point which is not necessarily to be granted), I don't see that it needs to beg for publicity. The fact in itself is all that matters, and you know its most important feature. Someone has won the jackpot, but why should you care to discover his identity? People who are less favored by fortune require your care."

But Don Camillo had the lottery prize on the brain and could find no rest until the mystery was solved. Finally a light shone upon his darkness. When the solution dawned upon him he was tempted to tug at the rope and ring the church bell. He managed to overcome this impulse, but he did go so far as to put on his cape and stroll about the village. When he came to Peppone's workshop he couldn't resist sticking in his head and wishing good-day to the mayor.

"Comrade Peppone, how do you do!"

Peppone looked up from his hammering and shot the priest a nervous glance.

"What's on your mind, Father?"

"Nothing. It just occurs to me that Pepito is a diminutive of Peppone. And I have an idea that by unscrambling all the letters of Pepito Sbezzeguti, the result would be something strangely like Giuseppe Bottazzi."

Peppone went right on hammering.

"Go give that to the Sunday puzzle page," he answered. "This is no place for anagrams; it's an honest man's workshop."

Don Camillo shook his head.

"I'm truly sorry that you're not the Pepito with ten millions in his pocket."

"I'm just as sorry as you are," said Peppone. "If I had them, I'd give you a couple just to persuade you to go home."

"Don't worry, Peppone, I'm happy to do you a favor free," said Don Camillo as he went his way.

Two hours later the whole village knew the meaning of an anagram, and in every house Pepito Sbezzeguti was dissected to see if he would yield up Giuseppe Bottazzi. That evening the Reds' general staff held a meeting at the People's Palace.

"Chief," said Smilzo, who was the first to speak, "the reactionaries have gone back to their old propagandistic device of spreading malicious slander. The whole village is up in arms over the suspicion that you're the winner of the ten million liras. We must make a quick comeback and nail the mud-slingers to the wall."

Peppone threw out his arms.

"To accuse a man of having won ten million liras isn't slander. It's slander to accuse a man of dishonesty. But there's nothing dishonest about winning a lottery prize."

"Chief," Smilzo insisted, "even the accusation of having done a good deed can constitute political slander. Slander is any accusation harmful to the Party."

"People are laughing behind our backs," put in Brusco. "We've got to stop them."

"We must post a printed statement for everybody to see," suggested Bigio, "a statement that makes the whole thing perfectly clear."

Peppone shrugged his shoulders.

"All right. We'll do something about it tomorrow."

Smilzo took a sheet of paper out of his pocket.

"Chief, in order to save you trouble, we've drawn up a statement for you. If you approve, we'll print it tonight and paste it up in the morning."

And he proceeded to read aloud:

"The undersigned, Giuseppe Bottazzi, hereby declares that he has no connection with Pepito Sbezzeguti, winner of ten million liras at the Lottery. It's useless for the reactionaries to slanderously link my name with that of the new millionaire.

Giuseppe Bottazzi."

Peppone shook his head.

"Until I see the accusation in print, I see no need for making a printed reply."

But Smilzo didn't agree.

"Chief, it seems to me foolish to wait for someone to take a pot shot at you before shooting in reply. The rule is to beat your enemy to the draw."

"The rule is to administer a swift kick to anyone who interferes in my personal affairs," said Peppone. "I don't need any defenders, thank you just the same. I'm quite capable of looking after myself."

Smilzo shrugged his shoulders.

"If that's the way you take it, there's nothing anyone can say."

"That *is* the way I take it!" shouted Peppone pounding the desk with his fist. "Every man for himself and the Party for all of us together!"

His henchmen went away without being convinced by anything he had said.

"This supine acceptance of the accusation seems very feeble to me," said Smilzo on the way home. "And then there's the complication of the anagram, too."

"Let's hope it turns out for the best," sighed Bigio.

After it had come out in gossip, the accusation finally did appear in print as well. The farm paper carried an italicized item which read: *Scratch a Peppone, and find a Pepito,* and this made everyone rock with laughter. As a result, Peppone's general staff held an emergency meeting and insisted that something must be done.

"Very well," said Peppone, "print the statement and plaster it up on the walls."

Smilzo made a beeline for the printer's and an hour later Don Camillo's friend, Barchini, brought a sheet of proof to the rectory.

"This is a black eye for the paper," Don Camillo said glumly. "If Peppone had won the millions, he wouldn't dare print so categorical a denial, unless he cashed them on the sly."

"He hasn't left the village for a single second," Barchini assured him. "Everyone has his eyes peeled."

It was late by this time and Don Camillo went to bed. But at three o'clock in the morning he was awakened, and the intruder was Peppone. He came in from the garden in back of the house, and paused in the hall to look back through the half-closed door.

"I hope no one saw me," he said. "I feel as if I were under watch the whole time."

"Are you stark crazy?" Don Camillo asked him.

"No, but I may be soon."

He sat down and wiped the perspiration off his forehead.

"Am I talking to the priest or to the town crier?" he inquired.

"That depends on what you have to say."

"I came to talk to the priest."

"Then the priest is listening," said Don Camillo gravely.

Peppone twisted his hat in his hands for a while and then came out with it.

"Father, I told a big lie. I *am* Pepito Sbezzeguti."

: [94] :

This bombshell hit Don Camillo so hard that he could hardly catch his breath.

"You won those ten million liras!" he exclaimed, after he had come to. "Why in the world didn't you say so?"

"I'm not saying it even now for public consumption," said Peppone. "I came to tell the priest, and all the priest should care about is the fact that I was guilty of a lie."

But Don Camillo couldn't resist this opportunity to preach to Peppone in no uncertain terms.

"Shame on you! So one of the comrades wins ten million liras! Why don't you leave those dirty deals to the bourgeois reactionaries? A good Communist should earn money by the sweat of his brow!"

"I didn't come here to joke, Father. Surely it's no crime to buy a lottery ticket."

"I'm not joking, and I never said it was a crime. I simply said that a good Communist wouldn't do it."

"Ridiculous! They all do."

"Too bad. And especially on your part, because you're a leader, with the guidance of the proletariat in your hands. Lotteries are one of the capitalists' most subtle weapons against the people, and one which costs them nothing. On the contrary it makes money for them. A good Communist ought to be dead set against lotteries, in any form whatsoever."

Peppone stared at him in amazement.

"Father, have you water on the brain?"

"No, but you have," said Don Camillo. "What is a lottery and how does it work? Imagine a thousand poor devils sentenced by a despot to hard labor in a prison camp, with only a miserable crust of bread for their daily pay. And what do they do to combat their hunger? Each one of them gives up a fifth of one day's ration to the despot, along with a piece of paper containing his own name. The despot puts all these papers into a hat and every Sunday draws one out. The bearer of the lucky name receives half the total amount of bread contributed by his companions and the despot keeps the other half for his trouble. So that nine hundred and ninety-nine poor devils have hopefully deprived themselves of a fifth of their daily bread for his enrichment. After all, the despot is the only one to steadily gain thereby. It's the same old story of capitalist exploitation."

Peppone shrugged his shoulders impatiently, but Don Camillo continued:

"Don't chafe at the bit, Comrade! Anything that makes the workingman believe there is any improvement of his lot outside the proletarian revolution operates against him and in favor of his enemies. In patronizing the lottery, you are betraying the cause of the people."

Here Peppone lost all patience.

"I'm not betraying anybody," he protested. "I know what I'm doing."

"I don't doubt that, Comrade Peppone. Since your aim is to win the people's cause and no one can hope that the capitalists are going to finance it, then it's logical to make money to finance it yourself. In other words, if you are a good Communist, then you play the lottery in a Communist spirit, in order to make money with which to carry on the class struggle. Of course, as a good Communist, you'll put those ten million liras in the Party coffers."

Peppone waved his arms.

"Look here, Father," he said, "do we have to turn everything into politics?"

"Comrade! What about the revolution?"

Peppone stamped angrily on the floor.

"I understand, Comrade," Don Camillo said with a smile. "You're right. Better ten million liras in your own pocket today than the revolution tomorrow!"

Don Camillo poked the fire for a minute or two and then turned again to Peppone.

"Is that all you came to tell me? That you had won the ten millions?"

Peppone was perspiring heavily.

"How can I cash them without letting anyone know?"

"Go straight to Rome."

"I can't. They're watching me too closely. And then my denial is coming out tomorrow."

"Send a trusted emissary."

"I can't trust a soul."

"Well, what can I say?" said Don Camillo, shaking his head.

"Then you go to collect the money for me."

Peppone got up and went away, leaving an envelope in front of Don Camillo. The priest went off the next morning and was gone for three days. He arrived late at night and on his way to the rectory stopped in the church at the main altar. With him he had a briefcase which he laid open on the altar rail.

"Lord," he said grimly, "here are ten packages, each one containing a hundred ten-thousand lira notes, in other words Peppone's ten millions. I'd only like to say that he is totally undeserving of any such prize."

"Tell that to the Lottery!" Christ advised him.

Don Camillo took the briefcase and went to the second floor of the rectory, where he switched the light on and off three times in succession, as he had previously agreed with Peppone. The latter was on the lookout, and signaled back with the light in his own bedroom, twice in succession. Two hours later he sneaked over to the rectory, with his coat collar up to the eyes. He came in through the garden and slipped the chain off the back door.

"Well?" he said to Don Camillo, who was waiting in his study.

Don Camillo pointed to the briefcase in reply. Peppone opened it with trembling hands and a burst of perspiration.

"Ten millions?" he asked in a whisper.

"Ten millions. Count them for yourself."

"No, no!" protested Peppone, staring at the money with fascination.

"Ten millions make a pretty pile, at least for the time being," said Don Camillo with a sigh. "But what will they be worth tomorrow? Just a little bad news, and their value is deflated, leaving nothing but a heap of worthless paper."

"They'd better be invested without delay," said Peppone anxiously. "Ten millions are enough to buy a sizable farm. Land always keeps its value."

"Land belongs to the people, Malenkov tells us. If Malenkov comes, he'll take your land away."

"Malenkov? Why should he come here? He's no imperialist."

"When I say Malenkov, I mean Communism. Communism is going to win, Comrade. The world's moving to the Left . . ."

Peppone was still staring at the money.

"Gold," he said, "that's the thing to buy. Gold can be hidden in the ground."

"And when it's hidden in the ground, what good will it do you? If Communism comes, everything will be rationed by the State and you won't be able to buy anything with your gold."

"Then I'd better send it abroad."

"Aha! Just like a capitalist, eh? You'd have to send it to America, because Europe is going Communist for sure. And when America is completely isolated, it will have to surrender."

"America's strong," said Peppone. "Communism will never get there."

"You can never tell, the future is in Malenkov's hands, Comrade."

Peppone sighed and sat down.

"My head's whirling," he said. "Ten millions!"

"Well, gather it up and take it home. But send back the briefcase; that belongs to me."

"No," said Peppone. "Just keep it all here, will you? We'll talk about it tomorrow. I can't think straight just now."

Peppone made his way home, and Don Camillo picked up the briefcase and went to bed. He was dead tired, but he didn't sleep for long because at two o'clock he was awakened. Peppone and his wife were standing, all bundled up, downstairs.

"Father, try to understand," said Peppone. "My wife wants to know—wants to know what ten million liras look like . . ."

Don Camillo fetched the briefcase and opened it up on the table. Peppone's wife paled when she saw the money. Don Camillo waited patiently for the spectacle to be over. Then he closed the briefcase and escorted the two of them to the door.

"Try to go to sleep," he said in farewell.

He went back to bed but at three o'clock Peppone roused him again.

"Isn't the pilgrimage over?" the priest asked.

"Father, I came to take the money."

"At this hour? Not on your life. I just stowed it away in the attic and I have no intention of bringing it down so soon. Come back tomorrow. I'm cold and sleepy . . . Don't you trust me?"

"It's not a question of trust. Imagine . . . just for instance . . . that you were to suffer an accident . . . How would I prove the money was mine?"

"Don't worry about that. The briefcase is locked and has your name on it. I've thought of everything."

"Of course . . . but it would be better to have the money in my own house."

There was something in his tone of voice that Don Camillo didn't like. And so he changed his tone to match it.

"What money do you mean?" he asked.

"My money! The money you got for me from Rome."

"You must be mad, Peppone, I never got any money of yours."

"The receipt was mine," panted Peppone. "Pepito Sbezzeguti, that's me."

"But it's plastered up all over the walls that you aren't Pepito Sbezzeguti at all. That's your own statement."

"But I am! Pepito Sbezzeguti is an anagram of Giuseppe Bottazzi."

"Not a bit of it. Pepito Sbezzeguti is an anagram of Giuseppe Bottezzi. And your name is Bottazzi. I have an uncle called Giuseppe Bottezzi and I bought the lottery ticket for him."

With a trembling hand Peppone wrote Pepito Sbezzeguti in the margin of a newspaper lying on the table. Then he wrote his own name and checked the letters.

"Damnation!" he shouted. "I put an *e* instead of an *a*. But the money's mine! *I* gave you the receipt!"

Don Camillo started upstairs to bed and Peppone followed him, calling for his money.

"Don't take it so hard, Comrade," said Don Camillo, climbing quietly into bed. "I shan't spend your money. I'll use it for your cause, for the cause of the People. In other words, I'll give it to the poor."

"Devil take the poor!" shouted Peppone.

"You reactionary swine!" exclaimed Don Camillo, settling down between the sheets. "Go away and let me sleep!"

"Give me my money or I'll kill you like a dog!"

"Take the filthy stuff and go away!" Don Camillo mumbled without even turning around.

The briefcase was on the chest of drawers. Peppone picked it up, hid it under his coat and hurried home. Don Camillo sighed when he heard the door slam.

"Lord," he said grimly, "why did you let him win? He's ruined for life! And the poor fellow didn't deserve such punishment."

"First you told me the money was an undeserved prize and now you say it's an undeserved punishment. I'm always rubbing you the wrong way, Don Camillo."

"Lord, I'm not really talking to you; I'm talking to the Lottery!" And at last Don Camillo fell asleep.

THE WHISTLE

AS USUAL, WHENEVER HE went hunting, Don Camillo started out from the orchard, and this time, in the farther field, behind the church, he saw a boy sitting on the stump of a tree and apparently waiting for him.

"Can I go with you?" the boy asked, as he got up and started to walk over.

Don Camillo looked hard and saw at a glance who the boy was.

"Go along with you," he answered brusquely. "You don't think I want one of you little devils for company, do you?"

The boy stood stock-still and watched the priest and his dog Thunder go on their way. Pino dei Bassi was not even thirteen years old, but he had already been enlisted by the Reds. They had signed him up in their youth organization and sent him out to distribute propaganda leaflets or to dirty the walls with diatribes against this, that and the other. He was the most active of the lot, because while the other boys had chores to do at home, he hung about the streets all day long. His mother, the widow of Cino dei Bassi, carried on her husband's trade. Every morning she hitched the horse to the wagon and went around the countryside selling pots and pans and cotton goods of every description. The boy had weak lungs and could not help her, so he was left in charge of his grandmother, who had a mere glimpse of him at noon, when he came home for something to eat. One day Don Camillo stopped the widow and told her she'd better keep an eye on the boy or else the company he was keeping would get him into trouble. But she answered tartly:

"If he goes with them, it's because it's more fun than going to church."

Don Camillo saw that there wasn't any use insisting. And he knew it was useless to preach at a good woman who wore herself out with hard work every day in order to keep body and soul together. Every time he saw the horse and wagon go by he thought of Cino dei Bassi, one of his very best friends, whom he had seen die before his eyes. And he thought of Cino again whenever he went hunting. If Cino had known Thunder, he would have been wild about him. Cino had hunting in his blood and was one of the best shots in the countryside. He had an unerring nose for game and an unerring eye for shooting, and his expeditions carried him to places no one had visited before. Whenever Cino went to a duck shoot or target competition, half the village tagged along behind, as if he were a one-man football team. He was Don Camillo's boon companion, and it was while they were out hunting together that Cino had stumbled into a ditch and by some mischance fallen on the trigger of his shotgun. He had sent a volley into his own chest and died in Don Camillo's arms.

This kind of death seemed to be written into the fate of the Bassi family. Cino's grandfather, who was a mighty nimrod in his time, had accidentally killed himself with a gun, and Cino's father had been shot in the course of a hunt. Then death came to Cino the same way. And he had left his gun to Don Camillo.

"You keep it," were his dying words, "and put it to good use."

Now the sight of Cino's son sharpened Don Camillo's memory of his old friend, and when the boy asked if he could come along, he wished violently that he could knock some sense into his head and wipe out the disgrace he was bringing upon his father's good name.

"Thunder," he said, relieving himself of his feelings to his dog, "the next time we meet the little rascal, we'll practically shave the hair off him. It's plain as day that they're training him to make trouble and sent him to pester me."

Thunder did not swerve from the path, but growled lightly in reply.

Four or five days later, Don Camillo found Pino waiting for him in the same place.

"I've quit," said the boy. "Can I go with you this time?"

"Quit? What do you mean?" asked Don Camillo.

"I'm not with them any longer. I resigned."

Don Camillo looked him over with a feeling of perplexity. The boy had a welt under his left eye and a slightly battered air.

"What did you do?" he asked.

"They beat me up. But I'm not with them any longer. Today, will you take me?"

"Why do you want to go?"

"I'd like to see some hunting."

Don Camillo walked on and the boy trailed him as silently as a shadow. He did not get in the way and his footsteps made no echo upon the ground. His pockets were stuffed with bread and he did not ask for a thing during all the hours they were walking.

: [103] :

Don Camillo did a good bit of shooting, and although he made no sensational hits he gave a very creditable performance and Thunder wasn't vexed with him too often. For when it came to his profession, Thunder was a strict taskmaster. He operated by the book and when Don Camillo made a whopping error he growled at him. On one occasion, early in their acquaintance, when the priest missed a hare almost the size of a calf, Thunder stood in front of him and bared his teeth.

Now Don Camillo had made a better-than-average record. He was ready to call it a day and go home, when suddenly Thunder showed signs of excitement.

"Can I have a shot?" whispered Pino, pointing to the shotgun.

"Of course not. You don't even know how to hold a gun to your shoulder."

Thunder took a few cautious steps forward and then froze into a pointing position.

"Give it here!" said the boy.

Don Camillo put the gun into his hands, but it was too late. A bird rose up out of the field, and only the kind of hunter that likes to hear the sound of his own weapon would have taken a shot at it. That is, only a perfect fool, or else a marksman of the caliber of the late Cino dei Bassi. The boy raised the gun to his shoulder and fired. And the bird fell like a stone, because this was Cino's son, wielding his father's gun.

Don Camillo broke out into perspiration and there was a tight feeling about his heart as he remembered that this gun was responsible for the death of Cino. Impulsively he snatched it. Meanwhile Thunder had streaked away and come back to deposit a quail at the boy's feet. The boy leaned over to pat his head, and a second later the dog raced off to the far end of the field to show off the power of his lungs and legs together. There he stopped and waited. At this point the boy gave out a whistle that Don Camillo hadn't heard since the days when Cino was his hunting companion, and the dog responded instantly. A shiver ran down Don Camillo's spine. Meanwhile the boy handed the quail over to him.

"You shot it, so it's yours," said the priest roughly.

"Mother doesn't want me to shoot," the boy mumbled, and two minutes later he had gone away.

Don Camillo stuffed the quail into his bag and walked homeward, with Thunder frolicking before him. All of a sudden the dog stopped in his tracks, bringing Don Camillo to a halt just behind. In the distance sounded Cino's special whistle, and Thunder was off like a shot in reply.

"Thunder!" Don Camillo shouted, causing the dog to pause and look around. "Thunder, come here!"

But the whistle sounded again, and after a brief whinny of explanation, Thunder ran on, leaving Don Camillo in the middle of the narrow road. The priest did not continue straight on his way. Instead of crossing the ditch, he walked along it for at least a quarter of a mile. The evening mist was descending, filling up the rents left in the sky by the dried branches of the bare trees. Beside the ditch, at a spot marked by a wooden cross, Cino had fallen, releasing the trigger of his gun. Don Camillo bowed his head, took the quail out of the bag and laid it at the foot of the cross.

"I see you're still in good form, Cino," he whispered, "but please don't do it again."

Don Camillo had no more taste for hunting. The episode of Pino had given him such a chill that merely to look at the shotgun hanging on the wall sent a tingle down his spine. And Thunder kept him company. The dog had received a major whacking and his demeanor was so humble that it seemed as if he must have understood every word, from the first to the last, of the little speech that had gone with it. If his master went out on the church square for a breath of air, he followed, but with his tail hanging. Then one afternoon, while the dog lay on the ground looking up at Don Camillo, who was pacing up and down with the usual cigar butt between his lips, the famous whistle sounded again. Don Camillo stopped and looked down at Thunder. Thunder did not budge. The whistle sounded again, and this time, although Thunder did not move, he traitorously wagged his tail and kept on wagging it until Don Camillo shouted at him. The confounded whistle sounded for the third time, and just as Don Camillo was about to grab his collar and pull him indoors, Thunder slipped away, jumped over the hedge and disappeared.

When he came to the field behind the church Thunder stopped to wait for further orders. Sure enough, he heard another whistle, which led him farther. The boy was waiting for him behind an elm, and they walked on together in the direction of an old mill which for the last fifty years had been nothing but a pile of stones beside a dried-up canal. When a dike had been thrown up to prevent floods, the course of the river had been changed, and the mill served no longer.

Now the boy climbed among the ruins, with Thunder at his heels. When they came to a half-collapsed arcade, he took away a few stones, revealing a long, narrow box behind them. Out of this he took an object wrapped in oily rags. Thunder looked on with a puzzled air, but in a minute he saw what it was all about. Enveloped in the rags was an old musket, as highly polished as if it had just come from the maker.

"I found it in the attic," the boy explained. "It belonged to my great-grandfather, who was a hunter in his day. It takes a while to load it, but it shoots perfectly well." With which, he proceeded to load it. Then he put the powder-horn in his pocket, hid the musket under his coat and led the dog away.

Thunder had very little confidence in this strange contraption. And when he heard a bird stir in the grass, he pointed without any particular enthusiasm. But when he saw the bird drop to the ground he put his heart into his work, because he knew that it was worthwhile. This boy shot as Thunder had never seen anyone shoot before, and when they came to tuck the musket away in its hiding-place at the old mill the boy's pockets were bulging with quail.

"I can't take them home, because if my mother and grandmother were to find out that I had been hunting, they would raise the roof," Pino explained. "I give my catch to a fellow from Castelletto who deals in poultry, and he lets me have powder, tow, buckshot and cartridges in exchange."

Thunder's reaction to the announcement of this trade was not expressed very clearly. But then boy and dog alike were true artists. They didn't hunt for the sake of garnishing spits or frying pans, or just because they had a barbaric taste for bloodshed.

From this time on Thunder led a double life. He stayed quietly at home for days on end, but whenever he heard Pino's whistle he threw off all restraint and made for the field back of the church. Eventually Don Camillo took offense and put Thunder out of the front door.

"You're not to set foot in my house until you've given up this shameful behavior," he said aiming a swift kick to underline his meaning.

And Thunder rejoiced, because his newly won independence favored the enterprise on which he had set his heart.

Pino got it into his head that he must bring down a pheasant.

"I'm tired of these small pickings," he explained to the dog. "Now I want to do some real shooting. We've got to find a pheasant. To have bagged a pheasant is the badge of a true hunter."

Thunder did the best he could, but even a blue-ribbon hunting dog can't find a pheasant where none is to be found. And yet there were some pheasants not too far away. They had only to go to the game preserve and worm their way through the wire fence. There thousands of pheasants awaited them. But three wardens reigned over the preserve, and they were no joking matter.

However the prospect of bringing down a pheasant was overwhelmingly attractive. And so one day Pino and Thunder found themselves up against the fence. They had chosen just the right sort of weather, for there was a mist in the air just thick enough to afford vision combined with invisibility and to muffle the sound of gunshot. Pino had a pair of pincers and he lay down on the ground to loosen just enough of the wire to allow himself and the dog to squeeze under. They stalked silently through the tall grass, and before they had gone very far Pino found a pheasant to shoot at. The bird came down like a ton of brick, but once it hit the ground it recovered sufficient strength to make a last flight which ended in a thicket. Thunder was just about to go for it when the boy called him back. Someone was running after them and calling upon them to halt or else. Pino ran like a demon, holding his head low, and Thunder followed after. The thickness of the mist and the general excitement caused the boy to strike the fence at a point slightly to the right of where he had made the hole. He realized this too late and lost time finding the right place. Just as he was bending down to slip through he was felled by the warden's gun.

He sank noiselessly to the ground and in spite of his ebbing strength tried to squeeze himself under. Just then the warden overtook him. Thunder stood in front of the boy, barking and baring his teeth. The man stopped short and when he saw the boy's bloodstained body on the ground he turned pale and did not know what to do. Pino was still trying to propel himself with his hands across the ground and Thunder, without taking his eyes off the warden, took the lapel of his jacket between his teeth and pulled him along. The warden stood there in a daze until at last he ran away. Pino had reached the other side of the fence, but he lay still and was apparently no longer breathing.

Thunder ran up and down, howling like one of the damned, but no one came by and finally he ran straight as an arrow to the village. Don Camillo was in the process of baptizing a baby when the dog rushed into the church, caught hold of his cassock and dragged him to the door. There Thunder let go, ran ahead, paused to bark, came back to take the priest's cassock between his teeth again, pull him forward and then dash on ahead to show the way. Now Don Camillo followed of his own free will, wearing his vestments and with his book in hand. And as he ran along the road, people from the village came after him.

Don Camillo brought the boy back in his arms, accompanied by a silent procession. He laid him down on his bed, while the old grandmother stared at him and murmured:

"There's fate for you! All of them died the same way."

The doctor said there was nothing to do but let him die in peace, and the onlookers lined up against the wall like so many statues. Thunder had disappeared, but he came back all of a sudden and took up his place in the middle of the room. In his mouth was the pheasant, which he had fetched from the thicket where it had fallen inside the preserve. He went over to the bed and put up his front legs and laid it on the boy's right hand which lay motionless on the bedcover. Pino opened his eyes, saw the bird, moved his fingers to stroke it and died with a smile on his face.

Thunder made no fuss but remained lying on the floor. When they came the next day to put Pino into his coffin they had to call upon Don Camillo to take the dog away, because he would not let anyone come near. Don Camillo put the body into the coffin himself and Thunder realized that if his master did it then it must be done. The whole village came to the funeral, and Don Camillo walked before the coffin, saying the office of the dead. At a certain moment his eyes fell upon the ground, and there was Thunder with the pheasant between his tooth. When they threw the first handfuls of earth over the coffin, Thunder let the pheasant drop among them. Everyone was scared by the dog's uncanny behavior and left the cemetery in a hurry. Don Camillo was the last to go, and Thunder followed him, with his head hanging low. Once they were outside he disappeared.

The three wardens of the game preserve were grilled for forty-eight hours by the carabinieri, but every one of them made the same reply: "I know nothing about it. There was a heavy mist, and I saw and heard nothing in the course of my rounds. Some other poacher must have shot him." Finally they were all dismissed for lack of proof.

Thunder lay all day in the rectory, but when night came he ran away and did not come back until dawn. For twenty nights in succession he did the same thing, and for twenty nights a dog howled under the window of one of the three wardens. He howled uninterruptedly and yet no one could find the place where he was hiding. On the twenty-first morning the warden gave himself up to the sergeant of the carabinieri.

"You may as well lock me up," he said. "I didn't mean to kill him, but the shot was mine. Do what you like with me, because I can't stand that confounded dog's howling."

After this everything returned to normal, and Don Camillo resumed his hunting. But every now and then, in the middle of some remote, deserted meadow, Thunder came to a sudden stop. And in the silence there rang out the whistle that was peculiar to Cino dei Bassi.

THE EXCOMMUNICATED MADONNA

ONE MORNING A YOUNG MAN
ode up on a bicycle to the square in front of the church and
egan to look inquiringly around him. Having apparently found
hat he wanted, he leaned his bicycle up against a pillar of the
rcade and unpacked the bundle on the carrier behind the sad-
le. He took out a folding stool, an easel, a paint box and a palette,

and a few minutes later he was hard at work. Fortunately the village children were all at school and he had a good half hour of peace and quiet. But gradually people crowded around and a hundred pairs of curious eyes followed his every brush-stroke. Just then Don Camillo came along, walking as casually as if he just happened to be passing that way. Someone asked him what he thought of the painting.

"It's too early to say," the priest answered.

"I don't see why he chose the arcade for a subject," said a member of the would-be intelligentsia. "There are far more picturesque scenes along the river."

The painter heard this remark and said without turning around:

"Picturesque scenes are for penny postcards. I came here to paint just because it isn't picturesque."

This statement left the villagers puzzled, and they continued to stare somewhat mistrustfully at the artist's work for the rest of the morning. At noon they went away and he was able to put in two solid hours without interruption. When the villagers returned they were so agreeably surprised that they ran to the rectory.

"Father, you must come and see. His picture's a beauty."

The painter was, indeed, a talented fellow, and Peppone, who happened to be among the onlookers, summed it up aptly by saying:

"There's art for you. I've been looking at that arcade for almost fifty years and I never realized that it was so beautiful!"

The painter was tired and packed his painting things away.

"Have you finished?" someone asked.

"No, I'll finish tomorrow. The light's changed and I can't get the same effects at this hour."

"If you'd like to leave your things at the rectory, there's plenty of room and I can answer for their safety," said Don Camillo, who saw that the young man didn't know what to do with his wet canvas.

"I knew the clergy would try to take him over," said Peppone disgustedly, as the artist gratefully accepted Don Camillo's offer

After the young man had put his things in the hall closet he asked Don Camillo to recommend some simple lodgings.

"You can stay here," said Don Camillo. "I'm happy to have an artist under my roof."

A fire was lit in the rectory and supper was on the table. The young man was cold and hungry, but after he had eaten the color came back into his cheeks.

"I don't know how to thank you," he said.

"You mustn't even try," said Don Camillo. "Will you be staying in these parts for long?"

"Tomorrow afternoon I must go back to the city."

"Has your enthusiasm for the river country suddenly left you?"

"No, it's a question of money," sighed the young man.

"Have you work waiting for you?" the priest asked him.

"Oh, I just scrape along from one day to the next," the artist told him.

"Well, I have no money," said Don Camillo, "but I can give you board and lodging for a month if you do some work in the church for me. Think it over."

"That's quickly done," said the young man. "It's a bargain. That is, if you let me have some time to paint for myself."

"Of course," said Don Camillo. "I need you for only a couple of hours a day. There's not so much to be done."

The church had undergone some repairs a month before and where the workmen had replaced some fallen plaster there was a gap in the decoration.

"Is that all?" asked the painter. "I can do that in a single day. You're offering me too much in return and it would be dishonest to accept it. You'll have to find something more for me to do."

"There is something more," said Don Camillo, "but it's such a big job, I haven't the courage to mention it."

"Let's hear."

Don Camillo went over to the rail of a side-chapel and threw on the light. A great spot filled the space above the altar.

"There was a leak," Don Camillo explained. "We caught onto it too late, and even though we mended the roof, the seepage had loosened the plaster. And so the painting of the Madonna was completely destroyed. The first thing to do, of course, is to replace the plaster. But I'm much more concerned over the repainting of the Madonna."

"You can leave that to me," said the artist. "Go ahead and get the plaster put in order, and meanwhile I'll make a sketch and have it ready to transfer to the wall when the mason gives me the word. I've had some experience in frescoes already. But I'll have to insist upon some privacy. You can see the job when it's done, but I can't bear to work with people staring at me."

Don Camillo was so pleased that he didn't have breath enough even to answer: "Yes sir!"

The young man had a genuine passion for painting, and the agreeable surroundings plus three square meals a day fired him to tremendous enthusiasm. When he had finished his widely admired picture of the arcade on the church square, he set off to explore the surrounding country and to find a model for the Madonna. He didn't want to paint a conventional figure, but to spiritualize a genuine face, which he hoped to discover in the vicinity of the village. During the first week he patched up the decorations in the main body of the church and restored an oil painting over the choir stalls. But he was restless and dissatisfied because he had not yet found his model. By the end of the second week the replastered chapel wall was ready for him to work on, but he was unable to begin. He had looked at hundreds of women in and around the village without finding a single face that interested him. Don Camillo became aware that something was wrong. The young man seemed listless and often came back in the evening without a single sketch in his notebook.

"Don't you care for this country any longer?" he asked. "There are all sorts of beauty you haven't yet discovered."

"Only one kind of beauty interests me just now," the artist complained. "And that I can't seem to find."

The next day the young man mounted his bicycle, making this resolution: "If I don't find what I'm after today, then I'm going home." He rode at random, stopping in farmyards to ask for a glass of water or some other trifle and looking into the face of every woman he saw along the way. But he was only confirmed in his disappointment. At noon he found himself in the settlement of La Rocca, a small place not far from the village, and rather than communicate his chagrin to Don Camillo he stopped for a bite to eat at the Pheasant Tavern. The big, low-ceilinged room with prints of characters from Verdi's *Othello* on the walls was completely deserted. An old woman appeared and he asked her for bread, sausage and a bottle of wine. A few moments later, when a hand deposited this simple fare on the dark table before him, he raised his eyes and was startled almost out of his skin. Here was the inspiration for which he had been searching. The inspiration was about twenty-five years old and carried herself with the nonchalance of eighteen. But what captured the artist's fancy was the girl's face, and he stared at it, hardly daring to believe it was true.

"What's the matter?" the girl asked. "Have I done something to annoy you?"

"Please forgive me . . ." he stammered.

She went away but returned a little later to sit down over some sewing at the door. At once the young man took a pad and pencil and began to sketch her. She felt his eyes upon her and broke in upon his work with a question:

"May I ask what you're doing?"

"If you don't mind, I'm drawing you."

"What for?"

"Because I'm a painter and take an interest in everything beautiful."

She gave him a pitying smile, shrugged her shoulders and went on with her work. After an hour she got up and went to look over the young man's shoulder.

"Do I really look like that?" she asked him, laughing.

"This is just a preliminary sketch. If you'll allow me, I'll come back to finish tomorrow. Meanwhile, how much do I owe you for lunch?"

"You can pay when you come back."

As soon as the artist got back to the rectory he shut himself up in his room to work. The next day he worked until noon, when he went out, locking the door behind him.

"I've got it, Father!" he exclaimed as he rode away.

When he reached the Pheasant he found things just as they had been the day before: bread, sausage, wine and his inspiration sitting at the door. This time, after he had worked for a couple of hours, the girl showed more satisfaction with what he had accomplished.

"It will be better yet if I can come back tomorrow," he sighed.

He came back for the two next afternoons and then no more, for he had reached another stage of his work. For three whole days he remained in his room and then, in agreement with the mason, started in on the chapel. No one could see what he was doing, because a board partition had been thrown up to protect him from the public view and he alone had the key to the door leading through it. Don Camillo was consumed with curiosity, but he contained himself and did no more than ask every evening:

"How's it going?"

"You'll soon see," said the young man excitedly.

Finally the great day came. The young man put a cloth over the fresco and tore down the boarding. Don Camillo rushed to the rail and waited, with his heart pounding. Then the young man took a pole and lifted the cloth off his "Madonna of the River." It was a most impressive painting, and Don Camillo stared at it with his mouth hanging open. Then all of a sudden something caught at his heart and perspiration broke out on his forehead.

"Celestina!" he shouted.

"Who's Celestina?" the young man asked.

"The daughter of the tavern-keeper at La Rocca."

"Yes," said the young man calmly. "She's a girl I found at the Pheasant Tavern."

Don Camillo took hold of a ladder, carried it over to the far end of the chapel, climbed up and draped the cloth over the fresco. The young man couldn't imagine what was wrong.

"Father, are you out of your head?" he asked him, but Don

Camillo only ran back to the rectory, with the young man at his heels.

"Sacrilege!" he panted, once he had reached his own study. "Celestina from the Pheasant Tavern! You mean you don't know about Celestina? She's the most ardent Communist anywhere around and to present her face as that of the Madonna is like painting Jesus Christ in the likeness of Stalin."

"Father," said the artist, recovering some of his calm. "I was inspired not by her political beliefs but by her beauty. She has a lovely face, and that was given her by God, not by the Party."

"But the black soul behind it came straight from the Devil!" shouted Don Camillo. "You don't appreciate the gravity of the sacrilege you've committed. If I didn't realize that you were completely innocent about it, I'd send you packing."

"I have nothing on my conscience," said the artist. "I gave the Madonna the most beautiful face I could find."

"But the portrait doesn't reflect your good intentions, it represents a damned soul! Can't you see the sacrilege involved? The only fitting title to the fresco is 'The Excommunicated Madonna!'"

The young man was in terrible distress.

"I put everything I had in me into bringing out the spiritual qualities of that face . . ."

"How do you expect to spiritualize the face of such a wanton creature? Why, when she opens her mouth, teamsters blush at the words that come out of it! No one can wish a face like that upon the Madonna."

The artist went to throw himself on his bed and did not come down to supper. About ten o'clock Don Camillo went up to see him.

"Well, are you awake now to the sacrilege you have committed? I hope that a second look at your sketches has revealed to you the essential vulgarity of that face. You're a young man and she's a provocative girl. She spoke to your senses, and your artistic discrimination went by the board."

"Father, you're misjudging and insulting me."

"Just let's look at your sketches together!"

"I've torn them all up."

"Then let's have another look at the chapel."

They went down to the empty church and Don Camillo took the pole to pull down the cloth covering the fresco.

"Look at it calmly and tell me if I'm not right."

The artist turned two powerful lights on the painting and shook his head.

"I'm sorry, Father," he said, "but there's nothing wanton or vulgar in that face."

Don Camillo stared at it again, scowling. The expression of the Madonna of the River was calm and serene and her eyes were pure and clear.

"Incredible!" exclaimed the priest angrily. "I don't know how you managed to get anything spiritual out of that creature."

"Then you admit that my picture has a spiritual and not a vulgar quality about it!"

"Yes, but Celestina hasn't. And anyone looking at it can't help saying: 'There's Celestina playing the part of the Madonna.'"

"Well, don't take it so tragically, Father. Tomorrow I can destroy it and start all over."

"We'll decide that tomorrow," said Don Camillo. "As a painting it's stupendous, and it's a crime to wipe it off the wall . . ."

Indeed, this Madonna of the River was one of the most stunning things Don Camillo had ever seen. But how could he tolerate Celestina in the guise of Our Lady? The next day he called five or six of his most trusted parishioners together, unveiled the fresco before them and asked for their honest opinion. Without exception they exclaimed:

"Marvelous!" and then a second later: "But that's Celestina from the Pheasant Tavern!"

Don Camillo told them of the painter's misadventure and concluded:

"There's only one thing to do: wipe the whole thing out!"

"Too bad, because it's a masterpiece. Of course, it wouldn't do for our Madonna to have an excommunicated Communist's face . . ."

Don Camillo begged the members of this little group not to say a word, and as a result the story spread like wildfire. People began to pour into the church, but the fresco was draped with a cloth and the entrance to the chapel barred. The news traveled outside the village and that evening, when Don Camillo was closing up the church he detected in the shadows the malicious face of Celestina in person.

"What do you want?" he asked gruffly.

"I want to see that idiot of a painter," she told him, and just then the idiot came upon the scene.

"Aside from the fact that you ate four meals at the Tavern without paying for them," Celestina said to him threatingly, "I'd like to know who gave you permission to misuse my face!"

The young man looked at her in amazement: here indeed was the face of which Don Camillo had spoken. He wondered how in the world he had seen anything spiritual in it. He started to make a hesitant reply, but she overrode him:

"You fool!" she exclaimed.

"Let's have less noise, my girl," Don Camillo interrupted. "We're in church, not in your father's tavern."

"You have no right to exploit my face and pin it onto a Madonna," the girl insisted.

"No one's exploited you," said Don Camillo. "What are you driving at, anyhow?"

"People have seen a Madonna with my face!" Celestina shouted. "Deny it if you can!"

"Impossible!" said Don Camillo. "But since it's true that some people see a slight resemblance, the fresco is going to be scraped away and done over."

"I want to see it!" Celestina shouted. "And I want to be present when you take my face out of it!"

Don Camillo looked at her ugly expression and thought of the gentle countenance of the Madonna of the River.

"It isn't your face," he said. "Come see for yourself."

The girl walked quickly to the chapel and came to a halt in front of the rail. Don Camillo took the pole and removed the cloth cover. Then he looked at Celestina. As she stood motionless, staring up at the picture, something extraordinary happened. Her face relaxed while her eyes lost their malice and became gentler and more serene. The vulgarity disappeared, and gradually she seemed to take on the expression of the painting. The artist gripped Don Camillo's arm.

"That's how I saw her!" he exclaimed.

Don Camillo motioned to him to be silent. A few moments later Celestina said in a low voice:

"How beautiful!" She could not take her eyes off the picture, and finally she turned to say to Don Camillo: "Please don't destroy it! Or at least, not too soon." And to his surprise she knelt down in front of the Madonna of the River and made the sign of the cross.

When Don Camillo was left alone in the church, he covered the fresco and then went to talk to the Crucified Christ over the main altar.

"Lord, what's going on?" he asked anxiously.

"Painting's not my business," answered Christ with a smile.

The next morning the young artist rode off on his bicycle to La Rocca. The tavern was empty, as usual, and Celestina sat, leaning over her sewing, at the door.

"I came to pay what I owe you," said the young man.

She raised her head, and he felt better because she had the gentle and serene expression of the painting on her face.

"You're a real artist!" she sighed. "That Madonna is a beauty. It would be a shame to take her away."

"I quite agree. I put my heart and soul into her, but people say an excommunicated Madonna won't do."

"I'm not excommunicated any longer," said Celestina with a smile. "I fixed that up this morning." And she proceeded to explain what steps she had taken.

Then she took advantage of the young man's surprise to ask whether it was his wife that kept his clothes so well mended and in such good order. He said that it wasn't, because he lived all alone and had no one to look after him. She observed with a sigh, that after a certain age, living alone was a tedious affair, even when a girl had any number of suitors. The time came when the thing to do was to settle down and have a family. He agreed on this point, but said that he had barely enough money to support himself. That, said Celestina, was because he lived in the city, where things were twice as expensive. If he were to move to the country, life would be much simpler, especially if he found a girl with a little house of her own and a parcel of land that only needed further development. He started to say something else, but just then the clock rang out noon. The hours have a way of flying when one engages in a conversation of this kind. Celestina went to fetch the usual bread, sausage and wine, and when he had finished eating he asked her:

"How much do I owe you?"

"You can pay tomorrow," she answered.

The Madonna of the River remained concealed for about a month longer. But on the day when the artist and Celestina were married, with all possible splendor, including organ music, Don Camillo drew the curtain and threw on the lights in the chapel. He was slightly worried about what people might say about the Madonna's resemblance to Celestina. But their only comment was:

"Celestina must wish she were equally beautiful! But she doesn't really look like Her at all!"

THE PROCESSION

DON CAMILLO WAITED PA-
tiently for things to come to a head, and although he waited a
long time, it was not in vain. One morning the man he was expecting turned up at the rectory.

"Is there any change in the program, Father," he asked, "or is
it just the same as other years?"

"Just the same," said Don Camillo, "except for one detail: no music in the procession."

This "one detail" made Tofini, leader of the local band, suffer considerable distress.

"No music?" he stammered. "Why not?"

"Orders from higher up," said Don Camillo, throwing out his arms helplessly.

Still Tofini couldn't believe it.

"Do you mean there's to be no more band-playing in any parades?"

"No," said Don Camillo, with icy calm. "It means that there's no more room in *my* procession for *your* band."

Tofini's collection of brasses was known as the "Verdi Band," but it was no great shakes from a musical point of view. However it was no worse than other bands in that part of the country and no one had ever dreamed of looking elsewhere for the musical accompaniment to a religious or patriotic display.

"If we suited you in previous years and now you don't want us any more, what's the matter?" asked the dismayed Tofini. "Have we lost our art?"

"That's something you never had. But you know the reason perfectly well."

"Father, I don't know a thing!"

"Then ask around until you find out who played the *International* in the village square two months ago!"

"We did," answered Tofini, "but I don't see anything wrong in that."

"I do, though."

"But you know us, Father. You know we don't go in for politics. We play for anyone that hires us. Two months ago the mayor asked us to play in the square and we put on a program of marches and operatic airs. Then people called for the *International,* the mayor said to play it, and we obliged."

"And if you'd been asked for the Fascist anthem, *Giovinezza,* or the *Royal March,* would you have played them too?"

"No. They're forbidden by law. But the *International* isn't forbidden."

"It's forbidden by the Church," said Don Camillo. "If you respect the laws of the State and not those of the Church, you may be a good citizen, but you're a very bad Christian. As a good citizen, you can go on playing in the square. But as a bad Christian, you can't play in a Church procession."

"Father, that's no way to reason. Everyone has his own way of making a living. And if everyone that works for the Communists were a bad Christian, where would we be now? Printers couldn't put out Communist papers, druggists couldn't sell medicine to Party members . . . When a man pursues his regular trade, politics and religion don't come into it. A doctor takes care of anyone that's sick, regardless of his party. And when we make music for money, we're simply dealing in the only commodity we have to sell. The *Overture to William Tell* and the *International* are all the same to us. The notes may be in different order, but they're still the same old A B C."

"Quite so," said Don Camillo, warming up to the debate. "One piece is as good as another, within the law. So if I'd come to the square on that occasion and asked for the anthem of the Christian Democrat Party, you'd have played that too?"

"Sure, if I wanted a beating," said Tofini with a shrug of his shoulders.

"It's not forbidden by law," said Don Camillo, "so why wouldn't you have played it?"

"If the Reds pay me, I can't very well play their opponents' song."

"When you say that, you're talking politics, after all. You appreciate the propaganda value of the *International* and you're a bad Christian to play it."

"Theory's one thing and practice is another," said Tofini. "A man's got to live."

"What matters more is that he's got to die. And our accounts with God are more important than those with any shopkeeper."

"God can wait," laughed Tofini, "the shopkeeper won't give me anything to eat until I pay."

Don Camillo threw out his arms.

"Are you reasoning like a good Christian?" he asked.

"No; like a poor devil that has to live as best he can."

"Very well, but there are other poor devils who manage to live very good Christians just the same. So why should I give you the preference? From now on the bands from Torricella, Gaggiolo and Rocchetta will play at funerals and all other religious processions. They're just as much out of tune, but at least they have more sense."

Tofini was so perturbed that he went to Peppone and a few hours later Peppone went to Don Camillo.

"Are fellows to be thrown out of work just because they played the anthem of a legally constituted party?" he shouted.

"Orders from higher up, Mr. Mayor," said Don Camillo regretfully. "Like you, I have to do what my superiors say."

"Even if their orders are stupid?"

"That's never been the case, where my superiors are concerned," said Don Camillo, calmly.

"Don't try to be funny," said Peppone, clenching his fists. "It hurts my conscience to see this man harmed through a fault of mine."

"There's no fault of yours. You didn't play the *International*. Tofini's band did, and that's why I must look for another."

"All right, then. You'll see," said Peppone, as he took his leave.

Don Camillo waited until the last minute to engage another band. And when he got around to it, he found that all three nearby bands had previous commitments. He searched farther afield, only to meet everywhere the same answer. Don Camillo smelled a rat, and sure enough he finally came upon a band leader willing to tell him the truth.

"Father, we're willing to play but not to take a beating."

"Did someone threaten you?"

"No, but we were given some friendly advice."

Don Camillo went home feeling considerably depressed. The procession of the Madonna was scheduled for the next evening and no band was to be found. He spent a night haunted by musical nightmares and woke up feeling even worse than when he had gone to bed. Around ten o'clock Tofini dropped by.

"I heard you were looking for me, Father," he said.

"You're wrong, Tofini. You were looking for me, but I wasn't in."

"Very well," said Tofini. "At your service, in case of need."

"You may serve the mayor," said Don Camillo, "but you won't serve me."

After noon the village was in a ferment. That was always the way during the hours preceding the nighttime procession of the Madonna. Every window was decorated with paper lanterns, luminous stars, candles and tapers, and out of every windowsill hung a rug, a piece of crimson damask, a garland of paper flowers, a bedspread, a linen sheet or a strip of lace or embroidery. The poorest houses were often the most artistically decorated, because ingeniousness took the place of money.

The village was in a ferment, then, during the afternoon, but toward evening, when the decoration was done, it grew calm. This year, however, the calm was only skin-deep, for everyone was curious. Would Don Camillo call upon Tofini or would he give up the idea of a band? And what about the People's Palace? The year before, the People's Palace was the only building which displayed no light. But at the last minute, just as the procession was getting under way, a red, white and green star appeared at a second-story window, only to disappear after the marchers had gone by. No one ever knew quite how that came about but everyone was speculating upon what would happen this year. Either there would be a star or there wouldn't. Or else the star would be all red, instead of a patriotic red, white and green. Don Camillo threatened a fourth hypothesis:

"If they show a red star with a portrait of Malenkov in the center, and they make me furious over the absence of music, I'll hold up the procession . . ."

But his hypothesis did not go any further. He knew that if the Reds deliberately provoked him, he would come to a halt. But he didn't know what he would do next. And this unknown worried him intensely.

Night fell, and when the bells rang, every window was illuminated, that is, all except those of the People's Palace. The procession began to move, and the voices of women and children sang out the hymn *Behold this Thy people*. But the song was a melancholy one without the re-enforcement of Tofini's band. Everyone felt uneasy, and as they approached the People's Palace, the uneasiness grew. It looked as if, this time, there would be nothing but grim darkness. The head of the procession was within twenty-five feet of the People's Palace when Don Camillo began to pray:

"Lord, let there be a star, no matter what the color! That dark, hermetically closed building gives me the impression of a world deprived of Your Divine Grace. Let some light be lit behind those dark windows in order to demonstrate Your presence. To tell the truth, Lord, I am afraid . . ."

Now the head of the procession was passing right in front of the People's Palace, and still there was no sign of life or light. All hope was gone, and the procession wound slowly on. The picture of the Madonna was about to pass by, but it was too late now to hope for a miracle. And no miracle happened. What happened was that all the windows were suddenly thrown open, flooding the street with light. A volley of fireworks went off in the sports field, and in the courtyard Tofini's band, flanked by the bands from Torricella, Gaggiolo and Rocchetta, burst into *Behold this Thy people*.

An atomic bomb could not have made any more of an impression. With their eyes glued to the fireworks and their ears deafened by the din of the music, the marchers were completely at a loss. Don Camillo was the first to recover his aplomb. When he realized that the procession had come to a stop and the Madonna was stalled in front of the People's Palace, he shouted:

"Forward!"

The procession went on, and a thousand voices rose as a single voice, because they had four rival bands to sustain them.

"Lord," said Don Camillo, raising his eyes to heaven, "they did it all just to spite me!"

"But if in spiting you they've honored the Holy Mother of God, why should you worry?"

"They don't mean to honor anyone, Lord. It's all a trick played upon poor, innocent people.

"They can't trick me, Don Camillo."

"I see, Lord. I was wrong, then, not to take the band that had played the *International* in the public square."

"No, you weren't wrong, Don Camillo. The proof is that four bands, instead of one, have gathered to give thanks to the Mother of God."

"Lord, this is just a deceitful game," Don Camillo insisted. "It's all because Russia's putting out peace feelers!"

"No, Don Camillo; I say it's all because Peppone isn't Russia."

Deep down in his heart, Don Camillo thought so too, and was thankful for geography.

HOLIDAY JOYS

IN RETALIATION FOR EXCOM-
munication, the Reds decided to abolish Christmas.

And so on Christmas Eve Peppone came out of the People's
Palace without so much as a glance at Bigio, who was waiting for
him at the door, and hurried home, avoiding the main square in
order not to run into the crowd returning from Midnight Mass.

Smilzo trailed after him in disciplined style, but got no reward for his pains, because Peppone slammed the door of his own house behind him without so much as a good-night. He was dead tired and lost no time in falling into bed.

"Is that you?" asked his wife.

"Yes," mumbled Peppone. "Who do you expect it to be?"

"There's no telling," she retorted. "With the new principles you've just announced, it might just as well be some other official of your Party."

"Don't be silly," said Peppone. "I'm not in a joking mood."

"Neither am I, after this very uninspiring Christmas Eve. You wouldn't even look at the letter your son had left under your plate. And when he stood up on a chair to recite the Christmas poem he learned in school you ran away. What have children to do with politics, anyhow?"

"Let me sleep, will you?" shouted Peppone, rolling over and over.

She stopped talking, but it took Peppone a long time to fall asleep. Even after he finally dozed off, he found no peace, for nightmares assailed him, the kind of nightmares that go with indigestion or worry. He woke up while it was still dark, jumped out of bed and got dressed without putting on the light.

He went down to the kitchen to heat some milk and found the table set just the way it was the evening before. The soup bowl was still there and he lifted it up to look for the little boy's letter, but it was gone. He looked at the spotted table cloth and the scraps of food upon it, remembering how his wife once decorated the table on past Christmas Eves. This led him to think of other Christmases, when he was a boy, and of his father and mother.

Suddenly he had a vivid memory of Christmas 1944, which he had spent in the mountains, crouching in a cave in danger of being machine-gunned from one moment to the next. That was a terrible Christmas, indeed, and yet it wasn't so bad as this one because he had thought all day of the good things that went with a peacetime celebration and the mere thought had warmed the cockles of his heart.

Now there was no danger, and everything was going smoothly. His wife and children were there right in the next room, and he had only to open the door in order to hear their quiet breathing. But his heart was icy cold at the thought that the festive table would be just as melancholy on Christmas day as it had been the evening before.

"And yet that's all there is to Christmas," he said to himself. "It's just a matter of shiny glasses, snow-white napkins, roast capons and rich desserts."

Then he thought again of Lungo's little boy, who had built a clandestine Manger in the attic of the People's Palace. And of the letter and poem of his own little boy, which had no connection with all the foodstuffs he had insisted were only the true symbols of the season.

It was starting to grow light as Peppone walked in his long black cape from his own house to the People's Palace. Lungo was already up and busy sweeping the assembly room. Peppone was amazed to find him at the door.

"Are you at work this early?"

"It's seven o'clock." Lungo explained. "On ordinary days, I start at eight, but today isn't ordinary."

Peppone went to his desk and started looking over the mail. There were only a dozen routine letters, and within a few minutes his job was done.

"Nothing important, Chief?" asked Lungo, sticking his head around the door.

"Nothing at all," said Peppone. "You can take care of them yourself."

Lungo picked up the letters and went away, but he came back soon after with a sheet of paper in his hands.

"This is important, Chief," he said. "It must have escaped our notice."

Peppone took the letter, looked at it and handed it back.

"Oh, I saw that," he said; "there's nothing unusual about it."

"But it's a matter of Party membership and you really ought to make an immediate reply."

"Some other day," mumbled Peppone. "This is Christmas."

Lungo gave him a stare which Peppone didn't like. He got up and stood squarely in front of his subordinate.

"I said it's Christmas, did you understand?"

"No, I didn't," said Lungo, shaking his head.

"Then I'll explain," said Peppone, giving him a monumental slap in the face.

Lungo made the mistake of continuing to play dumb, and because he was a strapping fellow, even bigger than Peppone, he gave him back a dose of the same medicine. With which Peppone charged like an armored division, knocked him onto the floor and proceeded to change the complexion of his hind-quarters with a series of swift kicks. When he had done a thorough job, he grabbed Lungo by the lapels and asked him:

"Did you understand what I was saying?"

"I get it; today's Christmas," said Lungo darkly.

Peppone stared at the little Manger Lungo's son had built.

"What does it matter if some people choose to believe that a carpenter's son, born two thousand years ago, went out to preach the equality of all men and to defend the poor against the rich, only to be crucified by the age-old enemies of justice and liberty?"

"That doesn't matter at all," said Lungo, shaking his big head. "The trouble is that some people insist he was the son of God. That's the ugly part of it."

"Ugly?" exclaimed Peppone. "I think it's beautiful, if you want to know. The fact that God chose a carpenter and not a rich man for a father shows that He is deeply democratic."

Lungo sighed. "Too bad the priests are mixed up in it," he said. "Otherwise we could take it over."

"Exactly! Now you've hit the real point. We must keep our heads and not mix up things that have no real connection. God is one thing and priests are another. And the danger comes not from God but from the priests. They're what we must seek to eliminate. It's the same thing with rich people's money. We must eliminate them and distribute their money among the poor."

Lungo's political education had not gone so far and once more he shook his head uncomprehendingly.

"That's isn't the essential question. The fact is that God doesn't exist; he's merely a priests' invention. The only things that really exist are those that we can see and touch for ourselves. All the rest is sheer fancy."

Peppone didn't seem to put much stock in Lungo's elucubrations, for he answered:

"If a man's born blind, how is he to know that red, green and the other colors exist, since he can't see them? Suppose all of us were to be born blind; then within a hundred years all belief in the existence of color would be lost. And yet you and I can vouch for it. Isn't it possible that God exists and we are blind men who on the basis of reason or experience alone can't understand His existence?"

Lungo was completely baffled.

"Never mind," said Peppone abruptly. "This isn't a problem that requires immediate solution. Forget about it."

Peppone was on his way home when he ran into Don Camillo.

"What can I do for Your Gray Eminence?" he asked gloomily.

"I wanted to offer you my best wishes for Christmas and the New Year," said Don Camillo blandly.

"You forget that we Reds have been excommunicated," said Peppone. "That makes your good wishes somewhat illogical."

"No more illogical than the care which a doctor gives a sick man. He may quarantine him in order to protect others from his contagious disease, but he continues to look after him. We abhor not the sinner but his sin."

"That's a good one!" said Peppone. "You talk of love, but you'd kill us off without hesitation."

"No, we'd be very poor doctors of men's souls if we killed them in order to obtain a cure. Our love is directed at their healing."

"And what about the violent cure you spoke of at the political rally the other day?"

"That had nothing to do with you and your friends," Don

Camillo answered calmly. "Take typhus for instance. There are three elements involved. The typhus itself, the lice that carry it and the suffering patient. In order to overcome the disease we must care for the patient and kill the lice. It would be idiotic to care for the lice and insane to imagine that they could be transformed into something other than a vehicle of contagion. And in this case, Peppone, you are the sick man, not the louse."

"I'm perfectly well, thank you, Father. You're the sick one, sick in the head."

"Anyhow, my Christmas wishes come not from the head but from the heart; you can accept them without reservation."

"No," said Peppone, "head, heart or liver, it's all the same. That's like saying: 'Here's a nice little bullet for you; it's a gift not from the percussion cap but from the barrel.'"

Don Camillo threw out his arms in discouragement.

"God will take pity on you," he murmured.

"That may be, but I doubt that He'll take pity on you. Come the revolution, He won't prevent your hanging from that pole. Do you see it?"

Of course Don Camillo saw the flagpole. The People's Palace was on the right side of the square and from his study window he could help seeing the pole sticking insolently up into the free air, with a shiny metal hammer and sickle at its summit. This was quite enough to ruin the view.

"Don't you think I may be a bit too heavy for your pole?" he asked Peppone. "Hadn't you better import some gallows from Prague? Or are those reserved for Party comrades?"

Peppone turned his back and went away. When he reached his own house he called his wife outside.

"I'll be back about one o'clock," he told her. "Try to fix everything in the usual Christmas way."

"That's already attended to," she mumbled. "You'd better be back by noon."

Shortly after noon, when he came into the big kitchen, Peppone rediscovered the atmosphere of Christmases gone by and felt as if he were emerging from a nightmare. The little boy's

Christmas letter was under his plate and seemed to him unusually well written. He was ready and eager to hear the Christmas poem but this did not seem to be forthcoming. He imagined it would come at the end of the meal and went on eating. Even when they had finished dinner, however, the child showed no intention of standing up in his chair to recite, in the customary manner. Peppone looked questioningly at his wife, but she only shrugged her shoulders in reply. She whispered something in the little boy's ear and then reported to her husband:

"Nothing doing. He won't say it."

Peppone had a secret weapon: a box of chocolates which he extracted from his pocket with the announcement:

"If someone recites a poem, this is his reward!"

The child looked anxiously at the chocolates but continued to shake his head. His mother parleyed with him again but brought back the same negative reply. At this point Peppone lost patience.

"If you won't recite the poem, it means you don't know it!" he said angrily.

"I know it, all right," the child answered, "but it can't be recited now."

"Why not?" Peppone shouted.

"Because it's too late. The Baby Jesus is born now, and the poem is about the time just before."

Peppone called for the notebook and found that, sure enough, the poem was all in the future tense. At midnight the stall at Bethlehem would be lit up, the Infant would be born and the shepherds would come to greet Him.

"But a poem's not like an advertisement in the paper," said Peppone. "Even if it's a day old it's just as good as it was to start with."

"No," the child insisted, "if Baby Jesus was born last night, we can't talk about him as going to be born tomorrow."

His mother urged him again, but he would not give in.

In the afternoon Peppone took the little boy for a walk and

when they were far from home he made one more attempt to bring him around.

"Now that we're all alone, can't you recite the poem?"

"No."

"No one will hear you."

"But Baby Jesus will know."

This sentence was a poem itself, and Peppone appreciated it.

The allotted number of days went by and then New Year's Eve arrived in the village. In the little world as everywhere else it was the custom to welcome the New Year with lots of noise. The irrepressible high spirits of the villagers found this an excellent excuse for letting go with every available firearm at midnight. So the New Year was started off right and the dying year killed off for good and all. Don Camillo had a hundred good reasons for disliking this custom, but this year he felt a perverse desire to kill the old year and have done with it. A few minutes before midnight he opened his study window and stood there, gun in hand, waiting for the bell in the church tower to ring. The lights were out but there was a fire in the fireplace and when Thunder, his dog, caught the gleam of the gun in Don Camillo's hand he was highly excited.

"Quiet there," Don Camillo explained. "This isn't my hunting gun. It's the old firing-piece I keep in the attic. It's a matter of shooting the old year out, and a shotgun won't answer the purpose."

The square was empty and the lamp in front of the People's Palace lit up the flagpole.

"It's almost as conspicuous by night as it is by day," muttered Don Camillo. "Seems as if they put it there just to annoy me."

The first of the twelve peals of midnight sounded, and at once the shooting began. Don Camillo leaned on the windowsill calmly and fired a single shot. Just one, because the gesture was a symbolic one and this was quite sufficient to give it meaning. It was very cold. Don Camillo carefully shut the window, leaned the gun against a chest and stirred the fire. All of a sudden he realized that Thunder wasn't there. Obviously he was so excited over the shooting that he had run out to join the fun. The priest was not particularly worried. The dog would slip back in just as easily as he had slipped out a few minutes before. Soon after this the door creaked and he looked up expectantly. The cause was not Thunder but Peppone.

"Excuse me," he said, "but the door was ajar and I came to pay you a call."

"Thank you, my son. It's always pleasant to be remembered."

"Father," said Peppone, sitting down beside him. "There's no doubt about it truth is stranger than fiction."

"Has something unfortunate happened?" asked Don Camillo.

"No, just a curious coincidence. Someone shooting into the air hit our flagpole just at the top, where the metal emblem is joined onto the wood. Don't you find that extraordinary?"

"Extraordinary indeed," Don Camillo agreed, throwing out his arms.

"And that's not all," Peppone continued. "In its fall the emblem very nearly hit Lungo on the head. He thought someone had thrown something at him on purpose and gave the alarm. We all went out to look, and although there was nothing on the ground we noticed when we looked up that the emblem was missing from the flagpole and that, as I told you, it had been clipped off very neatly. Now who do you think can have taken it away as a trophy from the deserted square?"

"To be quite frank," said Don Camillo, "I can't imagine who would be interested in a piece of junk of that kind."

Meanwhile Thunder had come back in and sat motionless between the two men. The hammer-and-sickle emblem was between his teeth and at a certain point he dropped it onto the floor. Don Camillo picked it up and turned it around in his hand.

"A poor quality of metal," he said. "From a distance it didn't look so frail. Take it home if it interests you."

Peppone looked at the emblem which Don Camillo was holding out to him and then looked into the fire. Since no hand was extended to take it, the priest threw it into the flames. Peppone gritted his teeth but said nothing. The emblem grew red hot, its joints melted and the various parts curled up like so many snakes.

"If Hell weren't just an invention of us priests . . ." Don Camillo murmured.

"It's the other way around," muttered Peppone. "Priests are an invention of Hell!"

While the priest poked at the fire Peppone went to look out the window. Through the glass he could see the decapitated flagpole.

"How many shots did it take you?" he asked without turning around.

"One."

"American model with telescope attachment?"

"No, a regular old ninety-one."

Peppone came to sit down again by the fire.

"That's still a good gun," he mumbled.

"Guns are ugly things at best," murmured Don Camillo.

"Happy New Year!" muttered Peppone as he went out the door.

"Thanks, and the same to you," Don Camillo answered.

"I was speaking to Thunder," said Peppone roughly.

And Thunder, who was stretched out in front of the fire, responded to the mention of his name by wagging his tail.

A LESSON IN TACTICS

$\mathbf{A}$ MASSIVE PIECE OF MACHIN-
ery distinctly resembling an automobile, with a "U.S.A." license
plate at the rear, drew up in front of the rectory, and a thin man,
no longer young, but of erect and energetic bearing, got out and
walked over to the door.

"Are you the parish priest?" he asked Don Camillo, who was
sitting on a bench just outside, smoking his cigar.

"At your service," said Don Camillo.

"I must talk to you," said the stranger excitedly, stalking into the hall for all the world like a conqueror. Don Camillo was momentarily taken aback, but when he saw that the stranger had reached a dead end and was about to descend into the cellar he moved to restrain him.

"This way!" he interjected.

"Everything's changed!" said the stranger. "I don't get it."

"Have you been here before, when things were differently arranged?" Don Camillo asked, leading him into the parlor, near the front door.

"No, I've never set foot in this house," said the stranger, who was still in a state of agitation. "But I still don't get it! Sermons won't cure the situation, Father. Nothing but a beating-up will teach those Reds a lesson."

Don Camillo maintained an attitude of cautious reserve. The fellow might be an escaped lunatic, for all he knew. But when a lunatic travels in a car with a "U.S.A." license and a liveried chauffeur, it is best to handle him with kid gloves. Meanwhile the stranger wiped his perspiring forehead and caught his breath. The priest scrutinized the somewhat hard lines of his face and tried to connect them with something in his memory, but to no avail.

"May I offer you some sort of refreshment?" he asked.

The stranger accepted a glass of water, and after he had gulped this down, apparently he felt a little more calm.

"You have no reason to know me," he said. "I come from Casalino."

The priest scrutinized him again, this time mistrustfully. Now Don Camillo was a civilized man and one ready to acknowledge his own mistakes; he had plenty of common sense and a heart as big as a house. Nevertheless he divided mankind into three categories: good people who must be encouraged to stay good; sinners who must be persuaded to abandon their sin and, last of all, people from Casalino, a village which from time immemorial had feuded with his.

In ancient times the struggle between the two villages had

been violent and men had lost their lives in it. For some years past it had degenerated into a cold war, but the substance of it was still the same. Politicians from Casalino had wormed their way into the provincial administrations and the national government, particularly the departments of public works and engineering. As a result, whenever there was any plan to do something for Don Camillo's village, these politicians blocked it or turned it to their own advantage.

So it was that although Don Camillo worked hard to keep good people good and to persuade sinners to abandon their sin, he left Casalino in God's care. When things got especially tense he would say to Christ, "Lord, if You created these people, there must be some reason for it. We must accept them like death and taxes, with Christian resignation. May Your infinite wisdom rule over them and Your infinite kindness deliver us from their presence!"

"Yes, I'm from Casalino," the stranger repeated. "And if I have humiliated myself to the point of coming here, you can imagine that I must be very angry."

This was easy enough to understand, but Don Camillo could not see the connection with the big American car.

"I was born in Casalino," the stranger explained, "and my name is Del Cantone. Until 1908, when I was twenty-five years old, I lived on a farm with my father and mother. We worked like dogs, because we had no peasants to help us. Then all of a sudden, those damned souls . . ."

He turned red in the face again and perspired profusely.

"What damned souls do you mean?" asked Don Camillo.

"If you, a priest, don't know that the Reds are damned souls, then you must be blind as a bat!" the stranger shouted.

"Excuse me," said Don Camillo, "but aren't you speaking of events of some forty years ago?"

"The Reds have been damned souls from the beginning, ever since Garibaldi invented that infernal red shirt . . ."

"I don't see much connection with Garibaldi," demurred Don Camillo.

"You don't? Wasn't the doctor who introduced socialism to this part of the world a follower of Garibaldi?" the stranger retorted.

"Didn't he put all sorts of ideas into people's heads and start subversive organizations?"

Don Camillo urged him to tell the rest of his own story.

"Well, in 1908 those damned souls made a big splash, with a farm-workers' strike and nonsense of that kind. They came to our place and insulted my father, and I took a shotgun and shot a couple of them down. No one was killed, but I had to run away to America. There I worked like a dog, too, but it took me a number of years to make any money. Meanwhile my father and mother died, in extreme poverty. All because of those damned souls . . ."

Don Camillo gently remarked that after all the shotgun was to blame. But the other paid no attention.

"When I heard about how Mussolini was taking care of the Red menace, I thought of coming back to settle my private account with them. But by that time, I was thoroughly tied up with a growing business. I did send someone to raise a gravestone to my parents in the cemetery. After that, more time went by, and now I'm in my seventies . . . Anyhow, here I am, after four decades of absence. And I haven't much time. I came back to do something more to commemorate my father and mother. A gravestone is something as lifeless as those that lie beneath it. What I wanted to do was to give their name to some charitable institution, a fine, modern building with plenty of grounds around it. And my idea was to have the building divided in two parts: one a children's home and the other a home for old people. Old people and children could share the grounds and come to know one another. The end of life would be drawn close to the beginning. Don't you think it's a good idea?"

"Very good," said Don Camillo. "But the building and grounds aren't all that's necessary—"

"I didn't come all the way from America to learn anything so elementary. You don't think I imagine that an institution can live on air, do you? I meant to endow it with a thousand-acre, self-supporting farm. In fact, for the whole project I have put aside a million dollars. I haven't much longer to live and there are no children to inherit from me. Taxes and lawyers' fees will eat up most of what I leave behind. And so I transferred the million dollars to this, my native land. But now I've decided to take them back to America."

Don Camillo forgot that the loss of this sum would be a loss to Casalino. In fact, with the notion of a million dollars earmarked for charity coursing through his mind he was willing to take the inhabitants of Casalino out of the category of untouchables and consider them in the same light as the rest of mankind.

"Impossible!" he exclaimed. "God inspired you with a truly noble idea. You mustn't go back on His inspiration."

"I'm taking the money home, I tell you," the stranger shouted. "Casalino shan't have a penny of it. I went there straight from Genoa, and what did I find? Red flags all over the village and on every haystack around! Red flags, posters bearing the hammer and sickle and threatening death to this one and that. There was a rally in the public square and the loudspeakers brought me every word of it. "Now let us hear from our comrade the Mayor," they were saying. And when they saw my license plate, they shouted at me: "Go back to Eisenhower! Go back to America!" One of them even damaged the top of my car. You can see for yourself if you don't believe me."

Don Camillo looked out the window and saw that this was indeed true.

"Well, I'm going back, never fear," concluded the stranger, "and taking my money with me. I'll give it to the Society for the Prevention of Cruelty to Animals, rather than to the damned souls of Casalino!"

"But not all of them are Reds," protested Don Camillo.

"They're all swine, though. The Reds because they're Reds, and the others because they're too weak to kick them out. Yes, I'm going back to America."

Don Camillo thought it was pointless to argue. But he wondered why the old man had come to him with this story.

"I understand your disappointment," he said. "And I'm ready to do anything I can to help you."

"Of course . . . I had forgotten the most important thing of all," said the stranger. "I came to you for a very good reason. I've money to burn and expenses don't matter. I'm willing to make this my legal residence or do whatever else is necessary, to organize a secret raid and enlist the devil himself to carry it out. But my parents can't be at rest in the cemetery of Casalino, and I want to bring their bodies here. I'll erect a new gravestone in your cemetery, a monument of colossal proportions. All I ask is that you take care of the whole thing. I'm content to pay."

And he deposited a pile of banknotes upon the table.

"Here's for your preliminary expenses," he added.

"Very well," said Don Camillo. "I'll do whatever's possible."

"You may be called upon to do the impossible," said the stranger.

Now that he had got all this off his chest, he seemed to be in a more reasonable frame of mind. He consented to drink a glass of sparkling Lambrusco wine, which brought back memories of his youth and restored his serenity.

"How are things here, with you, Father?" he asked. "Terrible, I suppose. I have an idea that the whole area is pretty much like Casalino."

"No," answered Don Camillo. "Things are quite different here. There are Reds, of course, but they aren't on top of the heap."

"Isn't your local government in Red hands?"

"No," Don Camillo said shamelessly. "They're on the village council, but not in the majority."

"Wonderful!" exclaimed his visitor. "How do you do it? You can't tell me that sermons have turned the tide."

"There you're wrong," said Don Camillo. "My sermons aren't without effect. The rest is a matter of tactics."

"What do you mean?"

"Well, it's hard to put into words, so I'll give you a concrete example." And out of a drawer he took a pack of cards. "Say each one of these cards is a Communist. Even a tiny child can tear them up one by one, whereas if they're all together it's almost impossible."

"I see," said the stranger. "Your tactics are to divide your enemies and overcome them one by one."

"No," said Don Camillo; "that's no it at all. My tactics are to

: [144] :

let the enemy get into a solid block in order to size up their strength correctly. Then when they're all together, I go into action."

So saying, he tore the pack of cards in two in his big, bare hands.

"Hooray!" the old man shouted enthusiastically. "That's terrific! Will you give me that pack of cards with your autograph on one of them? The only trouble with such tactics is that they require unusually strong hands!"

"Strong hands aren't lacking," said Don Camillo calmly. "We can handle a deck easily enough. But what shall we do when there are sixty or more? We're still on top, but they're working day and night to put us down. And they have powerful weapons."

"Weapons? And you haven't any? I'll send you plenty of those!"

"That's not the sort of weapons I mean. The Reds' chief weapon is other people's selfishness. People who are well off think only of holding on to their possessions; they show no concern for their neighbors. The richest people are often the most stingy; they fail to see that by clinging to their individual piles the whole lot of them will lose everything. But don't let's worry over that, Signor Del Cantone. Have another glass of wine."

"There's the Old World for you!" sighed the stranger, turning down the offer of a second drink. "I want to speak with the mayor right away. I see a way of killing three birds with one stone. I'll raise an enduring monument to my father and mother, save Western civilization and madden those damned souls of Casalino by making this village the seat of my institution."

Don Camillo saw stars. Then he hastily pulled himself together.

"The mayor's not here today. But I'll have him on deck here at the rectory tomorrow morning."

"Good. I'll be here. Remember I have very little time, and be ready to present your choice of a location. I have the building plans in my pocket. And my agent has rounded up several big farms for raising all the produce the institution can consume."

"No," said Peppone, "I won't take part in any such dirty comedy. I am what I am and I'm proud of it."

"There's nothing dirty about it," said Don Camillo. "All you have to do is pretend to be a decent sort of person."

"And there's no use your trying to be funny, either. I'm no puppet! I'll turn up at the rectory tomorrow morning, if you like, but with my red kerchief around my neck and three Party membership pins."

"Then you may as well save yourself the trouble. I'll tell him to hang onto his million, because the mayor has no use for it. Our mayor intends to build a children's and old people's home with the funds they send him from Russia. In fact, I'll have the whole story put into print so that everyone can know."

"That's blackmail!" said Peppone angrily.

"I'm only asking you to be quiet and let me do the talking. Politics shouldn't come into it. Here's a chance to do something for the poor, and we must make the best of it."

"But it's a fraud!" said Peppone. "Among other things, I have no intention of tricking that poor old man."

"All right," said Don Camillo, throwing out his arms. "Instead of tricking a millionaire, let's trick the poor! To think that you claim to be fighting for a fairer distribution of rich people's money! Come, come! Is there any trickery in persuading a madman that you're not a Communist, in order to obtain funds for the needy? I see nothing wrong. Anyhow, I leave it up to the Last Judgment, and if I am found guilty I shall pay. Meanwhile our old people and children will have shelter and a crust of bread. This madman wants to build something to commemorate his parents. Why shouldn't we help him?"

"No! I say it's dishonest and I won't have any part of it!"

"Very well," said Don Camillo. "You're sacrificing a cool million to Party pride. Perhaps tomorrow, when you're polishing up the weapons you've stowed away for the Revolution, a bomb will explode in your hands, leaving your son an orphan."

"I hope you explode first," retorted Peppone. "And my son will never beg for your reactionary charity!"

"That's true. He'll have your pension from Malenkov. But what if you live long enough to achieve second childhood and there's no old people's home to take you in?"

"By that time Malenkov will have fixed things so that every old person has a home of his own."

"What if Malenkov disappoints you?"

"I'm not worried about that. Meanwhile, I'll have nothing to do with this plan."

"All right, Peppone. I have to admit that you're right. I was so carried away by the idea of doing something for the poor that I lost my head completely, and it took a hardened unbeliever like yourself to remind me of God's law against lying. It's never permissible to sacrifice principle to profit. Come along tomorrow morning, and we'll tell that madman the truth. I have sinned and it's up to me to atone."

Don Camillo did not have the courage to speak to the Crucified Christ over the altar that evening. He slept uncomfortably and waited for the next morning to restore his peace of mind. Sure enough, the big American car pulled up in front of the rectory and the stranger walked in. Peppone, who was waiting outside with Brusco, Smilzo and Bigio, followed after.

"Here are the mayor and three members of the village council," said Don Camillo.

"Good!" said the old man, shaking hands all around. "I suppose that Don Camillo has already told you my story . . ."

"Yes," said Peppone.

"Splendid. I presume you belong to the clerical party."

"No," said Peppone.

"We're independents," put in Smilzo.

"So much the better!" said the old man. "I don't hold particularly with the priests. If you're free and independent, then of course you're against the Reds. Castor oil and a beating, those are the only treatments for them. Don't you agree?"

His slightly wild eyes were fastened upon Peppone.

"Yessir," Peppone answered.

"Yessir," echoed Bigio, Brusco and Smilzo.

"These cursed Reds . . ." the old man continued, but Don Camillo broke in.

"No more!" he said firmly. "This comedy has gone far enough."

"Comedy? What comedy do you mean?" the old man asked in amazement.

"You were so excited when I saw you yesterday, that in order to calm you down I said some things that are not exactly true," explained Don Camillo. "Things are just the same here as they are at Casalino. The mayor and most of the members of the Village Council are Reds."

"Did you want to make a fool of me?" the stranger asked with a grim laugh.

"No," answered Peppone calmly. "We simply wanted to help the poor. For their sake we were willing to stoop to almost anything."

"And what about those famous tactics of yours?" the stranger said ironically to Don Camillo.

"They're still valid," the priest answered determinedly.

"Then why don't you explain them to the mayor?" the old man asked vindictively

Don Camillo gritted his teeth and took a pack of cards from a desk drawer.

"Look," he said. "Even a tiny child can tear them up one by one, whereas if they're all together it's almost impossible . . ."

"Just a minute," said Peppone. And taking the pack out of Don Camillo's hands he tore it in two with his own.

"Amazing!" exclaimed the old man. "Record-breaking!" And he insisted that Peppone give him a split card with an autograph upon it.

"I'll display them both in the window of my shop in America," he said, putting the whole pack in his pocket. "On one side the priest's and on the other the mayor's. And in between their story. The fact that both of you can split a pack of cards is important," he added. "Likewise the fact that you can league together for the good of the village against an outsider. I still have the same low opinion of you cursed Reds. But I don't care if they burst with envy at Casalino; this is the place where I want to build my institution. Draw up a charter for it by tomorrow and choose a board of directors with no politicians among them. All decision made by this board must be approved by two presidents, who have a lifelong term and the power to choose their successors. The first two men to hold this office shall be Don Camillo and (if I have the name right) Giuseppe Bottazzi. Before we American businessmen embark upon any enterprise we obtain a thorough report on the people and places with which we expect to be concerned. Yesterday, when your priest told me that the local government was not predominantly Communist in character, I had a good laugh. Today I didn't find it quite so funny. But I have learned something I didn't know before and I shall go home happy. Push this thing through fast, because I want to settle it tomorrow. I'm buying the farm today."

Don Camillo went to kneel before the Crucified Christ over the main altar.

"I'm not especially pleased with you, Don Camillo," Christ said. "The old man and Peppone and his friends behaved themselves more creditably than you did."

"But if I hadn't stirred up the situation a bit, nothing would have come out of it," protested Don Camillo weakly.

"That doesn't matter. Even if some good comes out of your evildoing, you're responsible to God for what you did. Unless you understand this, you've misunderstood God's word completely."

"God will forgive me," murmured Don Camillo, lowering his head.

"No, Don Camillo, because when you think of all the good which your sin has done for the poor you won't ever honestly repent."

Don Camillo threw out his arms and felt very sad, because he knew that Christ was quite right.

PEPPONE HAS A DIPLOMATIC ILLNESS

THIS IS AN OUTRAGEOUS hour," grumbled Don Camillo when Peppone's wife came to the rectory.

"I thought priests and doctors were available twenty-four hours a day," she answered.

"All right, all right, but say what you have to say without sitting down. That way you won't stay too long. What is it you want?"

"It's about the new house. I want you to bless it."

Don Camillo clenched his fists.

"You've come to the wrong counter," he said sternly. "Goodnight."

The woman shrugged her shoulders.

"You must forgive him, Father. He had something on his mind."

Don Camillo shook his head. The matter was too serious to be forgotten, even after six months had gone by. Peppone had had an irresistible impulse to make a change; he had sold his shabby, run-down workshop, borrowed money until he was in debt up to his ears and built himself a new house just outside the village, on the main road running parallel to the river. The workshop was as well equipped for making repairs as that of any big city garage, and there were living quarters on the second floor. He had acquired the franchise for a well-known brand of gasoline, and this promised to bring him many customers from the heavy highway traffic.

Of course Don Camillo couldn't resist his curiosity, and one fine morning he went to see. Peppone was deep in a disemboweled motor and decidedly not in talkative mood.

"Fine place you've got here," said Don Camillo, looking around.

"Yes it is, isn't it."

"A big courtyard, an apartment on the second floor, a gasoline pump and everything," Don Camillo continued. "There's only one thing missing."

"What's that?"

"Once upon a time, when a man moved into a new house he called upon the priest to bless it . . ."

Peppone drew himself up, wiping the sweat off his forehead.

"Here's the holy water of our day and age," he said aggressively, "consecrated by good hard work instead of by one of your priestlings."

Don Camillo went away without saying a word. There was something alarming in Peppone's words, something he had never

: [151] :

heard before. Now this request from Peppone's wife carried him back to the feeling of disgust he had suffered six months before.

"No," he told her.

"You've simply got to come," she said, no whit discouraged. "My husband's not the only one in the house. There's myself, and my children. It's not our fault if Peppone was rude to you. If Christ were to . . ."

"Christ doesn't come into it at all," interrupted Don Camillo.

"He does, though," she insisted.

And so, after pacing for several minutes around the room, Don Camillo answered:

"All right, then. I'll come tomorrow."

"No, not tomorrow," she said, shaking her head. "You must come right now, while Peppone's out. I don't want him to know, or the neighbors to see and report to him, either."

This was too much for Don Camillo.

"So I'm to be an underground priest, am I? Perhaps in order to bless a house I should disguise myself as a plumber. As if it were something shameful that had to be hidden! You're more of a heathen than your wretched husband!"

"Just try to understand, Don Camillo. People would say that we were having the house blessed because we're in trouble."

"Because you're in trouble, eh? And actually you want it blessed for some totally different reason. Out with it, woman!"

"Because we *are* in trouble, to tell the truth," she explained. "We've had bad luck ever since we moved into the new house."

"So because you don't know where to turn, you thought you might try God, is that it?"

"Well, why shouldn't I? When things go well, we can look out for ourselves, without bothering God Almighty."

Don Camillo took a stick out of the pile beside the fireplace. "If you aren't at least as far away as the square in the next two seconds, I'll break this over your head!" he told her.

She went away without a word, but a second later she stuck her head through the door.

"I'm not afraid of your stick," she shot at him. "I'm afraid of your unkindness and bad temper."

Don Camillo threw the stick onto the fire and watched it go up in flames. Then brusquely he threw his overcoat over his shoulders and went out. He walked through the darkness until he came to Peppone's house and there he knocked on the door.

"I knew you'd come," said the wife of Peppone.

Don Camillo took the breviary out of his pocket, but before he could open it, Peppone came like a whirlwind into the hall.

"What are you doing here at this hour?"

Don Camillo hesitated, and Peppone's wife spoke up: "I called him to come bless the house."

Peppone looked at her darkly. "I'll settle accounts with you later. As for you, Don Camillo, you can go at once. I don't need you or your God either."

This time Peppone's voice was hardy recognizable. To tell the truth, Peppone was not the man he had been before. He had bitten off more than he could chew, and in throwing himself into this new venture he had borrowed on everything he had and some things he hadn't. Now he was in really hot water and didn't see how he was ever going to get out of it. That evening, for the first time in his life, he had surrendered and asked for help.

After Don Camillo had left, Peppone exploded. "So you'd betray me too, would you?"

"I wouldn't betray you. There's a curse on this house and I wanted to break it. I didn't do anything wrong."

Peppone went into the large kitchen and sat down at the table. "Bless the house, indeed!" he shouted. "He didn't come to bless the house; he came to spy on us, don't you understand? To see how things are going and dig up some proof of our desperate situation. If he'd got into the workshop, he'd have noticed that my new lathe is gone . . ."

"Tell me, what happened?" his wife broke in.

"Well, the lathe's taken care of, and no one saw me carrying it away."

"Someone will notice tomorrow," his wife sighed. "The first man to come in will see that it's not there."

"No one will see a thing," Peppone reassured her. "With the

money I got for the lathe, I paid off our two most pressing creditors, and tomorrow I won't open the shop for business. I've taken care of that too."

His wife looked at him questioningly.

"I called the village council together and told them that I was ill and needed a long rest. I'm going to shut myself up in the house and not let anyone see me."

"That won't do any good," she answered. "Notes will fall due, no matter how tightly you shut yourself up."

"The notes will fall due in another month. Meanwhile, the lathe is gone, and that's a fact we must cover. There are all too many people who'd be happy to know that I'm in trouble."

Then Peppone asked his wife for a big sheet of paper and printed on it in big letters:

WORKSHOP TEMPORARILY CLOSED
DUE TO ILLNESS OF OWNER

"Go stick that on the door," he ordered.

His wife took a bottle of glue and started out, but Peppone stopped her.

"That won't do," he said sadly. "*Owner* is far too bourgeois a word."

He sought in vain for some less reactionary term and finally had to content himself with a vague:

CLOSED, DUE TO ILLNESS

As a matter of fact, the whole business was sick, and not just Peppone.

Peppone did not stick his nose outside, and his wife explained to everyone that he was in a state of exhaustion and mustn't be disturbed until he got better. Ten days went by in this way, but on the eleventh day there was bad news. In the local column of the farm paper there was an item that ran:

LOCAL CITIZEN IN THE LIMELIGHT

We are happy to say that the popularity of our mayor, Giuseppe Bottazzi is always on the increase. Today's list of called-in promissory notes carries three mentions of his name. Congratulations on the well-deserved publicity.

Peppone ran a genuine temperature and went to bed, asking his wife to let him completely alone.

"I don't want to see any letters or newspaper. Just let me sleep."

But three days later she came sobbing into the room and woke him up.

"I've got to tell you something," she said. "They've seized all the new tools in your workshop."

Peppone buried his head in the pillow, but he heard what she was saying. He sweated all the fever he could out of him and then suddenly decided to jump out of bed.

"There's only one thing to do," he exclaimed. "I'll have to go away."

"Just forget about the whole thing," his wife begged him, in an attempt to bring him back to reason. "Let them seize and sell whatever they like. There's a curse on the whole business. We still have the old house and the old workshop. Let's start all over."

"No!" Peppone shouted wildly. "I can't go back to the old place. That would be too humiliating. I must go away, that's all. You can say that I've gone to the mountains on account of my health, and meanwhile I'll try to think up a solution. I can't concentrate in these surroundings, and there's no one to advise me. I'm not breaking off for good; I'll leave everything as it is. If things continue to go badly, they'll blame it on my poor health. But I can't bear to take a step backward and give satisfaction to my enemies."

"Whatever you say," his wife conceded.

"I still have my truck," said Peppone. "That's something. I don't know where I'll go, but you'll be hearing from me. Don't breathe a word to a soul, even if they kill you."

At two o'clock in the morning, Peppone started up the truck

and drove away. No one actually saw him, but he was the subject, even at this late hour, of many conversations.

"His creditors have jumped on him just because he's sick," some people were saying.

"That illness of his is just an excuse to cover up his crimes," said others.

"He's a coward."

"Serves him right!"

"The main thing is for him to get well and come back to his job as mayor."

"If he has any decency, he ought to resign."

Peppone's name was on hundreds of mouths, and all the while he was hurrying away in his old truck, pursued by the "complex of bourgeois respectability," whose influence is felt in every class, including the proletariat.

The days went by and after the news of the seizure came an announcement of a public auction of Peppone's new tools and machinery.

"Lord," said Don Camillo, pointing to the newspaper, "here's proof that God does exist!"

"You're telling Me!" Christ answered.

Don Camillo lowered his head. "Forgive my stupidity," he murmured.

"The stupid things you say are entirely forgivable. I know how that tongue of yours is always getting you in trouble. But what worries Me is your way of thinking. God doesn't care about seizures and auctions. Peppone's bad luck has nothing to do with his demerits, any more than a rascal's rapid rise to riches has anything righteous about it."

"Lord, he has blasphemed Your Name, and ought to be punished. All the decent people of the village are sure that it's because he refused to have the house blessed that he ran into difficulty."

Christ sighed. "And what would these decent people say if Peppone had prospered? That it was because he turned down the blessing?"

Don Camillo threw out his arms impatiently.

"Lord, I'm only telling you what I hear. People—"

"'People'? What does that mean? 'People' as a whole are never going to get into Heaven. God judges 'people' individually and not in the mass. There are no 'group' sins, but only personal ones, and there is no collective soul. Every man's birth and death is a personal affair, and God gives each one of us separate consideration. It's all wrong for a man to let his personal conscience be swallowed up by collective responsibility."

Don Camillo lowered his head. "But, Lord, public opinion has some value . . ."

"I know that, Don Camillo. Public opinion nailed Me to the Cross."

On the day of the public auction, a flock of vultures arrived from the city. They were so efficiently organized that for a mere pittance they divided up and carried away the worldly goods of Peppone. Don Camillo was somewhat depressed when he came back from the sale.

"What are people saying, Don Camillo?" Christ asked him. "Are they happy?"

"No," Don Camillo answered; "they say it's too bad that a man should be ruined because he's ill and far away and can't defend himself."

"Be honest with me, Don Camillo, and tell me what people are actually saying."

Don Camillo threw out his arms. "They're saying that if God really existed, such things wouldn't happen."

Christ smiled.

"From the 'Hosannas!' of the acclaiming crowd to the same crowd's cry of: 'Crucify him!' there isn't so very far to go. Do you see that, now, Don Camillo?"

That same evening there was a stormy meeting of the village council. Spiletti, the only councilman belonging to the Opposition, raised the subject of the mayor.

"For two months we've had no news of him. He's lost all interest in the village and even in his own private affairs. Where is

: [157] :

he, and what's he doing? On behalf of a large number of my fellow-citizens, I demand a definite answer."

Brusco, who was serving as deputy mayor, got up to reply.

"I shall give you a detailed answer tomorrow."

"I'm not inquiring into any top secret, am I?" objected Spiletti. "I demand an answer right away. Where is the mayor?"

Brusco shrugged his shoulders.

"We don't know," he admitted.

There was a grumbling protest from all those present. The thing was simply incredible.

"Nobody knows the whereabouts of the mayor!" Spiletti shouted. "Then let's put an ad in the paper: *Reward to anyone who can find one Red mayor, two months missing.*"

"It's not so funny as all that," said Brusco. "Not even his wife knows where he is."

Just then a voice boomed out from the back of the room.

"I know," said Don Camillo.

Everyone was silent, until Brusco spoke out: "If you know, tell us."

"No," said Don Camillo. "But I can bring him here tomorrow morning."

In a gloomy section of the suburbs of Milan, Peppone was shoveling scrap iron and plaster from a recently demolished building into his truck. When the noon whistle sounded, he threw down his shovel, took a sandwich and a copy of the Communist paper, *Unity,* out of the pocket of his jacket and went to sit down with his back against a fence, alongside his fellow-workers.

"Mr. Mayor!"

The shrill voice of Spiletti brought him to his feet with a single bound.

"There aren't any mayors around here," he answered.

"And the trouble is we have no mayor in our village, either," said Spiletti. "Can you tell me where to find one?"

"That's none of my business," said Peppone, sitting down on the ground.

"You look to me as if you'd recovered your health," Spiletti insisted. "You must be well enough to send us a postcard."

"You don't catch me sending a postcard to you, you tool of the clergy! How happy I am not to have you on my mind!"

"That's no way for a mayor to talk!" Spiletti protested.

"I'm speaking as a free man."

"Well said!" said the other workers, who had left their lunch to gather around Peppone.

"If you want to be free, then resign from your position!" Spiletti shouted.

"Just to please you, eh?" grumbled the workers. "Hold on to it, Comrade!"

"Well, if you're not resigning, we'd like at least to know your intentions."

Peppone shrugged his shoulders.

"If you'd rather have fun in Milan than do the job to which you've been appointed, then you've simply got to give up the job."

"We'll take *your* job away, that's what," threatened the workers. But Peppone turned around.

"Easy, boys," he said authoritatively. "This is a democratic country, and threats don't go."

Meanwhile Brusco, Bigio and the rest of Peppone's henchmen had appeared upon the scene and sat silently down around him.

"Chief," said Brusco sadly, "why did you desert us?"

"I'm not deserting anybody."

"What are we to do about the new road? Here's a letter from the Ministry of Public Works."

And Brusco held out a sheet of paper, which Peppone proceeded to read.

"As long as there's a certain crowd in the government, we'll never get anywhere," he observed.

"Never mind about the national administration!" Spiletti shouted. "It's up to you to make a concrete proposal."

"We made one, long ago," Bigio put in.

"That was just propaganda!" Spiletti shouted. "There was nothing concrete about it."

Smilzo had a word to put in at this point, and so did Peppone. Soon they were in the middle of a heated discussion. Amid the refuse from a demolished building in Milan, they held one of the most unusual village council meetings ever to be seen. When five o'clock came and they were still debating, the night watchman said he must close the gate and send them away. The whole council, including the Opposition, transferred the debate to Peppone's truck.

"Let's go find a quieter place," said Peppone, starting up the motor.

There was no telling how it happened, perhaps because none of them knew the layout of the city too well, but soon the truck was rolling down the highway. Peppone bent with clenched teeth and tense muscles over the wheel. There was something on his mind, which for a long time he had been unable to say. All at once he threw on the brakes. One of those cursed hitch-hikers was standing practically in front of the truck and signaling that he wanted a lift in the same direction. He had a cake and a toy balloon in one hand and a priest's hat on his head. Smilzo got down from the seat beside Peppone and went to sit in the back of the truck, along with the rest of the village council. Don Camillo climbed up to take his place, and Peppone started off with a jolt like that of a tank.

"Do certain people always have to be hanging around?" he grumbled.

The truck was traveling like a racing car, and the roar coming out of the motor was like the orchestra of Toscanini. All of a sudden, over the crest of the river embankment, they saw the church tower.

"Ah!" Peppone exclaimed ruefully.

"'Ah' doesn't make the first two letters of 'happy,'" observed Don Camillo.

"Yes, it does, even if the letters aren't in the right order," said a voice that only Don Camillo could hear.

A BALL BOUNCES BACK

WHEN WOMEN GO IN FOR
politics they're worse than the most rabid of the men. The men
throw their weight around for the sake of "the cause," whereas
the women direct all their wiles toward the discomfiture of the
enemy. The same difference as there is between defending one's
country and going to war in order to kill as many people as possible on the other side.

Jo del Magro was up to her ears in politics, and because of her fiery temperament she did not only her share but that of her husband as well. He died, poor fellow, leaving her with a three-year-old son, but her grief for his loss must have been to some degree compensated by the fact that she ignored the priest and carried him to the grave to the muted notes of the Red anthem.

Jo was good-looking enough, in her way, and could perfectly well have found a second husband to look after her. But she clung obstinately to her hard lot, feeding upon it the embitteredness which held the place of faith in her heart. She supported herself by heavy farm work—sowing, reaping, threshing and wine-pressing—in the summer, and in the winter by making reed baskets which she peddled about the country. She worked fiercely, as if weariness were an end in itself and her only satisfaction. And even the boldest men took care not to bother her, because she was not only strong-armed, but had a vocabulary coarse enough to put theirs to shame.

The little boy grew like a weed. When he wasn't left alone in their isolated shack but was allowed to trail after his mother, she set him down in the farmyard where she was working and told him to shut up and "keep out of her hair." When he was five years old he could throw stones as well as a boy of ten and destroy a laden fruit-tree in less than half an hour. He nosed about like a hunting-dog among the chicken coops, leaving a mess of broken eggs behind him; he strewed bits of glass on the roads and perpetrated other tricks of the same kind. His only distinction lay in the fact that he was a lone wolf and preferred to operate on his own rather than to run with the pack. When two gangs of boys were engaged in battle he hid behind a bush or tree and threw stones indiscriminately at both factions. He was anti-social by nature and had an extraordinary ability to disappear from the scene of his misdemeanors. The evening of the grape-gathering festival he let the air out of the tires of some fifty bicycles and threw the valve caps away. No one could lay hands on him, but everyone was saying:

"It must be that confounded little Magrino!"

A few days later some well-meaning ladies went to call on his mother and tactfully intimated that instead of letting him run wild she should turn him over, during her working hours, to the day nursery. Jo grew red in the face and shouted that rather than give her son over to a priestly institution she'd leave him with certain women whose reputation they knew all too well.

"Tell Don Gumshoe Camillo to look after his own business!" she said, adding a volley of oaths which caused the well-meaning ladies to pull up their skirts and run. Their leader reported the upshot of their visit to Don Camillo, concluding:

"Father, I can't repeat the name that unfortunate creature fastened upon you!"

"I know it already," he answered gloomily.

The weather was fine and the children of Don Camillo's day nursery were out on the playing field most of the afternoon. The swings and see-saws had been restored to good order and even the grumpiest children were all smiles. Don Camillo lay in a deck chair, smoking his cigar and enjoying the warm sun, when he had a sudden feeling that something was wrong.

The playing field bordered, on the river side, on a field of alfalfa, from which it was separated by a galvanized wire fence. Now Don Camillo was struck by an unaccustomed ripple in the alfalfa, and his hunter's instinct told him that it was neither a dog nor a chicken. He did not move, but half closed his eyes in order to observe without being detected. Slowly something rose out of the grass and Don Camillo felt Magrino's eyes converging upon him. He held his breath while Magrino, feeling sure that he was not watched, transferred his gaze to another objective. He was following the children's game and such was his curiosity that at one point he forgot himself and raised his whole head above the alfalfa. No one noticed, and of this Don Camillo was glad. All of a sudden his head disappeared. A big ball, with which some of the bigger boys were playing, had been kicked over the fence and they called out to ask Don Camillo if they could go get it. The priest pretended to wake up with a start.

"Is the ball out of bounds again?" he shouted. "I've told you to be more careful. That grass can't be trodden down. No more ball-playing today. You can go get the ball tomorrow, and meanwhile let me sleep!"

The boys grumbled a bit; then they found another ball and played with that, while Don Camillo pretended to be sleeping. Actually, he was more alert than ever. Ten minutes later the alfalfa stirred again, but this time the line of rippling moved farther and farther away. Magrino was leaving, but he was following an odd course, which for the moment led him to the center of the alfalfa field.

"He must be cutting across diagonally," thought Don Camillo, "in order to emerge along the hedge parallel to the canal."

Instead, Magrino stopped short and made an abrupt turn to the left. Obviously he had found the ball, picked it up and now was carrying it away.

"Rascal!" muttered Don Camillo. "You've pulled off the trick handsomely. But when you reach the row of trees at the end of the alfalfa you'll have to show yourself!"

But Magrino knew better. When he was out of the tall grass he slid on his stomach until he came to a ditch which ran at right angles to the trees and afforded him perfect cover.

"Lord," Don Camillo murmured, "how can a five-year-old boy have learned to be so tricky?"

"Don Camillo," the Lord answered, "how do fish learn to swim? By instinct, of course."

"Instinct?" Don Camillo exclaimed gloomily. "Are men instinctively evil?"

Don Camillo bought the boys another ball and made no mention of the escapade of Magrino. He hoped that the stolen ball would act like bait and bring Magrino back later. Every day he scanned the field of alfalfa, but there was no ripple. Then someone told him that Magrino was ill and confined to the house. As a matter of fact, Magrino had come down with a fever the night after he had taken the ball. The ditch was full of water, and in crawling through it he was chilled to the bone. Then, before going into the shack he had buried the ball in a hole. His mother came home late, and found him shivering all over. At first it seemed like nothing at all, at least nothing that couldn't be cured with a few pills and a hot-water bottle. Then things took a turn for the worse and one evening he became half delirious. He muttered something over and over, and finally Jo understood him to mention a big rubber ball.

"Don't worry," she said. "Hurry up and get well, and I'll buy a ball for you."

Magrino quieted down, but the next night, when his fever rose again, he resumed his insistence upon the ball.

"Take it easy!" said Jo. "I told you I'd get it as soon as you're well."

"No . . . no . . ."

"Do you want me to get one right away?"

"No . . . no . . . The ball . . ."

Evidently he couldn't take his mind off it. But the doctor said there was no use looking for a meaning in the ravings of a delirious child. And so, on the third night, Jo simply answered:

"All right . . . Whatever you say . . ."

He raved until one o'clock when the fever went down sufficiently for him to sleep. Then, at last, the exhausted Jo was able to go to bed.

The next morning at five o'clock Don Camillo stood shaving in front of the mirror hanging from the sash bolt of his window. It was a clear, cool day, and he took his time, looking out over the fields to the row of poplars along the river bank and beyond them the gleaming river. Directly below him lay the playing-field, empty and silent at this hour, but soon to be overrun by the day nursery. He smiled to himself at the thought of all the freshly washed little faces.

As his glance fell upon the field of alfalfa and the wire fence, he murmured to himself: "The little rascal! . . ." Then he started as a moving white object caught his attention. Only when it was within a few yards of the fence did he recognize it. It was little Magrino, bundled up in a long white night-shirt, which his father had formerly worn by day, weaving in and out of the tall grass, like a drunkard or a sleepwalker. He stumbled and fell, but stood up again and went on, clutching all the while a big rubber ball. When he reached the fence he threw it up in the air, but the

: [165] :

fence was too high and it fell back on the same side. He threw it again and it hit the wire. Don Camillo's forehead was covered with perspiration.

"Lord," he prayed, "give him the strength to throw it over!"

Magrino was tired out and the tiny arms sticking out of the shirtsleeves seemed to have lost all their former skill. He staggered in order to remain erect and paused for several minutes before making another try. Don Camillo shut his eyes, and when he opened them the ball was in the playing field, while Magrino lay motionless among the alfalfa. The priest went like an avalanche down the stairs. When he picked up the little boy the lightness of his burden struck terror into his heart. Magrino's eyes flickered open, and finding himself in the enemy's grasp he whispered:

"Don Gumshoe . . . the ball's inside . . ."

"Good fellow!" said Don Camillo.

The bell-ringer, who went to tell Jo, found her beside herself over the disappearance of her son. When she saw him lying on a couch before the fire in Don Camillo's study her amazement knew no bounds.

"I found him in a dead faint among the alfalfa, just twenty minutes ago," Don Camillo told her.

"And what in the world was he doing there? My head is completely woozy."

"Always has been, hasn't it?" asked Don Camillo.

The doctor told Jo not to dream of taking the boy away but gave him an injection and left precise instructions for his care. Meanwhile Don Camillo was in the sacristy, preparing for Mass.

"Lord," he said to the Crucified Christ as he stood before the altar, "how did it all happen? After the upbringing that boy's had, how could he know the difference between good and evil?"

"Don Camillo," said Christ, "how do fish learn to swim? By instinct. And conscience is instinctive in the same way; it's not something that can be transmitted from one person to another. It's not like taking a light into a dark room. The light is burning all the time, covered by a thick veil. When you take the veil away, the room is lit."

"Very well, Lord, but who unveiled the light in that boy's soul?"

"Don Camillo, when the darkness of death is impending, everyone instinctively searches within himself for a ray of light. And now, don't you bother your head about how it came about; just rejoice in it and thank God."

Magrino stayed for a fortnight in the rectory and Jo came morning and evening to see him; that is, she knocked at the window and when Don Camillo opened it, she said:

"I've come to see the prisoner."

Don Camillo made no reply but let the two of them talk together. After a fortnight had gone by he came home one day to find Magrino letting the air out of his bicycle tires. He gathered together the boy's few clothes and took him to the door saying:

"You're cured. Go along home!"

That evening Jo came boldly to the door.

"How much do I owe you?" she asked.

"Nothing. The most that you can do for me is to stay out of my sight forever, *per omnia saecula saeculorum*."

"Amen," mumbled Jo.

But out of sheer spite she appeared at eleven o'clock Mass the following Sunday, sitting in the front pew, with Magrino beside her. Don Camillo shot her a terrifying glance, but from the bold way in which she stared back at him he knew perfectly well that she was saying to herself:

"Don Gumshoe, don't make those ferocious eyes at me. I'm not the least bit afraid!"

THE CARD SHARPS

SMILZO HAD THE POST OF-
fice job of taking around special delivery letters, and now he
braked his bicycle in breakneck Mao Tse-tung style right in front
of the sunny bench where Don Camillo was quietly reading his
paper.

The method of stopping a bicycle by sliding off the saddle toward the rear and at the same time jerking up the handlebars in such a way as to lift the front wheel off the ground and produce the effect of a bucking broncho had been known until recent years as "Texas Cowboy" style. Now, for obvious political reasons, this reactionary Western name had given way to an appellation from the proletarian and revolutionary East.

Don Camillo raised his eyes and viewed Smilzo's cyclonic arrival distrustfully.

"Does a certain Jesus Christ live here?" Smilzo asked, pulling a letter out of the bag hanging over his shoulder.

"Someone lives here that may give you a swift kick," Don Camillo answered tersely.

"Due respect must be paid to all officials engaged in the public service," said Smilzo. "The address on this Special Delivery letter is: *Jesus Christ, Parish House.* If no such person resides there, then I write: *Unknown at the above address,* and that's all there is to it."

Don Camillo took hold of the letter, and sure enough, the address was just what Smilzo had represented it to be.

"I'll take it," he said. "It will give me grounds for a complaint to the postal authorities. They have no right to encourage such a piece of sacrilegious imbecility."

"The postal authorities are only doing their duty," said Smilzo. "The parish house exists, and they don't have to know who's inside. A man can have anyone in his house he wants to. And the name doesn't matter; it may be an alias for all we care."

Don Camillo bent over with studied indifference and the intention of taking off his shoe to serve as a missile, but Smilzo rode off like a flash, before he could reach it.

The joker who had written the sacrilegious address had added the word *Personal,* and underlined it, and Don Camillo went to give vent to his indignation before the Crucified Christ over the altar.

"Lord," he exclaimed, "won't You tell me who pulled off this disgraceful trick? Won't You enable me to go wring his neck and force him to eat the letter?"

"Don Camillo," Christ answered with a smile, "we must respect

: [169] :

the privacy of the mails. We can't go against the principles of the Constitution."

"Then, Lord, are we to allow these fellows to blaspheme You with the written word as well as the spoken one?"

"How do you know that the author of the letter is a blasphemer?" Christ asked. "Mightn't he be a simple-minded man or a mad one? You'd better read it before you condemn him."

Don Camillo threw out his arms in resignation, tore open the envelope and took out a sheet of paper with words printed in capital letters upon it, which he read slowly to himself.

"Well, Don Camillo? Is it as dreadful as you imagined?"

"No, Lord; it's the work of a madman, who deserves only compassion."

Don Camillo stuffed the letter into his pocket and started to go away, but Christ called him back.

"What does this madman ask of Me, Don Camillo?"

"Nothing in particular. His letter's a mass of chaotic sentences, with no order or meaning."

"All well and good, but you mustn't pass such a quick judgment upon the expression of a troubled mind. Madness has a logic all its own, and the understanding of this leads to a discovery of the cause of the trouble."

"Oh, the trouble is a vague sort of affair," said Don Camillo hurriedly. "It's impossible to understand it."

"Read it to Me, Don Camillo."

Don Camillo shrugged his shoulders in resignation, drew the letter out of his pocket and read it aloud.

"Lord, I beg you to illuminate the mind of a certain priest and convey to him that he is carrying his political activity too far. In fact, if he carries it much farther, he may find his hind quarters in contact with a hickory stick. To exercise the priesthood by vocation is one thing, and by provocation is another. Signed—A friend of democracy."

"What priest do you suppose he means?" Christ asked at the end of the letter.

"I haven't the slightest idea," said Don Camillo.

"Do you know any priest who carries his political activity too far?"

"Lord, I get around so very little . . . All the priests in this part of the country are quiet, well-balanced fellows . . ."

"What about yourself, Don Camillo?"

"Lord, we were speaking of priests in this part of the country. If the letter had referred to me, it would have said 'the local priest,' or 'the priest of this parish,' instead of 'a certain priest.' As You so rightly remarked, madness has a logic all its own, and I am trying to reason along the lines of this logic."

"Don Camillo," Christ sighed, "why are you trying to keep the truth from Me? Why don't you admit that you are the priest in question?"

"Lord, do You pin Your faith on poison-pen letters and anonymous accusations?"

"No, Don Camillo, but I'd pin My faith on any accusation you care to make against yourself."

"Lord, the election is very near, and we're waging an important battle. I must be loyal to the parish priest. I can tell him to be careful, but I can't bring any accusation against him."

"You mean you'll advise him to keep his hind quarters out of contact with a stick, is that it?"

"No, Lord, I'm concerned not with my body but with my soul."

With which Don Camillo went to meditate in his study, and as a result the next day Smilzo brought a Special Delivery letter to Peppone.

"What are we to do with this, Chief?" he asked.

Peppone saw that the address on the envelope was: *Mr. Malenkov, People's Palace.* Undaunted, he took out the letter and read the printed text:

"Mr. Malenkov, please inform your follower known as 'a friend of democracy' that his interesting letter will be photographed for reproduction in the local reactionary press. Gratefully yours, A Certain Priest."

Peppone turned purple with anger, but Smilzo calmed him down.

"Chief, you'll just have to take it and let the whole thing blow over. He's maneuvered himself into a favorable position."

"He's got himself out of range of a hickory stick," roared Peppone, bringing his massive fist down on the desk. "But if I beat him up with a branch of elm or acacia, then no one will suspect me."

"Naturally, Chief. There are dozens of ways you can get the better of him, without giving yourself away by the use of hickory. All nature is on the People's side!"

The publication of the letter aroused considerable talk and everyone accused the Reds of its authorship. In self-defense Peppone decided to relax the general tension by organizing a "Poker Tournament for the Peace Crusade." In this part of the world, which is cut off by the winter fog from the rest of humanity, poker is not so much a game as it is a vital necessity and a tournament of this kind, even if it was organized under the shadow of the wings of Stalin's Peace Dove, was bound to be a success.

Tournament headquarters was set up at the Molinetto tavern, which was filled every evening with people of every class and condition. The match grew more and more exciting as poor players were eliminated and undisputed experts held the field. At last it came to a final showdown, which brought two champions face to face. Don Camillo informed Christ of the latest developments.

"Lord, this evening brings the last round. Everyone's excited, because as always happens in these parts, politics has entered the situation. I shouldn't be surprised if fists were to fly before the evening's over."

"How does that happen, Don Camillo?"

"Lord, politics has a way of changing the aspect of everything it touches, and so the last round of the tournament has turned into a duel between the People's champion and the champion of Reaction. The finalists are Farmer Filotti and Peppone. If Filotti wins, then it is a victory for Reaction, and if, instead, Peppone manages to beat him, then the proletariat will rejoice."

"This is all very silly," said Christ. "What interests are tied up in this game?"

"It's just a matter of prestige. Foolish, if you like, but in politics it makes a big difference. Anyhow, we're certain to be defeated. I say 'we' because the Reds are our natural enemies. But it had to end this way. Peppone isn't coming up against our best player. Filotti may be good, but he's not our top man. And Peppone's such a schemer that he's not above pulling off some funny business with the cards. Now, it may be blasphemous to speak of 'Justice' in something so frivolous as a game of poker. But, if I may be allowed to say so, it's unjust that victory should go to someone who doesn't deserve it . . ."

"Don't take it too hard, Don Camillo," Christ interrupted. "You said yourself that it's a frivolous matter. As a matter of fact, all such games are bad for a man, even if they are played for nothing more than fun. Card-playing is a vice, just like everything else that serves merely to kill time."

"Of course," said Don Camillo, with a bow. "But if it's legitimate to draw up a scale of values among all these vicious games, I should say that poker was the least harmful of the lot, because it's based on reason and provides mental gymnastics as well as wholesome recreation."

"Don Camillo, you talk like a real fan."

"No, just like someone that knows the game. Like a very mediocre player, but one that could beat three Peppones to a frazzle . . . But of course it's unthinkable for a priest to mingle with card-players in a tavern, even if he is motivated by a noble desire to prevent a leader of godlessness from carrying off an undeserved victory."

"Quite right," Christ answered. "A priest must never set foot in a tavern simply in order to take part in some petty game. Priests serve the King of Heaven, not the kings of clubs and diamonds."

It was late by now, and Don Camillo started off to bed. Meanwhile the crowded Molinetto tavern was the scene of the final battle. Peppone was in good form; indeed, he seemed to have a calculating machine in the place of his brain. The last game won him deafening applause. Filotti threw his cards down on the table and called for a glass of white wine.

"Let's have a drink on it," he said. "There's nothing else I can do."

Peppone was the winner and the Reds were so wild with joy that they began to shout for a speech. Amid general silence Peppone took the floor.

"Comrades! In the battle of sport as well as the battle of labor, the workingman must win. This victorious tournament, played under the auspices of . . ."

But at this point he stopped short, because someone was knocking at the window which gave onto the street. Smilzo prudently opened it, and there behind the grating was the face of Don Camillo. There was a dramatic silence.

"What do you want?" Peppone asked threateningly.

"I want to play," answered Don Camillo.

"To play? Play with whom?"

"Anyone that's not afraid to play with me."

Peppone shot him a pitying glance.

"I'm not afraid of anybody. But the tournament is over. If you wanted to play, you should have signed up for it."

"I did sign up," Don Camillo explained. "If you look at the list, you'll find a registration under the name of *Il Calmo*, or 'The Calm Man.'"

"That doesn't mean anything," retorted Peppone. "Anyone can come along and claim to have signed up under that name."

"No, because *Il Calmo* is an anagram for 'Camillo.'"

"This isn't an anagram contest or a Latin lesson; it's a serious card game."

Don Camillo explained the nature of an anagram, and after Peppone had counted the letters he had to admit that Camillo and *Il Calmo* came to the same thing.

"Of course if His Honor the Mayor is afraid of coming a cropper, then I'll go away."

"Come on in," shouted Peppone.

"I can't do that," said Don Camillo; "it wouldn't be proper. I'll stay here and we'll play on the windowsill."

"That may be a good idea," said Peppone. "You'll feel safer that way."

Don Camillo grasped two bars of the grating in his hands and twisted them back.

"That makes it more convenient," he explained, "but if the fresh air bothers you, you can fix it the way it was before."

"It does bother me," said Peppone, grasping the bars and pulling them back into their original position.

The crowd had never seen a more formidable sight. People held their breath the way they do at the circus when two tight-rope walkers advance to the roll of drums. Peppone took a pack of cards and laid it on the windowsill; Don Camillo picked it up and shook his head.

"Those are too thin and frail for a temperament like mine," he objected. And taking the pack in his big hands, he tore it in two. Peppone paled, and Smilzo came up with another pack of cards.

"Will this do?" asked Peppone.

"No," said Don Camillo.

"I don't like it myself," said Peppone, picking up the pack and mangling it in exactly the same way.

Someone offered them a third pack.

"It has to be brand new and in its original wrapping," Don Camillo insisted. "Trust is all very well, but mistrust is better."

Smilzo brought out a pack of cards still wrapped and sealed in cellophane paper, which Peppone examined carefully and then handed to Don Camillo.

"I'm satisfied," he said. "What about you?"

"It's all right with me," said Don Camillo, turning the cards over in his hands and giving them back to Peppone. "Go ahead and shuffle, but keep your hands out of mischief."

Peppone gritted his teeth, shuffled the cards and laid them on the windowsill.

"The tournament's over, and I won it," he said. "The Cup goes to the Party, and no one can take it away. But in order to make this a good game and lend it some social significance, I'll put up my shotgun as stakes. What about you?"

A murmur went through the room. Peppone's gun was the finest for miles around and everyone knew how he prized it. He would have cut off a leg rather than give up that precious gun. Everyone waited for Don Camillo to make a fitting reply. And he did not disappoint them.

"I'll put up my dog!" he said boldly. And everyone knew that the dog was the apple of Don Camillo's eye.

The game that followed was of an epic character. If Homer's heroes had played poker they would have played it in just the same way. The two men fought with all their wits until the bitter end, and Don Camillo won. No one dared applaud him. Finally Don Camillo tipped his hat.

"Thanks for the good game, and good-night. Gambling debts are due within twenty-four hours."

Don Camillo went straight to the rectory, without passing through the church, but Christ's voice overtook him.

"At this late hour, Don Camillo!"

"I went to look in at the last round of the tournament. But I didn't set foot in the tavern; I stayed just outside the window. And just as I thought, Peppone was the winner."

"Did that cause any trouble?"

"No, everything went smoothly, and there was general agreement that the best man won."

"Don Camillo, this game of poker interests me. I gather from what you say, that it must be played with a pack of brand-new cards, in their original wrapping."

"That's a wise precaution, especially if you're playing with nimble-fingered fellows who may connive with the tavern-keeper to use marked cards."

"I see. So a pack of new cards is brought out; the first player examines it and passes it to the second, who then slips it into his pocket and puts in its place another identical pack, inconspicuously marked with his thumb-nail and rewrapped in the original paper. Isn't that the system?"

"Oh, I wouldn't put it that way," said Don Camillo.

"Then what have you got in your pocket?"

"I can't imagine how in the world it got there," stammered

Don Camillo, pulling out a pack of new cards and laying it on the table.

"Peppone gave it to you and you slipped his pack into your pocket and gave him back another pack which you had brought with you."

"Obviously there was a mix-up of some kind," said Don Camillo.

"Yes, you mixed up right and wrong and added to the immorality of a gambling game. But you're the real loser, Don Camillo."

Don Camillo was wiping the perspiration off his forehead when Peppone came into the room. He took his famous shotgun out from under his coat and handed it over.

"Gambling debts are paid promptly," he said, "but if you're an honest man, you'll give me a chance for revenge."

Then he noticed the pack of cards on the table.

"This is luck," he added. "Here's a brand-new pack, which guarantees a fair game. Open it and shuffle the cards."

They sat down at the table and Don Camillo opened the pack and shuffled. The game was just as Homeric in character as the one that had gone before, but this time Peppone won.

"Shall we play a third game to break the tie?" he suggested.

Don Camillo did not answer, because he was fingering the cards.

"Aha!" he said all of a sudden. "So you mark the ace like this, do you?"

Peppone did not blench. He pulled another pack of cards out of his pocket and searched for the seven.

"And your mark is these two fine lines, isn't it?" he countered.

Don Camillo picked up Peppone's pack and threw it onto the fire. And Peppone did the same thing with Don Camillo's.

"Well, we're even," said Peppone as he got up to leave.

"No," said Don Camillo; "I'm the loser."

And he said it so sorrowfully that Peppone was touched.

"Father, don't take it too hard. In a game of poker the prospect of winning addles a man's brain and he can't help himself. I'll

: [177] :

lend you my gun to go hunting, and you can lend me your dog in return. How about it?"

After Peppone had gone, Don Camillo stared into the fire.

"Don Camillo, I said that you were in the service of the King of Heaven, not of the kings of clubs and diamonds. You ought to be ashamed!"

Don Camillo threw out his arms, raised his eyes to heaven and exclaimed:

"Lord, I know I'm in the wrong. But you heard what he said about the game and how it addles a man's brain."

Then something caught Don Camillo's eye. It was Peppone's deck and the flames of the fire were just beginning to curl round it. In a moment it would be too late to find out how an expert like Peppone marked the kings and queens.

Christ sighed.

"Don Camillo, who's going to save you from burning in Hell?"

Don Camillo did not answer, but he sat quite still and did not go up to bed until the glowing coals had turned to ashes.

HUNGER STRIKE

SMILZO'S MOTHER HAD PARA-
lyzed legs, but she also had a head on her shoulders, and even
though she had been confined to a chair for five or six years, she
knew exactly what was going on. When she was present Smilzo
and his wife didn't dare talk politics, but she had a keen ear and
heard much of what they didn't even say. They thought they

: [179] :

had everything under control but a few days after their son was born the old woman came out and said:

"It's time to baptize him."

Smilzo was taken by surprise and stood there gaping, but his wife jumped into the breach.

"There's no hurry," she said. "Let's wait at least until this cold spell is over."

The old woman said nothing, but two days later she attacked again.

"Well, is he going to be baptized or isn't he?"

With the passage of time she became more and more insistent, and finally Smilzo screwed up his courage to say: "Don't let's hear any more talk about this business of baptism. Times have changed in a great many ways that you don't know."

The old woman shook her head. "From the day when Jesus Christ started this business of baptism, times have changed over and over and any number of things have happened, but newborn babies have always been baptized."

Smilzo muttered something about political parties and excommunications but the old woman knew what she was talking about and stuck to it.

"Newborn babies aren't party members. And so they've got to be baptized."

Smilzo repeated that she didn't understand, but she went on shaking her head.

"I understand perfectly well. Your father was worse than you are when it comes to political notions, but you were baptized shortly after you were born."

"Things were different in those days," Smilzo's wife exclaimed.

"And wives were different too!" retorted the old woman.

"Wives were different? What do you mean? What have you got against me?"

"The fact that you're a silly girl."

"All right, then," the wife shouted. "I won't have my baby baptized for certain. If when he's older, he feels like being baptized, then he can do something about it."

The old woman looked at her son, but he failed to agree with her.

"It's putting something over on children to baptize them when they don't know what it's all about," he mumbled.

"Very well," said the old woman. "From now on, I'm not eating. I shan't eat until the baby's been baptized."

"You'll starve for years, then," said her daughter-in-law with a mocking laugh.

Smilzo said nothing, but brought his fist down on the table and went out of the house.

The next day the old woman did not drink her usual cup of milk for breakfast and at noon she sat quietly in her chair, watching the others eat their lunch. It was the same thing at supper, and finally Smilzo lost his patience.

"You've behaved quite long enough like a spoiled child," he said. "Go ahead and eat, instead of trying to upset me."

"She'll eat when she's hungry," his wife reassured him. But another day went by in the same way, and the daughter-in-law began to be worried.

"We must call the doctor," she said, "tell him what's happened and have her taken away. Otherwise, if she dies of starvation, we'll be blamed for it. Can't you see her little game? She wants to ruin our reputation."

At this point the old woman spoke up.

"Give me pen and paper and I'll write down that I'm dying of my own free will. I'm not trying to ruin your reputation; I simply want to save my grandson's soul."

Smilzo's wife had an attack of nerves and began sobbing: "She hates me! I won't have any milk for the baby if she goes on this way."

"What of it?" said the old woman. "Snake's milk won't do him any good."

Smilzo ran out of the house in despair. But he could just as well have stayed home, because the old woman did not open her mouth to speak again. The third day she chose to stay in bed.

"I'd rather die in this position," she explained. "Please call the priest."

"No!" shouted her daughter-in-law. "No!"

"It doesn't really matter," said the old woman. "God will listen to me just the same."

"You'll die with a curse upon you!" shouted her daughter-in-law. "It's a clear-cut case of suicide, because you won't eat."

"No, you've prevented me from eating by refusing to have the baby baptized."

She closed her eyes and sank back on the pillows, while her daughter-in-law withdrew uneasily. Smilzo had been listening just outside the door.

"Something must be done in a hurry," he said.

"Are you going to give in to the priests?" his wife panted. "They've thrown you out of the Church and you ask them to baptize your son? That doesn't go very well with the beliefs you profess in public."

"Take it easy!" said Smilzo. "We've got to find a way to kill two birds with one stone. I'm going to see Peppone."

Peppone was in his workshop when Smilzo burst in upon him.

"Chief, you've got to help me. I'm in hot water." He proceeded to tell his thorny story and concluded: "Chief, I don't want to betray my political principles, but I can't let my mother die. Suppose I get a fancy, lace-trimmed baptismal dress; you put on your best clothes and come for us in your car. We'll have the baby all rigged out in white and show him to his grandmother, with you in a godfather's role. We'll drive to the People's Palace, sneak in through the courtyard, drink a bottle of wine and then go back and say to my mother: 'Here he is, fresh from the font, just as you wanted!' Then she'll start eating again and my conscience will be clear."

"I see," said Peppone. "But what if she ever finds out?"

"She won't," said Smilzo curtly. "And the main thing just now is to get her to eat."

Peppone shrugged but agreed to cooperate and while Smilzo went to buy a robe he put on his best clothes. Half an hour later they were at Smilzo's house. The house was in a lonely spot and there was a heavy fog in the air, both of them favorable circumstances. Smilzo's wife ran to wake up the old woman.

"If you really don't want to ruin our reputation, then get up for a minute. The baby's godfather is here."

"His godfather?" exclaimed the old woman, opening her eyes wide.

"Yes, the mayor himself, who's honored us by consenting to present him for baptism."

Voices rang out downstairs, and the old woman pulled herself into an upright position and threw a shawl around her shoulders.

"Where's the baby?" she asked.

"They're dressing him now."

"Is he fitted out properly?"

"You'll soon see."

There was a knock at the door, and Smilzo came in, carrying the baby wrapped in the most elaborate outfit that can be imagined. Behind this dazzling white vision was the massive figure of Peppone. But the old woman had eyes only for the baby.

"What a little beauty!" she sobbed, raising her gaunt hands as if before some miraculous apparition.

Even the mother was amazed to see her child in such festive array. She snatched him out of Smilzo's arms in order to smooth out the pleats and straighten the bows of the baptismal robe and put the cap at the proper angle on the tiny pink head.

"How are you?" Peppone asked the old woman.

At last she managed to take her eyes off the baby and look at Peppone.

"What an honor you are paying us, Mr. Mayor!" she exclaimed, grasping one of his big paws. "God bless you! I know it's thanks to you that my son came around to reason. But never mind about that; it's all over . . ."

Peppone tried to free his hand, but she held it in an iron grasp.

"Don't say that!" he replied. "Your son doesn't need advice from anybody. He's a fine man. And the honor of being his child's godfather is all mine . . . But tell me how you are feeling."

"Splendid, thank you," she answered. "I had a touch of flu, just like everyone else this winter, but I'm quite well now."

"Take good care of yourself!" Peppone admonished her in an

authoritative tone. And after this he could find nothing else to say.

"We must hurry along," put in Smilzo. "The priest is waiting."

The old woman insisted on looking at the baby again and laid a finger on his forehead.

"He's smiling!" said Peppone. "Seems as if he knew you already."

The baby had clutched the old woman's hand and for a moment he would not let it go.

"He wants me to come along," she sighed, "but I'm in no condition to go. When I hear the church bells ring I'll be happy."

"You may not hear them at all," mumbled her daughter-in-law nervously. "There's a fog outside so thick you could cut it with a knife."

"I've a keen ear, and besides, I'll open the window," the old woman answered, smiling.

In the bar of the People's Palace, there was no one but Bigio, who was engaged in going over some accounts. He was startled to see Peppone and Smilzo come in, bearing the decked-out baby.

"Pull down the blinds," said Peppone, "and bring us a bottle of dry white wine."

Bigio brought the bottle of wine and three glasses.

"Aren't you having a drink too?" asked Smilzo.

"Well, there are three of us, aren't there? And I've brought three glasses."

"What about the fourth?" asked Smilzo, pointing with a laugh at the white bundle on the table.

"I don't get it," Bigio said.

"A proletarian baptism!" explained Smilzo, raising his glass. "To the health of a new comrade!"

Bigio and Peppone drained their glasses. Then, while Peppone told Bigio what it was all about, Smilzo dipped his finger into the wine and held it up to the baby's lips.

"Look how he sucks it!" he said proudly. "It's plain he'll grow up to be a very fine fellow!"

The others made no answer, and Smilzo drank down another

glass of wine. For several minutes he was absorbed in his thoughts, but finally he said:

"The church bells! She wanted to hear them ringing!"

Just then the church bells actually rang, and the three men jumped as if in the presence of something supernatural.

"Oh yes," said Bigio. "Today they were going to baptize the druggist's baby."

Smilzo gave a roar of joy.

"She wanted to hear the church bells, did she? Well, there they are! What luck!"

The bundle on the table began to wriggle and Peppone touched the baby's warm, rosy forehead with his enormous hand. The baby took hold of his middle finger and would not let it go. Peppone reflected that a short time before the baby had held his grandmother's old hand in the same way. Now the baby held fast again. Meanwhile Smilzo drank a third glass of wine.

"We can go home now," he said, slamming the empty glass down on the table.

Peppone and Bigio did not move.

"Ring down the curtain!" said Smilzo. "The play is over, and I'm a perfect swine."

Peppone and Bigio had never heard what the Party calls confession couched in such very honest and appropriate terms.

"Go to it, Bigio," said Peppone, "and make it snappy."

And Bigio was off like a shot.

"What's this?" asked Don Camillo, going over to the baptismal font.

"My son!" said Smilzo, straightening the ribbons which stuck out of the bundle on Peppone's arm.

"Poor boy!" sighed Don Camillo. "Couldn't he have chosen a better father?"

The baby was in good form by now and proceeded to grasp Don Camillo's middle finger. "Brat!" Don Camillo said severely. "Are you trying to take other people's belongings away from them so soon?"

Smilzo wanted to say something, but Don Camillo drowned out his voice.

"Silence! As you know, no convinced Communist can serve as a godfather. Are you a convinced Communist, Peppone?"

"No sir!" said Peppone.

"God only knows whether you are telling the truth, and He'll call you to account for it on Judgment Day."

After the ceremony was over and Peppone had gone out to the car, in which Bigio was waiting before the church, Smilzo went up to Don Camillo.

"How much do I owe you for your trouble?" he asked.

"Nothing. You too can settle your accounts with God Almighty." Smilzo looked at him with mistrust.

"You won't get my next baby, though!" he said defiantly.

"The future is in God's hands, my son!" said Don Camillo, throwing out his arms. "But get out of here in a hurry, because the present might be in my feet!"

This was a theory just like any other. But Smilzo knew the size and strength of Don Camillo's feet and so he took it into due consideration.

PEPPONE GOES BACK TO SCHOOL

PEPPONE DECIDED TO GO ALL out against clerical interference in the primary schools and an announcement to this effect came out in the bulletin nailed to the wall of the People's Palace. In it was the proposal that a supervisory committee be set up and empowered to visit the schools at any time to make sure that the teaching was in accord with democratic principles.

Of course, the next day, the bulletin of the Opposition printed a reply:

"We don't for a moment criticize our Mayor for the fact that he never finished school. We believe that ideas are much more important than good grammar. But for purposes of the present discussion we must note that it seems singularly inappropriate for primary instruction to be in the hands of someone who never finished his own. Let the Mayor hand over this job to Smilzo, who stayed two years in first grade and three years in both second and third, thus acquiring considerably more experience in the field of education."

This piece caused considerable talk in the village, and Don Camillo made a copy of it which he took to read to the Christ over the altar.

"I am still of the same opinion," Christ told him. "This was written by a man just as stupid as the one who penciled the word 'Donkey!' on the margin of some other declaration by Peppone."

"But, Lord," Don Camillo objected, "this is an entirely different matter. Isn't it stupid of a man with one leg to insist on entering a race?"

"Don Camillo, you're not playing fair! A man with only one leg can't acquire another in its place, but a man who doesn't know grammar can always learn it. If you know the person who wrote these words, tell him that they are very stupid."

"I'll try to explain," said Don Camillo, throwing out his arms, "but it's going to be uphill work, because he honestly believes he's in the right."

"He can't honestly believe that, when he's out of harmony with God's law. You know that perfectly well, because I've told you."

"Don Camillo is always in hot water," the priest sighed.

Peppone couldn't take the counter-attack lying down, and so he brought out another broadside:

"We can confidantly state that if our unknown adversary were to look after his priestly affairs instead of the affairs of other people, it would be a very good thing. There are two kinds of ignorance: the ignorance of those who for obvious reasons have not been able to continue their schooling and that of persons like the ignorant priest in question, who has studied a great deal but learned nothing. He reminds us of a shiny copper pot, with a hole in the bottom, looking down at a tarnished old pot, which is obviously much more serviceable for cooking."

This was only the beginning, and the rest was couched in much grosser terms. When Don Camillo went to kneel in front of the altar, Christ asked him if he had read Peppone's new innuendo.

"Yes, Lord."

"And have you resisted the temptation to reply?"

"Yes, Lord."

"Will you be able to keep up your resistance?"

Don Camillo threw out his arms.

"The future is in God's hands," he answered.

"But the draft of your reply is in your right hand pocket, and so in this case the future is in the hands of Don Camillo."

Don Camillo took the sheet of paper out of his pocket and burned it in the flame of a candle.

"The election is just around the corner," he observed, "and to my mind these are mistaken tactics, from a political point of view."

"That may be, Don Camillo. But don't worry about the election. I'm not for or against any ticket. I won my battle a long time ago."

When Peppone was beside himself with political passion, he proceeded with about as much delicacy as a Sherman tank, and so, naturally enough, this piece of prose which began with the famous "confidantly" was full of errors. People laughed immoderately at it, even without any instigation on the part of Don Camillo, and Peppone's pride was deeply injured. He tried throwing a few punches around and received a few from persons upon whom he had not inflicted any, but he was aware that this did not alter the situation and that his grammar was just as stumbling as ever. And so he dropped the fight for a supervisory committee and fastened his energies upon the fulfillment of a very ambitious dream. No one except his wife knew anything about it. Every evening, when he set off on his motorcycle, she gave an anxious sigh, and toward midnight, when he returned she immediately asked:

"How did it go?"

"It's tough sledding, but I'll make it."

This went on for three and a half months, until one night, upon his return from the mysterious trip, Peppone announced:

"This is it! I'm taking the plunge!"

"What if you don't succeed?"

"I must, that's all."

"Think how those wretched people will laugh if you fail. Couldn't you do it in the city, where nobody knows you and if you don't make the grade, it doesn't matter?"

"No, if I did it anywhere else, they'd say there was something tricky or dishonest about it. It's got to be done in the light of day, with everything legal. I'm putting in an application tomorrow."

"Well, be sure not to make any mistakes in the application!"

"You don't need to worry about that," Peppone reassured her. "I've got the application all ready. They typed it up for me in the city!"

"I, Giuseppi Bottazzi, etc., etc., respectfully ask permission of the Board of Education to take the eighth-grade examinations . . ."

The bomb burst with a noise almost atomic in intensity and Smilzo ran to Peppone's house with his eyes popping out of his head.

"Chief, people are saying that you want to take the eighth-grade examinations!"

"Well, what's so remarkable about it?"

"Chief, the eighth grade is tough!"

"Good! 'Live dangerously!' must be our motto."

"Chief, if you flunk it, you're a goner!"

"Verdi flunked out of the Conservatory, and then did pretty well."

In the face of such confidence, Smilzo could find nothing to say. With all the nonchalance of a gentleman flicking an ash off the end of his cigarette, Peppone added:

"If I haven't got an inferiority complex, why should you have one?"

This was the last straw. If Peppone knew the meaning of an inferiority complex, then he must be up to his ears in culture.

"Chief," Smilzo stammered, "have you been studying all these months? It must have cost you an awful lot of money?"

"Why? I took a cramming course at a night school in the city, for adults and children together. At the desk next to mine there was a twelve-year-old boy called Mario Bibelli, a little fellow that didn't come up to my shoulder. He'll pay me a visit here some Sunday."

"Amazing!" exclaimed Smilzo. "It sounds like an old-fashioned, romantic novel."

"Reality is the true romanticism of both yesterday and today," said Peppone didactically. "Both De Amicis and De Sico are neo-realists, even if the former did his writing a century ago."

Smilzo went away completely convinced of one thing: Peppone had turned into an intellectual.

"It wouldn't surprise me if he were to write for some literary magazine," he said to Brusco, Bigio and the rest of Peppone's henchmen. "This is going to be a bitter pill for some people to swallow."

It was a bitter pill for Don Camillo, who was burning up with eagerness to talk to Peppone and size up his new education. Peppone seemed to be avoiding him, and this exasperated his curiosity all the further. Finally he did get hold of him, by means of a personal visit to the workshop. Peppone greeted him with gentlemanly indifference.

"What can I do for you?" he asked.

"I was just passing by," said Don Camillo, "and wanted to inquire about the health of our mayor."

"There's no mayor here. Here you have only Giuseppe Bottazzi, the blacksmith, descendant of the blacksmith of the same name who brought the family to this village several centuries ago and was beheaded because he stripped a priest of his ill-gotten gains. There's the nemesis of history for you!"

"The nemesis of history? How do you mean?" asked Don Camillo in utter astonishment.

"I mean that maybe this time there'll be a different ending and Giuseppe Bottazzi will not only strip the priest of his ill-gotten gains, but kill him!"

"Ill-gotten gains? But I have no more money than a jumping jack-rabbit!"

"I'm not speaking of money. You've captured the confidence of a great many ignorant people, and we shall take it away!"

The conversation was taking an unpleasant turn, but Don Camillo swallowed his pride for the sake of acquiring further information.

"What will be, will be," he said. "How about the examinations?"

"Trifles!" answered Peppone. "The important examination is the one I take every day with this hammer and anvil. And I pass it, time after time."

As Don Camillo was going away he saw Peppone's wife at the door.

"Did you come to needle him?" she said aggressively. "It's eating you up, isn't it, that you can't brand him as someone that never graduated from primary school?"

"No," said Don Camillo. "But it's still too early to say. We'll see what happens when he's put to the test."

Don Camillo went home in a gloomy state of mind.

"Lord," he said to the Christ over the altar, "that poor fellow is so swollen with pride that he deserves to fail every single subject."

"I don't know about that, Don Camillo. I'm not on the examination committee. That's for them to decide."

"God is everywhere," objected Don Camillo, "and He'll be in the schoolroom where that country bumpkin comes to make a fool of himself."

"Certainly, Don Camillo, God is everywhere. Right now He's here listening to the stupid things you are saying."

Don Camillo threw out his arms in discouragement.

"For some time now, I haven't been able to say the right thing!"

The matter of examining Mayor Peppone was a headache to the Board of Education. Things had to be conducted with such scrupulous care that no one could find an excuse for saying that either success or failure was due to the candidate's political office or party affiliation. A special commission was made up of the board's director and two teachers from another township, one a stiff, elderly woman and the other, a middle-aged man. Peppone was in a radiant mood, with no doubts at all as to his ability to get through. When he received notice that the examinations would be held the next day he burst out with:

"It's about time! I was beginning to be thoroughly bored."

He went to bed in a good humor and got up in one that was even better. Immediately he put on his best suit, filled his fountain-pen, tested it on a piece of paper and started to leave the house.

"I'll go with you as far as the school," his wife suggested.

"Don't let's be silly about it!" said Peppone.

"Your son insists on going," she told him.

"Don't make me look ridiculous; I'd seem like a schoolboy, and all those wretched people will be staring out their windows at me."

And so Peppone went off alone, but when he reached the school, his wife and son were already there, lurking behind a hedge, all red in the face from having run across the fields to beat him. As he started up the steps into the schoolhouse, they waved to him and he waved back at them with his hand hidden halfway down his back. The commission welcomed him with icy politeness.

"Sit down," said the director. "You will have written examinations in arithmetic and composition. Remember that the allotted time is four hours."

Then they set before him four sheets of officially stamped examination paper, two for a rough copy and two for the finished product.

"Shall we begin?" asked the director, after Peppone had sat down and taken out his pen.

"By all means," said Peppone.

"Then take this down: 'Problem: A cement basin of parallelepiped form has a base 40 by 60 centimeters in size and is fed by two taps. The first tap pours in 8 liters of water a minute and the second tap 5 liters of water every other minute. In thirty minutes the flow from the second tap alone fills two fifths of the basin. How long will it take to fill the whole basin if both taps are open? How high is the basin?'"

As Peppone diligently wrote down the problem, he noticed that his hand had begun to tremble. "I shouldn't have done so much hammering last night," he said to himself. "It has tired my hand." Meanwhile the director told him to shift to another sheet of paper and take down the composition theme set for him by the woman teacher.

"Theme: Narrate some event, either recent or long ago, which made a strong impression upon you."

Peppone took this down with some difficulty, for his hand continued to tremble. Then he ran a handkerchief over his perspiring forehead. He looked over the two sheets, and reread the arithmetic problem. A parallelepiped—what the devil was that? Two minutes earlier, he had known perfectly well, but now it had gone out of his head completely. The tap whose flow sufficed to fill two-fifths of the basin filled him with confusion. What could be meant by two-fifths of a parallelepiped? And what about the other tap, which poured in water continuously?

His head was empty, as he looked again at the theme for a composition. What was an event? What events had he witnessed, and how could he tell the story of any one of them? He thought back to his night school classes and tried to fish out of his memory some of all that he had heard there in the last three and a half months. But not a single word could he recapture. Then he thought of his wife and son waiting for him outside, and there was an ache in his heart.

The three examiners sat around a table at the far end of the room, as stiff as statues. Peppone wiped the perspiration off his brow. The clock in the church tower rang ten. How perfectly terrible! He looked out the window to make sure he had heard correctly. Yes, the hands were pointing to ten, and so were those of the clock in the schoolroom. He had barely written down the questions, and it was ten o'clock already. And those damned taps were still pouring water into that damned parallelepiped!

The old charwoman brought the news to the rectory.

"Father, I saw him with my own eyes. He's been staring for a whole hour and a half at the paper, and perspiring as if he had a high fever. Not a single word has he written!"

Don Camillo listened to her with satisfaction.

"That's what he gets for being so stuck-up" he exclaimed.

"He looked just like a schoolboy," the old gossip continued. "He came up the road alone, but he got his wife and son to walk along parallel to him, behind the hedge. They met him at the schoolhouse door and waved goodbye."

With that the charwoman went away, promising to come back later. She came at eleven o'clock, even more excited than before.

"Things are still exactly the same," she reported. "He's still perspiring, and still staring at the paper. In two more hours, time will be up. His wife and child are still hiding behind the hedge. She's chewed up half a handkerchief, she's so nervous. Father, I only wish you could see the state that big bully is in now!"

And Don Camillo thought he had every right to see the big bully brought so low.

The two strokes of half-past eleven rang out, and Peppone was thinking that he had only an hour and a half more. Just then the charwoman came to call the director. The director went out into the hall and met Don Camillo.

"Excuse me," said the priest, "but even if the mayor is playing schoolboy he can't neglect his municipal duties. There's a poor woman who may die if he doesn't sign the papers authorizing her immediate removal to a city hospital." And he held out a sheet of paper, adding: "Will you give it to him?"

"That's not regular," the director stammered.

"I know, but it would be still more irregular for a poor woman to die simply in order not to disturb an examination. I don't think this will upset your examinee."

The director shrugged his shoulders.

"Father," he said in a low voice, "it's positively nerve-wracking: all he's done is perspire!"

Don Camillo smiled.

"All these boys are the same way. Outside school they go in for a lot of big talk, but in class . . ."

The director took the sheet of paper and started to go back into the classroom. Then he changed his mind.

"Father, I'll send him out here and let you give it to him in person. I'll leave the door open."

Don Camillo glimpsed the sad state of Peppone and calmly waited for him. Meanwhile after Peppone had heard what the director had to say, he slowly got up and came out into the hall.

"Forgive me, Mr. Mayor," said Don Camillo, "but it's an urgent matter."

Peppone took the sheet of paper and read: "I, Angiolina Pateri, widow, without means of support, state as follows . . ."

"I've already told you that I can't do anything for her, he said, handing the paper back to Don Camillo. "I had this same statement in my hands two weeks ago."

"Two weeks ago, things were different," Don Camillo shot back at him. "Please read on. Here you have the notarized signature of the doctor."

Just then the director came out into the hall again.

"Mr. Mayor," he said, "since you're called upon to decide an important matter, this time won't be counted. The commission has noted the exact hour at which you left the room."

"Thank you," said Don Camillo. "I shouldn't want to have on my conscience the theft of time from a mathematics exercise or a literary masterpiece."

Peppone gritted his teeth and shot a bitter glance at Don Camillo.

"Come, Mr. Mayor, hurry!"

Peppone reopened the paper and scrutinized the declaration: "The undersigned certifies that Angiolina Pateri is in a desperate condition and must be sent away for a surgical intervention; *meanwhile, ten minutes from now, you ask for permission to go to the toilet.*"

He reread the last two lines, fearing that he had misunderstood them. Then he looked at Don Camillo and asked:

"Why?"

"If the doctor says so, then it's got to be done," answered Don Camillo. "Just sign here."

Peppone signed the paper and handed it back. When he returned to the classroom the commission took note of the hour. Don Camillo thanked the director and then said to him in a whisper: "He may not seem to be so very bright, but you'll see. He's a slow starter."

"Very slow indeed, Father," said the director with a low laugh.

Ten minutes went by, and then suddenly Peppone raised the thumb and forefinger of his right hand.

"Go right ahead," said the director. "And smoke a cigarette while you're there, if you want to. We'll subtract the time."

Peppone walked unsteadily to the toilet, which was at the end of a long hall. A window looked out over some empty fields.

"Psss!"

Peppone nailed his face to the grating over the window. Just below there was a pile of dried grass and sticks, and this was the source of the whistle.

"Hurry up, you jackass! Light a cigar and pretend to take it easy. Quick, tell me the problem!"

Peppone told him the problem between one puff of smoke and another.

"Parallelepiped. . . . Basin . . . 40 by 60 centimeters . . ."

"What's 40 by 60 centimeters?" came the voice from outside.

"The base . . . two taps . . . one 8 liters a minute . . . other 5 liters every two minutes, but in 30 minutes fills two fifths of the basin . . ."

"And what do they want to know?"

"How long it would take to fill the basin with both taps running. And the height of the parallelepiped."

"Jackass! That's child's play."

Don Camillo proceeded to explain it to him.

"Do you get it?" he said in conclusion.

"No, but now that you've given me a hint, I'll try to think it out."

"Beat it, then!"

Peppone jumped.

"How about the composition?"

"What's the theme?"

"An event which made a strong impression upon me."

"Well, you'll have to work that out yourself. What do I know of your affairs?"

"But I can't remember a single thing! What shall I tell?"

From the pile of grass came a suggestion, and Peppone took it back with him to the classroom. He thought hard over what Don Camillo had told him about the arithmetic problem, and having caught onto the general idea he was able to work it out on paper. He was still perspiring, but in a different way. And the trembling of his hand was not the same, either. The director's voice aroused him:

"It's one o'clock and allowing you ten minutes for each of the two interruptions, you've only twenty minutes left."

Peppone fell once more into a panic. Twenty minutes to make clean copies of both the problem and the composition! He looked around in search of help and his eye fell on the clock in the church tower.

"It isn't yet one o'clock," he exclaimed. "It's twenty minutes to."

The examiners remarked that the hands of the classroom clock pointed to one.

"But I came with the tower clock and it's only fair that I leave with it too."

"Very good," said the director, who wanted above all to have everything proceed smoothly.

Peppone copied first the problem and then the composition, and when the tower clock pointed to one-eighteen he handed in both papers. Don Camillo was watching with spyglasses from the bell tower, and when he saw Peppone coming down the steps he adjusted the mechanism of the clock.

"Now try to catch up on those twenty minutes I set you back!" he murmured.

Looking out again through his spyglass, he saw Peppone jump over the hedge and start home with his wife and son.

"Wretched creature!" the priest murmured. "I wonder if at the oral examinations tomorrow, you'll find another shady character to help you the way I did today!"

But the next day Peppone did very well without any help whatsoever and the old woman teacher felt impelled to say:

"Allow me to congratulate you not only on your thorough preparation but on your good manners and sensitivity as well."

Her fellow-examiner and the director both agreed, and Peppone went triumphantly home, not across the fields, this time, but down the street, with his head held high. Don Camillo sat in the church square, smoking his usual cigar butt, and Peppone marched decisively over to him.

"Did you get your diploma?" Don Camillo asked.

"Yes," said Peppone gloomily. "But you were your usual perfidious self to suggest "The Day of my First Communion" as subject for a composition. I was down and out, and you took advantage of me."

"I can see that it puts you in real danger," admitted Don Camillo. "If Malenkov comes this way and this composition gets into his files, then you're done for! That's what you get for your pursuit of culture!"

As Don Camillo was passing in front of the main altar, Christ's voice stopped him.

"Where were you yesterday morning, Don Camillo?" Christ asked. "You were away from here for some time."

"Lord, please let it go by for the moment, will You? Later on we'll draw up accounts, and I'll pay up what I have to pay."

"You're shamefully lucky, Don Camillo," Christ said with a sigh. "Even when that time comes you'll find Someone to overlook what you owe Him and give you more credit."

"Forgive us our debts as we forgive our debtors," said Don

Camillo, throwing out his arms. Then he remembered how Peppone's wife and child had waited for him behind the hedge.

"I did it for the sake of those two, Lord," he said.

"For the sake of those three," Christ corrected him.

"Oh well, one more or less doesn't matter," concluded Don Camillo.

A BABY CONQUERS

PEPPONE WOKE UP AT FOUR o'clock that morning. He had gone to bed the night before with something on his mind, and hence there was no need of any alarm clock to arouse him. A little before midnight, when he was just about to retire, he had received news that the clerical group was holding a meeting at the house of Filotti. His informant, who was on watch in the vicinity, had overheard one of the big shots say in a loud voice as he came away from the meeting: "We'll have a good laugh tomorrow."

What could be going to happen? Peppone had no idea, and after cudgeling his brain in vain he had decided that the wisest thing was to go to bed and get up early the next morning in order to meet trouble wherever he found it.

Now, at a quarter past four, he left the house and made an inspection of the sleeping village. Apparently there was nothing new. The posters on the wall were the same as the day before, and so were the electoral pennants and banners. This was in a way reassuring, but in another it wasn't. If his rivals' latest trick were not connected with propaganda, what could it be? Perhaps it would come out in the newspaper, and in this case there was nothing to do but await the paper's arrival.

Peppone crossed the square in the direction of the People's Palace. His head hung low, heavy with thought, and when he raised it to fit the key into the lock he leaped back with surprise. On the step at the foot of the door was a suspicious looking bundle, which made him think immediately of a time-bomb. But this hypothesis proved false a few seconds later, when the bundle emitted a cry and waved a tiny hand.

Peppone moved cautiously nearer, and having lifted up a corner of the black cloth covering, discovered that the tiny hand was attached to a tiny arm and the tiny arm to a tiny baby. Never had he seen such a beautiful specimen. It couldn't have been more than three or four months old, and lacked only a pair of wings to be mistaken for an angel. On the clothes there was pinned a piece of paper with a scrawled message which read: "If yours is the poor people's party, then this is the poorest creature in the world, being possessed of absolutely nothing, not even a name. It is brought to you by an unhappy mother."

He read this incredible message several times over, remained no longer than necessary with his mouth hanging open and let forth a piercing cry. People ran out from everywhere, with sleepy eyes and nothing on but their nightclothes. And when they had read the note they were equally taken aback.

"Is it really possible that in our atomic age something of this sort can happen?" Peppone shouted. "It seems to come straight out of the Middle Ages."

"Except that in the Middle Ages, children were left on the steps of the church," put in Smilzo, who had just arrived upon the scene.

Peppone turned around and looked at him with perplexity.

"Just what do you mean by that?" he mumbled.

"I mean that times have changed," Smilzo explained unctuously. "Nowadays an unmarried mother no longer puts her baby into the hands of the priests, but . . ."

Peppone grabbed the lapels of his jacket and pulled him toward the door without waiting for the end of the sentence.

"Pick up the baby and come on in!" he ordered.

Smilzo bent over to pick up the bundle and followed him.

"Chief," he said when they had reached Peppone's private office, "why did you treat me so roughly? Have I said something wrong?"

"Smilzo," said Peppone excitedly, without stopping to answer this question, "take pencil and paper and get that idea down in writing without a single second's delay. We'll be the ones to laugh last today."

The wife of Lungo was called in to look after the baby, and Smilzo hastened to develop his idea. He worked over it for a whole hour, and then read the result to Peppone:

"Fellow citizens! Very early this morning, under the cover of darkness, an unknown woman abandoned her baby on the steps of the People's Palace, where Comrade Giuseppe Bottazzi found it. Pinned to its clothes was a note reading: 'If yours is the poor people's party, then this is the poorest creature in the world, being possessed of absolutely nothing, not even a name. It is brought to you by an unhappy mother.'

"Although we condemn this reckless gesture on the part of the mother, we cannot help calling attention to the social injustice by virtue of which the rich have more money than they can use and the poor have not enough to feed their helpless young.

"The mother forced to abandon her child was a commonplace of the feudal society of the Middle Ages. But today the poor no longer think in medieval terms. In those days babies were left at the church door, but now they are brought to the People's Palace. This signifies that people have lost confidence in the priests and now pin their hopes on the Communist Party, which looks upon all men as equal and entitled to an equal place in the sun.

"And so, fellow-citizens, while we take charge of the abandoned baby, we urge you to vote all together for our candidates in the coming election.

Local Group of the Italian Communist Party"

Peppone had him read the statement again, discussed a few commas and then sent him to order Barchini, the printer, to make five hundred copies. That same afternoon the posters were ready and the paste-pot squad plastered them all over.

Almost at once there was trouble. That is, Peppone received a visit from the sergeant of the carabinieri.

"Mr. Mayor, is this Communist story true?"

"Why, Sergeant, you don't suppose I'd make it up, do you? I found the baby myself."

"And why didn't you report your discovery?"

"Well, five hundred posters are reporting it!"

"Yes, but you should have come to the police in person to make a signed statement, which we must, in turn, amplify and send on. A woman who abandons her child is guilty of a crime. And how can you be sure that the baby really belongs to the woman who wrote the note? You don't even know that the writer is a woman. What if the baby was kidnapped and then disposed of in this way?"

As a result, Peppone made the require statement, the sergeant questioned other witnesses and drew up his own official account of the story.

"Where is the baby now?" he asked when this was completed.

"In his new home, the People's Palace."

"And who has charge of him?"

"The Communist Party. We've adopted him."

"But a political group can't legally adopt a baby or even hold one in temporary care. The baby has to be turned over to the proper institution. We'll get in touch with a place in the city and you can take the baby there tomorrow."

Peppone looked at the sergeant with exasperation.

"I'll not take that baby anywhere. I'm adopting him myself, personally."

The sergeant shook his head.

"Mr. Mayor, I take my hat off to your generosity. But you can't do that until we have made the necessary investigation."

"Well, while you're investigating, the baby may as well stay with my wife and myself. We're experienced parents. It isn't as if you were putting him into the hands of the firstcomer. After all, I am the village's number one man."

The sergeant could find no more objections. "Let's go take a look at the creature," he suggested.

"Don't inconvenience yourself. I'll have him brought here and you can turn him over to me officially."

Shortly after this, Lungo's wife came with the baby in her arms. And when the sergeant saw him, he exclaimed, "What do you know about that! What a handsome little fellow! I don't see how anyone could abandon him."

Peppone sighed.

"No matter how handsome a baby may be, he can't live on thin air."

The sergeant's investigation didn't have to go too far. That very evening he was called to Toricella, a couple of miles away, where a woman's dead body had been found on the railroad track. In her bag was a note saying: "Mine is just the same old story of a girl left all alone in the world and then jilted by her lover . . ." There were also identification papers, which made it possible to write to the police of the city whence she had come for further information. A reply was soon forthcoming and brought news that this girl was, as she claimed, quite alone in the world and had registered the birth of a baby without the father's name.

"Now the way is clear," the sergeant said to Peppone. "If you want to proceed with the formalities for adoption, you can go do so. Of course, if you've changed your mind . . ."

"Of course I haven't changed my mind," said Peppone.

The baby was a very handsome one indeed, and everyone admired him. A wealthy couple by the name of Bicci, whose only misfortune was that they had no child, took a special fancy to him and went to Don Camillo about it.

"He'd be a godsend to us," they told him. "And you're the only one that can swing it. Peppone wouldn't listen to anyone else."

So Don Camillo went to knock at Peppone's door. Peppone gave him an unpromising welcome.

"Politics?" he asked ill-humoredly.

"No, something much more serious than that. I came to see you about the baby."

"I'd like even politics better. The baby doesn't need a thing. If you must know, he's already been baptized. His mother gave him the name of Paolo."

"I know all that. But it's not true that he doesn't need a thing. First of all, he needs a father and mother. And you don't really need another child."

"That's none of your business, Father. I'm quite capable of looking after my own family affairs. I've come to love that baby as much as if he were my own."

"I know that, too. That's why I've come. If you really love him, then you ought to give him all the advantages you can. The Biccis have neither child nor relatives. They're anxious to adopt the child and leave him everything they have."

"Is that all you came to say?" asked Peppone.

"Yes."

"Then the door's down there to the right."

But Don Camillo had a parting shot ready.

"I see. The baby is useful to you as political propaganda. You don't really care about his future."

Peppone left his anvil and came to stand squarely in front of Don Camillo.

"Look, I'd be justified in knocking you over the head with a hammer. But that wouldn't serve any purpose other than that of throwing me into a criminal role. And that's a role I prefer to save for you. Let's go see the carabinieri together."

Peppone went out the door and Don Camillo, with his curiosity aroused, followed after. They found the sergeant at his desk.

"Sergeant," said Peppone, "is it true what they said in the papers, that the poor girl left a note in her handbag?"

"Of course," said the sergeant cautiously. "It was addressed to the judicial authorities and I transmitted it to them."

"So nobody else knows what is in it, is that right?"

"Nobody."

"Well, I do."

"What's that?" exclaimed the sergeant. "Will you kindly explain?"

"Before the girl threw herself under the train she posted from Toricella a letter identical to the one found in her bag. And that letter was addressed to me."

"To you? Did you know her, then?"

"No. The letter was addressed: 'Director of the People's Palace,' and it was delivered to me in person."

The sergeant smiled incredulously. "It does seem likely enough, since that's where she left her baby, that she should have written to you about it. But how can you be sure that letter is an exact copy of the note found in her bag?"

"Because she wrote on it: 'I have sent an exact copy of this letter to the judicial authorities.' I have the original letter of hers in safekeeping. But I've brought with me a typed copy, which I shall now read to you. 'Mine is just the same old story of a girl left all alone in the world and then jilted by her lover. My betrayer is a rich but egotistical and dishonest man. Before dying I wish to leave my son in the hands of people who are against the dishonesty and egotism of the rich. I want him to be educated to combat them. My desire is not for revenge but for justice.' Now tell me, isn't that the exact text?"

"Don't ask me," said the sergeant. "I passed the note on to the proper persons, and only they can answer."

"Very well, Sergeant. Meanwhile, I have a signed letter addressed 'Director of the People's Palace.' I could have had this letter reproduced and used it for campaign purposes . . ." Peppone turned and gave Don Camillo a withering look. "Now, do you see what material I had there for propaganda? . . . And you, Sergeant, don't you agree?"

"Mr. Mayor, that's not up my alley. I have said all I have to say."

Don Camillo and Peppone walked away in silence, until Peppone said:

"Now, wasn't I justified in wanting to knock you over the head with a hammer?"

"No, only God has a right to take away human life."

"All right. But isn't it God's duty to take away the life of the priest of this parish?"

"God has rights, not duties. Duties are what men have in relation to God."

"Perfect!" shouted Peppone. "And before God, what is my present duty? To give the baby to the Biccis and let them bring him up to be a little egotist like themselves?"

"Or to bring him up in the school of hate to which you belong?" retorted Don Camillo.

They had reached Peppone's house and now they walked in. There was a cradle in the kitchen, and in it the baby lay sleeping. When the two men drew near he opened his eyes and smiled.

"What a beautiful child!" exclaimed Don Camillo.

Peppone wiped the perspiration off his forehead and then went to fetch a paper.

"Here's the original letter from the mother," he said. "You can see for yourself that I was telling the truth."

"Don't give it to me!" said Don Camillo, "or else I'll destroy it."

"Never mind!" Peppone answered. "Go ahead and look!"

As he handed it across the cradle, a tiny hand stretched out and grabbed it.

"Lord help us!" said Don Camillo, with his eyes wide open in astonishment.

Just then Peppone's wife came in.

"Who let the baby have that paper?" she shouted. "It was written with an indelible pencil, and if he puts it in his mouth he'll be poisoned!"

She snatched the paper away and threw it into the fire. Then she picked up the baby and raised him into the air.

Turning to Don Camillo she said, "Isn't he a handsome fellow? I'd like to see if your De Gasperi could produce his equal!"

And she spoke as if the baby were her very own. Don Camillo did not let this remark upset him, but took his leave with a polite farewell greeting.

"Goodbye, Mr. Mayor; goodbye, Signora Bottazzi; goodbye, Baby Bottazzi!"

And Baby Bottazzi answered with a gurgle which filled Don Camillo's heart with comfort and hope.

THE ELEPHANT NEVER FORGETS

THUNDER, OF COURSE, WAS
Don Camillo's dog. And Antenore Cabazza, known as "Thunderer," was a follower of Peppone. The dog was the brainier of
the two, which fact is noted simply in order to give some picture
of his two-legged namesake, with whom we are concerned in this
story.

Thunderer was an enormous fellow, who, once he got into motion, proceeded with all the grace and implacability of an elephant. He was the ideal man to carry out orders but for some reason Peppone took especial care not to entrust him with their execution. And so most of Thunderer's Communist activities took place at the Molinetto tavern, where he went to play cards whenever he wasn't working. He was an enthusiastic poker player, and his phenomenal memory made him a formidable opponent. Of course memory isn't always the deciding factor in a card game, and every now and then Thunderer took a trouncing. But the experience he had one Saturday with Cino Biolchi was worse than anything that had ever happened to him before. He sat down to play with five thousand liras, and five hours later he was left without a penny. Now Thunderer couldn't stomach the idea of going home in this condition.

"Give me my revenge!" he panted, grasping the cards with shaking hands.

"I've given you I don't know how many thousand chances for a revenge game," said Cino Biolchi. "But now I've had enough."

"Let's have just one game, for all or nothing," said Thunderer. "That way, if I win, I get back my five thousand liras."

"And what if you lose?" asked Cino Biolchi.

"Well, you can see I haven't got any more money," stammered Thunderer, wiping the perspiration off his forehead, "but I'll stake anything you say."

"Don't be a donkey," said Biolchi. "Go on to bed and forget about it."

"I want my revenge!" Thunderer roared. "I'll put up anything . . . anything at all. You name it!"

Biolchi was an original fellow. And now, after a moment of thought, he said:

"All right; I'm with you. Five thousand liras against your vote."

"My vote? What do you mean?"

"I mean that if you lose, you promise to vote for whatever party I say in the next election."

Gradually Thunderer was convinced that the other meant just what he was saying. And he had accepted the terms in advance.

So it was that Biolchi put a five-thousand lira bill upon the table and gave Thunderer a pen and paper.

"Just write: 'The undersigned Antenore Cabazza solemnly swears to vote on June 7 for such-and-such a party . . .' You can leave the name of the party blank, and I'll put it in when I feel like it."

Thunderer wrote it duly down and then shot Biolchi a look of resentment.

"It's strictly between ourselves," he said. "And sometime between now and election day, on June 7, you have to play off the game."

"That's a bargain," Biolchi replied.

Peppone was just leaving the People's Palace when Thunderer loomed up before him.

"Chief, I've just lost everything I have to Biolchi in a card game."

"Too bad. But that's none of my business."

"Yes, it is, too. Because I lost something else; I lost my vote."

Peppone laughed after Thunderer had told him the story.

"You don't have to worry," he said reassuringly. "After all, we have a secret ballot, and once you're in the booth you can vote for whom you please."

"No I can't," said Thunderer ruefully. "I signed a paper."

"Devil take the paper! That doesn't bind you."

"I gave my word of honor, and we shook hands on it. And I'm not the kind of a fellow that breaks his word."

Yes, Thunderer had the character of an elephant rather than a jack-rabbit. He had a motor in place of a brain, and the motor ran with a logic of its own, which no one could stop without causing breakage. Peppone realized that the matter was more serious than he had thought, and that Thunderer was adamant on the subject of his honor.

"Keep your shirt on," he said. "We'll talk it over tomorrow."

"At what time, Chief?"

"At ten thirty-five," muttered Peppone, meaning: "Devil take you for your stupidity!"

But at exactly ten thirty-five the next morning Thunderer turned up at the workshop, saying:

"It's ten thirty-five."

It was obvious that he hadn't slept a wink, and he stood there with bewildered, drooping eyes. Peppone's first impulse was to hit him over the head with a hammer. And when you come down to it, that impulse was a healthy one. But he felt sorry for the fellow and threw his hammer down on the floor instead.

"You ass!" he shouted. "I ought to expel you from the Party. But elections are coming up and we can't let our opponents use this story. Here are five thousand liras; now go tell Biolchi to release you from your word. If he won't do it, let me know."

Thunderer pocketed the banknote and disappeared, but he came back no more than a quarter of an hour later.

"He won't do it."

Peppone put on his jacket and cap and hurriedly went out.

"Wait for me here!" he tossed over his shoulder.

Biolchi greeted him politely.

"What can I do for you, Mr. Mayor?"

"Never mind about the mayor part of it. I've come about that stupid Thunderer. He must have been drunk last night. Anyhow, take the money and release him from his word."

"He wasn't drunk at all. In fact, he was in full possession of his mental faculties. And he was the one to insist on my choice of a stake. Our agreement is crystal-clear. And I'm ready anytime between now and June 7 for the return game."

"Biolchi, if I were to go to the police about this, they'd lock you up. But since I don't want to make a public scandal, I'm here to tell you that unless you give me back the paper I'll flatten you out against the wall like an electoral poster!"

"And who'd go to the police, then? That would be very unwise, Peppone!"

Peppone clenched his fists, but he knew that Biolchi had him cornered.

"All right, then. But if you have any decency, you'll play the return game with me instead of with that idiot, Thunderer."

Biolchi shut the door, took a pack of cards from a drawer and sat down at the table, with Peppone across from him. It was a desperately hard-fought game, but at the end, Peppone went away minus his five thousand liras. That evening he met with his henchmen in the People's Palace and told them the story.

"That rascal doesn't belong to any particular party, but he's against us, for sure. We must settle this business quietly, or else he'll turn it into a tremendous joke. Has anybody a suggestion?"

"Well, we can't settle it at cards, that's certain," said Smilzo. "Biolchi can play all of us under the table. Let's try offering him ten thousand liras instead of five."

Although it was late at night, they went in a group to Biolchi's door. He was still up and in a restless mood, as if something out of the way had happened. In answer to Peppone's proposition, he regretfully threw out his arms.

"Too late!" I just played cards with Spiletti, and he won fifteen thousand liras off me, plus Thunderer's paper."

"Shame on you!" said Peppone. "It was agreed that the matter was strictly between you."

"Quite right," said Biolchi. "But Thunderer was the first to spill the beans, when he went to you about it. This simply makes us even. Anyhow, I got Spiletti to promise that he wouldn't tell the story and that before June 7, he'd give Thunderer a chance for revenge."

A pretty kettle of fish! The paper was in the hands of the head of the clerical party and there was no telling what use he would make of it. Peppone and his gang went back to headquarters, where Thunderer was anxiously waiting.

"This is no time for talking," said Peppone. "We've got to act, and act fast. Tomorrow morning we'll post news of Thunderer's expulsion from the Party."

"What's that?" said Thunderer, pitiably.

"I said that the Party is purging you for undignified behavior. And I'll date the expulsion three months back."

Peppone braced himself for an explosion of anger. But there was nothing of the sort.

"You're quite right, Chief," said Thunderer in a voice that was anything but thunderous. "I deserve to be kicked out like a dog." And he laid his Party membership card meekly on the table.

"We're not kicking you out like a dog!" exclaimed Peppone. "The expulsion is just a pretense, to stave off an attack from the opposition. After the elections, you can make your little act of confession and we'll take you back into the fold."

"I can confess right now," Thunderer said mournfully. "I'm a donkey, and after the elections I'll still be a donkey. There's no use hoping I can change."

Thunderer went dejectedly away, and the spectacle was such that for several minutes Peppone and his henchmen could not settle down to business.

"We'll prepare the announcement," said Smilzo, "but don't let's post it tomorrow. Perhaps Spiletti will keep his word."

"You can't know him very well!" said Peppone. "But just as you say."

For the next two days nothing unusual happened, and it seemed as if the silence would remain, for a while at least, unbroken. But toward evening Thunderer's wife came in a state of agitation to the People's Palace.

"He's stark mad!" she burst out. "For forty-eight hours he hasn't eaten. He lies flat on the bed and won't look at a soul."

Peppone went to survey the situation, and sure enough he found Thunderer in bed immobile. He shook the fellow and even insulted him, but could not get him to say a single word or to abandon for even a second his pose of absolute indifference to the world around him. After a while Peppone lost patience.

"If you're really mad, I'll call the asylum, and they'll take care of you, all right."

With his right arm Thunderer deliberately fished for an object between the bed and the wall. And his eyes seemed to be saying: "If they come from the asylum, I'll give them a proper welcome."

Inasmuch as the object in his right hand was an ax, there was no need of words. Finally Peppone sent everyone else out of the room and said sternly:

"Surely you can tell me confidentially what's got into you to make you behave this way."

Thunderer shook his head, but he put down the ax, opened a drawer of the bedside-table and took out a pad on which he wrote with considerable effort: "I've made a vow to the Madonna not to speak, eat, move or get up for any purpose whatever until I recover that paper. Signed: Antenore Cabazza."

Peppone put this note in his pocket and went to call Thunderer's wife and daughters.

"Don't let anyone into the room unless he calls. Leave him strictly alone. It's nothing serious, just an attack of simple psychosis, a sort of spiritual influenza, which requires rest and a severe diet."

But he came back the next evening to inquire after the patient.

"Exactly the same," said his wife.

"Good," said Peppone. "That's the normal course of the affliction."

Things were still stationary on the fourth day, and so Peppone went from Thunderer's bedside to the rectory. Don Camillo sat at his desk, reading a typewritten paper.

"Look," said Peppone, "do you know the story of this fellow who lost his vote over a game of cards and . . ."

"Yes, I happen to be reading it this minute," answered Don Camillo. "Someone wants to make it into a poster."

"Oh, it's that rascal Spiletti, is it? He gave his word of honor that he'd make no use of it before election day, and that he'd give the loser a revenge game."

"I don't know anything about that. All I know is that we have here an interesting document signed by the loser's own hand."

Peppone took out the sheet of paper he had torn off Thunderer's pad.

"Then read this authentic document as well. That will give you the whole story, and it may be even more interesting if the signer starves himself to death, as seems quite likely." And he went away, leaving the paper in Don Camillo's hands.

Spiletti came to the rectory a quarter of an hour later.

"Father, was there anything you didn't like in my draft?"

"No, but the trouble is that Thunderer came around here to demand his return game."

"His return game? Nonsense! I'm giving him nothing of the sort. This document is entirely too precious, and I have no intention of relinquishing it."

"What about your promise?"

"Why should we have to keep a promise made to one of that mob which deals exclusively in lies?"

"I see your point. But Thunderer is quite a menace when he's well, and now he's half crazy. If you deprive him of his revenge, he's capable of bumping you off like a fly. And although propaganda is important, it's more important for you to stay alive."

Spiletti thought it over and was forced to admit that Don Camillo was right.

"Let's play the game, then. But what if I lose?"

"You mustn't lose, Spiletti. If you beat Cino Biolchi, then you ought to make mincemeat out of Thunderer."

"The truth is that I didn't beat Cino Biolchi, Father. I didn't win the paper away from him; he gave it to me so as to get rid of Peppone . . . Look here, Father, why don't you play in my place? I'll say that now the document is yours, and I doubt if Thunderer will come anywhere near you."

Don Camillo was a shark at cards, and so he said laughing:

"If he plays with me, I'll demolish him! And he won't dare say a word. Never fear, Spiletti, we shall win!"

The next day Don Camillo went to see Peppone.

"The document is now in my hands. If your fasting friend wants it back, then I'm his opponent. If he refuses, then it will go on public display."

"What?" said Peppone indignantly. "How can a poor wretch who's had nothing to eat for almost a week stand up to you at a game of cards?"

"You're just as much of a wretch as he is, although you eat a large meal every day. If you like, I'll play with you."

"Good enough!"

"Then it's five thousand liras against the famous paper."

Peppone put a banknote on the table and Don Camillo covered

it with the incriminating document. It was an exceedingly fierce game, and Peppone lost it. Don Camillo put the money into his pocket.

"Are you satisfied?" he asked. "Or do you want a return game?"

Peppone put up another five-thousand lira bill. He fought hard but played a miserable game. However, Don Camillo's game was even more miserable, and Peppone won.

"Here's Thunderer's paper, Comrade," said Don Camillo. "I'm satisfied with the money."

Peppone had been present for a whole hour at Thunderer's "Liberation dinner," when Don Camillo appeared upon the scene.

"Thunderer," said the priest, "you lost five thousand liras to Biolchi, didn't you?"

"Yes," the elephant stammered.

"Well, thanks to Divine Providence, here they are. Remember that when the elections come around, and don't vote for God's enemies."

"Yes, of course that was understood in my vow," sighed the unhappy Thunderer.

Peppone waited for Don Camillo outside the door.

"You're a snake in the grass! You built up the reputation of Divine Providence with my money!"

"Comrade, infinite are the ways of Divine Providence!" sighed Don Camillo, raising his eyes to heaven.

THE BEST MEDICINE

PEOPLE COULDN'T GET OVER the fact that Don Camillo was in such a state over Thunder.

"After all," they said, "a dog's only a dog."

But it's the last straw that breaks the camel's back. And at this time, that was Don Camillo's situation.

The day before the official opening of the hunting season,

Thunder went out of the house around noon and failed to return in the evening. He didn't turn up the next day, either, and Don Camillo searched wildly for him until night. When he came home empty-handed he was too miserable to eat supper. "Somebody's stolen him," he thought to himself, "and by this time he's probably in Piedmont or Tuscany." Then all of a sudden he heard the door creak, and there was Thunder. It was obvious from his humble look that he was aware of having done something very bad. He didn't have the nerve to come all the way in, but stood half outside, with only his nose sticking around beyond the door.

"Come in!" shouted Don Camillo, but the dog did not budge. "Thunder, come here!" the priest shouted again.

The order was so definite that Thunder obeyed, coming forward very slowly, with his head hanging low. When he reached Don Camillo's feet, he stopped and waited. This was the last straw. For it was then that Don Camillo discovered that someone had painted Thunder's hindquarters bright red.

Love me, love my dog; if you insult my dog, I am insulted. This is especially true of a hunter. And in this case, nothing could have been more cowardly. Don Camillo felt a grinding pain deep down inside and had to go take a breath of fresh air at the open window. There his anger passed away, giving place to melancholy. He leaned over to touch the dog's back and found the paint already dry. Evidently it had been applied the day before and Thunder had been afraid to come home.

"Poor fellow," said Don Camillo. "You were caught just like an innocent puppy."

Then he stopped to think that Thunder wasn't the kind of dog to let strangers get too near him or to fall for the offer of a chunk of meat. Thunder was a thoroughbred, and didn't take to all-comers. He trusted only two people, and one of these was Don Camillo.

This shed more light on the situation, and Don Camillo impulsively decided to clear it up completely. He went out, calling Thunder, and Thunder followed somewhat shamefully after. Peppone was still in his workshop when Don Camillo appeared, like a ghost, before him. He went right on hammering, while

Don Camillo went to stand on the far side of the anvil to ask him a question.

"Peppone, have you any idea how Thunder got into this condition?"

Peppone looked over at the dog and shrugged his shoulders.

"How should I know?" he said. "Perhaps he sat down on some bench that was freshly painted."

"That could be," said Don Camillo calmly. "But I have a notion you're mixed up in it, somehow. That's why I came straight here."

Peppone grinned at him.

"I'm a blacksmith and mechanic," he said. "The dry cleaner is on the other side of the square."

"But the fellow who asked me to lend him my dog to go hunting and then painted the dog red because I refused him is right here before me!"

Peppone dropped his hammer and stood up to Don Camillo with his hands on his hips, defiantly:

"Now, exactly what do you mean?"

"That your revenge was abject and unworthy!"

Don Camillo was panting with indignation. He heard Peppone shout something at him but could not catch the words. His head was whirling strangely and he groped for the anvil in order to keep his balance. Peppone eyed him coldly.

"If you've been drinking, you'd better go sleep it off in the rectory, where it's cooler."

Don Camillo managed to grasp this last sentence and started reeling home, where he arrived without knowing how he had done so. Half an hour later Thunder's incessant barking drew the attention of the sacristan. He noticed that the rectory door was open and an electric light burning inside. And a moment later he cried out in astonishment. Don Camillo lay stretched out on the floor and Thunder was howling beside him. The priest was bundled into an ambulance and taken to a hospital in the city. And the villagers did not go to bed before the ambulance came back and they had some news.

"Nobody knows what's wrong," said the driver. "It seems as if his heart and liver and nervous system were all involved. Then

: [221] :

he must have given his head a nasty crack when he fell. All the way to the city he was delirious, raving about how someone had painted his dog red."

"Poor Don Camillo!" the villagers murmured as they went to bed. The next day they found out that the dog really had been daubed up and that Don Camillo's raving was by no means as delirious as it had seemed. And although they were still just as sorry that he had been stricken, they found his concern over Thunder exaggerated. "A dog's only a dog," they were saying.

This was because they didn't realize that the last straw can break the camel's back.

Every evening someone brought back the latest news from the city. "He's not at all well. They won't allow anyone to see him." And early every morning Thunder came to Peppone's workshop, lay down in the doorway and fixed his melancholy eyes upon Peppone. He stayed there until eight o'clock, when the square began to fill up with people going about their daily occupations. Peppone paid him very little attention, but after this performance had been repeated for twenty-five days in succession, he lost patience and shouted:

"Can't you let me alone? Your master's ill, that's all. If you want to know more than that, you'll have to go see him."

The dog did not budge an inch and Peppone still felt those melancholy eyes upon him. At seven o'clock he could not stand it any longer. He washed up, put on his best suit, got on his motorcycle and rode away. After he had gone a mile he stopped to see how he was off for gasoline. He found the tank full, and proceeded to check the oil and the pressure of the tires. After this, he scribbled something in a notebook. A few seconds later Thunder caught up with him, his tongue hanging out with exhaustion, and jumped into the side car.

"Devil take you and your master!" grumbled Peppone as he started the motor.

At eight o'clock he arrived in front of the hospital and left Thunder to watch over the machine. But at the door they told him that it was entirely too early for a visit. And when they heard which patient he wanted to see, they told him it was no use waiting. Don Camillo's case was so serious that no visitor could be admitted to his room. Peppone did not insist. He remounted his bicycle and rode off to the Bishop's Palace. Here, too, he was refused admittance, but finally his persistence and his big hands caused the secretary to grant him a stay.

The Bishop, older and tinier and whiter-haired than ever, was walking about his garden, admiring the bright hues of the flowers.

"There's some sort of ruffian outside who says he's Your Grace's personal friend," the secretary explained breathlessly. "Shall I call the police?"

"What's that?" said the Bishop. "Do you hold your Bishop in such low esteem as to think that his personal friends are wanted by the police? Let the fellow in."

A few seconds later, Peppone torpedoed his way into the garden, and from behind a rose bush the old man held him off with the end of his cane.

"Forgive me, Your Grace," stammered Peppone, "but it's a serious matter."

"Speak up, Mr. Mayor. What's wrong?"

"Nothing's wrong with me, Your Grace. It's Don Camillo. For over three weeks . . ."

"I know all about it," the Bishop interrupted. "I've been to see him already. Poor Don Camillo!" He sighed.

Peppone twisted his hat between his hands.

"Something's got to be done, Your Grace."

"Only God Almighty can do it," said the Bishop, throwing out his arms in resignation.

But Peppone had an idea of his own.

"There's something you can do, Your Grace. You can say a Mass for his recovery, for instance."

The Bishop looked at Peppone incredulously.

"Your Grace, please try to understand. I'm the one that painted his dog red."

The Bishop did not answer, but walked down the garden path. Just then his secretary came to tell him that lunch was ready.

"No," said the Bishop. "Not just yet. Leave us here alone."

At the far end of the path was the Bishop's private chapel.

: [223] :

"Go down there and ask them for an altar boy," said the Bishop.

Peppone shrugged his shoulders.

"I can serve at the altar. I did it often enough as a boy . . ."

"A very special Mass, with a very special altar boy," said the Bishop. "Go on in and lock the door behind us. This is something that must remain strictly between ourselves. Or rather, between ourselves and God."

When Peppone left the Bishop's Palace, he found Thunder on guard in the side car. He jumped onto the saddle and rode back to the hospital. Again they were unwilling to let him in, but Peppone bullied his way through.

"We can't be responsible for what happens," the nurses told him. "If he takes a turn for the worse, then you're to blame."

They led him to the second floor of one of the pavilions and left him in front of a closed door.

"Remember, as far as our records are concerned, you made your way in by sheer force."

The room was flooded with light, and as he opened the door, Peppone drew back in alarm at the sight of Don Camillo. Never had he imagined that twenty-five days of illness could lay a man so low. He tiptoed over to the bed. Don Camillo's eyes were closed, and he seemed to be dead but when he opened them he was very much alive.

"Have you come to claim an inheritance?" he said in a thin voice. "I have nothing to leave you but Thunder . . . Every time you see that red behind of his, you can think of me . . ."

"The red's almost all gone now," said Peppone, in a low voice with his head hanging. "I've scrubbed him with turpentine every day."

"Well, then, you see I was right to bring him to you rather than to the dry cleaner," said Don Camillo with a wan smile.

"Forget about that . . . Thunder's downstairs. He wanted to come see you, but they won't let him in . . ."

"Funny people they are," sighed Don Camillo. "They let you in, and you're much more of a dog than he."

Peppone nodded assent.

"Sounds to me as if you were getting better. You're in high spirits, that much is certain."

"Soon they'll be so high that they'll carry me up into the blue beyond. I'm done for; my strength is all gone. I'm not even strong enough to be angry at you."

Just then a nurse came in with a cup of tea.

"Thank you," said Don Camillo, "but I'm not hungry."

"This is something to drink."

"I'm not thirsty, either."

"You really must make an effort to get something down."

Don Camillo sipped at the cup of tea. Once the nurse was out of the room he made a face.

"Soups and slops, for twenty-five days, without interruption. I'm beginning to feel as if I were a bird . . ." And he looked down at his gaunt, white hands. "It's no use offering to match fists with you now."

"Don't let yourself worry," said Peppone, lowering his head.

Don Camillo slowly closed his eyes and seemed to fall asleep. Peppone waited for a few seconds and then started to go away, but Don Camillo reached out a hand to touch his arm.

"Peppone," he whispered, "are you a dastardly coward or an honest man?"

"I'm an honest man," Peppone replied.

Don Camillo motioned to him to lower his head and whispered something into his ear. He must have said something very terrible, because Peppone drew himself up abruptly, exclaiming:

"Father! That would be a crime!"

Don Camillo looked into his eyes.

"Are you going to let me down?" he panted.

"I'm not letting anybody down," said Peppone. "Is it a request or an order?"

"An order!" murmured Don Camillo.

"Let your will be done!" Peppone whispered as he left the room.

The maximum speed of Peppone's motorcycle was fifty-five miles an hour, but on this occasion it made seventy. And on the way back it didn't roll over the ground, it positively flew. At three o'clock in the afternoon, Peppone was back at the hospital. Smilzo was with him, and the attendants made an attempt to block the two of them at the door.

"It's a serious matter," explained Peppone. "It's concerned with an inheritance. That's why I brought a notary along."

When they came to Don Camillo's door, Peppone said, "You stay out here and don't let anyone in. You can say that he's making his confession."

Don Camillo seemed to be asleep but he was only dozing and quickly opened his eyes.

"Well then?" he asked anxiously.

"Everything's just as you wanted it," answered Peppone, "but I still say it's a crime."

"Are you afraid?"

"No."

Peppone proceeded to take a parcel out from under his jacket and unwrap it. He put the contents on the bedside table and then pulled Don Camillo into a sitting position, with the pillows at his back. He spread a napkin over the priest's lap and moved the contents of the parcel onto it: a loaf of fresh bread and a plate, of sliced salame. Then he uncorked the bottle of red Lambrusco wine. The sick man ate and drank deliberately, not in order to prolong any gluttonous enjoyment but simply to get the full savor of his native earth. For you must realize that Lambrusco is no ordinary wine but something unique and particular to that section of the river valley. Every mouthful made him homesick for the river and the misty sky above it, the mooing of the cattle in their stalls, the distant thumping of tractors and the wail of threshing machines in the poplar-bordered fields. All these seemed now to belong to another world, from which he had been taken away by a succession of malevolent medicines and insipid soups. When he had finished his meal he said to Peppone:

"Half a cigar!"

Peppone looked fearfully at Don Camillo, as if he might stiffen and die before him.

"No, not a cigar!"

Eventually he had to give in, but after a few puffs Don Camillo let the cigar drop to the floor and fell into a deep sleep.

Three days later Don Camillo left the hospital, but he did not return to the village for three months, because he wanted to be in perfect health for his arrival.

Thunder gave him a wildly enthusiastic welcome, turning around in circles and chasing his tail in order that Don Camillo might see that his hindquarters were in perfect condition. Peppone, who happened to be passing in front of the rectory, was attracted by Thunder's barking and asked Don Camillo to note that there was not a trace of red left upon him.

"Quite so," said Don Camillo. "He's all right. Now to get the red off the rest of your dogs."

"You're yourself again, all right," mumbled Peppone. "Almost too much so, in my opinion."

ONE MEETING AFTER ANOTHER

"LORD," DON CAMILLO SAID
to the Christ over the altar, "this is our great day!"

Christ was obviously surprised.

"What do you mean, Don Camillo?"

"Lord, it's written in letters three inches high on posters plastered all over the countryside. The Honorable Betio is making a speech in the village square this afternoon."

"And who might the Honorable Betio be?"

"Lord, he's one of the big shots of our party."

Christ seemed even more surprised than before "Are we enrolled in a party? Since when, may I ask?"

Don Camillo smiled and shook his head.

"Lord, I didn't express myself clearly. By 'our party,' I meant the party which supports us."

Christ sighed.

"It's all very sad, Don Camillo. To think that we have a party to help us keep the universe in order, and we didn't even know it! We're not as omniscient as we used to be. God Almighty is slipping . . ."

Don Camillo lowered his head in humiliation.

"Lord, I failed utterly to put across what was in my mind. When I said 'our party' I meant the party of all those good Christians that rally around the Church and seek to defend it against the forces of the anti-Christ. Of course, these good Christians aren't so presumptuous as to claim that they help God run the universe."

Christ smiled.

"Don't worry, Don Camillo I can read your heart like an open book, and I shan't judge you merely by what you say. Just tell Me this: is this party of good Christians a large one? How many people belong?"

Don Camillo replied that the party was quite strong and gave the approximate number of its members

"Ah!" Christ sighed. "Unfortunately there aren't nearly as many good Christians as there are bad ones!"

Don Camillo told Him that beside the enrolled party members there were a lot of sympathizers. He mentioned more figures.

"But there aren't so many of them, either," Christ exclaimed. "Good, honest people are a minority compared to the number of bad, dishonest people that belong to other parties or sympathize with them. Don Camillo, you've given Me very sad news! I thought there were a great many more good people than that. But let's make the best of it. The idea of gathering all good people into one group makes our job a comparatively simple one. Those who are actually enrolled in the good party will go straight to Heaven, the sympathizers to Purgatory and all the rest can be bundled off to Hell. Please oblige Me with the exact figures."

Don Camillo threw out his arms helplessly.

"Lord, punish me! I've said too many stupid things."

"No," Christ answered. "I'm concerned not with your words but with your intentions. Your heart's in the right place, even if your tongue does trick you. Watch that tongue of yours, Don Camillo; it has a way of getting you into trouble."

Don Camillo thanked Christ for his indulgence, and feeling somewhat reassured he went out into the village. Everything was going the way it should. Busloads of people were arriving to hear the speech and their numbers were rapidly filling the square.

"Efficiency, that's what did it," someone said behind Don Camillo.

Don Camillo turned around and found just the person he was expecting, that is, Peppone, flanked by Smilzo, Brusco and three or four other members of his general staff.

"Were you speaking to me, Mr. Mayor?" asked Don Camillo.

"No sir," Peppone said with a smile. "I was speaking to Smilzo. I was saying that the success of the meeting is due to the efficiency of the postal system. If it weren't for that the pink notification cards wouldn't produce such a remarkable result."

Don Camillo took the cigar butt out of his mouth and flicked the ashes away with his little finger.

"Take it from me, Mr. Mayor," he said heartily, "an efficient postal service isn't the whole story. Sometimes an organization can send out thousands of cards and yet get no more than two hundred and twenty-seven people together."

Peppone gritted his teeth. The last meeting he had summoned, the "Peace Assembly," had been a complete flop, with no more than two hundred and twenty-seven people present.

"I don't agree with you," he retorted, "on the matter of the relationship between the number of notices sent out and the number of people actually in attendance. You can count those that turn up for the meeting, but how can you know how many notices were distributed?"

"That's easy," said Don Camillo, pulling a notebook out of his cassock: "two thousand nine hundred and fifty-seven!"

Peppone turned indignantly to his henchmen.

"There you are!" he shouted. "See what's become of the privacy of the mails!"

"Thanks for bearing out the exactness of my calculations!" said Don Camillo slyly.

"Exactness, my eye!" shouted Peppone. "We sent out exactly two hundred and thirty!"

Don Camillo put the notebook back in his cassock.

"Good! That shows the privacy of the mails is inviolate and the anonymous information given me was all wrong. As far as we're concerned, there's nothing to hide. We sent out two thousand four hundred and seven postcards, exactly."

"Six thousand nine hundred and forty-three!" shouted Peppone.

Don Camillo looked at him with a preoccupied air.

"I can draw only one of two conclusions: either the privacy of the mails has been violated or else you're telling a lie."

Peppone paled. He had fallen into the trap like a perfect simpleton.

"I heard mention of some such figure," he muttered. "I'm only telling you what people say."

"Just as I thought," said Don Camillo triumphantly. "The number of notices sent out is two thousand four hundred and seven, as I was saying a short time ago. I'm very happy to see that about three times as many people have chosen to come And they're not all here yet."

Peppone turned around to go away, but Don Camillo called him back to look at a mimeographed sheet.

"Here's something that just happened to fall into my hands," he explained. "This is a copy of the notice of today's meeting. Since your notice wasn't very effective, I'll let you copy this one. I have an idea that the secret of success is in the letterhead. If you put 'Christian Democrat' in the place of 'Communist Party,' you might have better luck."

Peppone let Don Camillo speak without opening his mouth to

reply but his general staff had to lay hold of him and drag him away.

The square was crowded to capacity, and when the Honorable Betio appeared in the grandstand, he was greeted by a thunderous ovation. He began by speaking of the general political situation and the platforms of the various parties. When it came to the royalists, he pulled out all the stops:

"Speaking of the royalists, who want to overturn our democratic republic and restore a monarchy which in its time betrayed us, let them take note that the sovereign people . . ."

But here he was interrupted by the loud notes of the "Royal March." He tried to protest against this seditious act, but the music rang out from somewhere overhead, all the louder. Meanwhile the vastly annoyed public was aroused to commotion. Some people started to sing the republican song, "Brothers of Italy," while others embarked upon the Christian Democrat party anthem. The resulting confusion made it difficult to identify the place from which the disturbance had come. Actually it came from the fourth-story window of the very house against which the grandstand was erected, and therefore was a real stab in the back of the republic. At least, so the Honorable Betio defined it.

Once the window was identified, a carabinieri sergeant ran up to locate the door of the apartment to which it belonged. He found it easily enough, but it was so strong and securely locked that he could not smoke out the offender and decided to call upon the blacksmith to help him. He turned around and found the blacksmith at his elbow. Peppone had availed himself of his office of mayor to come through the barrier which the sergeant had hastily thrown up at the downstairs door in order to prevent mob justice from taking over a governmental function. Now he stood on the landing, with Smilzo at his side.

"For heaven's sake, open that door!" the sergeant exclaimed excitedly.

"In my capacity as mayor or in my capacity as blacksmith?" asked Peppone.

"As blacksmith," the sergeant answered promptly.

While the criminal behind the armored door went merrily on playing a record of the "Royal March" Smilzo dashed off to fetch the proper tools from Peppone's workshop. Because of the crowd in the square, it took him some time to get there, but he finally made it. When he came back, Peppone peeled off his jacket and hesitantly fingered the tools.

"Why don't you get to work?" the sergeant asked him.

"The blacksmith in me is arguing a point with the mayor," said Peppone, "and they can't seem to reach an agreement."

"Mr. Mayor," the sergeant muttered, "tell the blacksmith that if he doesn't hurry he'll find himself in trouble with the police."

Peppone set to work at taking the door off its hinges, while the record went right on playing the provocatory tune. At last, when the door was unhinged, the sergeant made his way in. But in the presence of the disturber his anger faded to irritation. For Colonel Mavelli, an eighty-year-old retired army officer, had nothing of a dangerous rebel about him.

"Stop that gramophone, and come along with me," the sergeant ordered.

The old man obeyed, but when he had removed the record he broke it over one knee, as if it were a sword, and consigned it to his captor

"Sergeant," he said, in a voice that seemed to come straight from the front lines, "do your duty!"

Before this unexpected demonstration of nineteenth-century heroics, the sergeant was so embarrassed that he thought it was his duty to draw himself to attention. And he was not altogether mistaken. Finally, however, he remembered the circumstances and recovered his aplomb sufficiently to tell the colonel to hold himself at the disposal of the law. And Peppone, before going downstairs, managed to whisper into the rebel's ear:

"As mayor, I told the blacksmith he'd better open your door if he didn't want to get in trouble with the police. Now, as an ordinary citizen, I shall request the mayor to order the blacksmith to repair it."

Don Camillo was thoroughly indignant.

"Lord," he said to the Christ over the altar, "that old fool of a Monarchist ruined a magnificent meeting. I can't see where he got the idea of debating a point by means of a gramophone record."

"I'm sure I don't know," Christ answered. "Unless he got it from someone I know who once rang the church bells when the Red commissar was speaking and thereby wrecked the rally."

Don Camillo bowed his head and walked back through the sacristy.

"For they have sown the wind, and they shall reap the whirlwind," Christ called after him.

Naturally enough, Peppone wanted his revenge, and he tried to work it out so as to kill two birds with one stone. He organized a mammoth meeting, to be addressed by an important speaker who had previously come to celebrate the Red victory in the last local election. It was upon this occasion that Don Camillo had interrupted the speech by ringing the church bells.

"I want the meeting to be of historical proportions," Peppone told his henchmen. "I want to crush the enemy to a pulp."

He worked over it for a month, until finally the great day came. The speech was scheduled for four o'clock in the afternoon, but the square was teeming by three. At half-past three Don Camillo was striding nervously up and down the empty church. Finally he stopped and looked up at the altar.

"Lord," he said, "don't You think I might go look out the window?"

"Of course," Christ answered, "but as far as I know, the rose window above the main door of the church is the only one with a view over the square."

"There is one other," said Don Camillo, "but it's up in the bell tower."

"I wouldn't go up there," said Christ. "For one thing, it's very drafty."

"Oh, I've plenty of warm clothes on," said Don Camillo reassuringly.

"I appreciate the fact, Don Camillo, but I'd be sorry to see you repeat what you did last time and ring the bells in the middle of the speech."

Don Camillo spread out his arms in rueful assent.

"*Errare humanum est, diabolicum perseverare,*" he admitted.

"Let's hope you don't forget that on your way up the stairs."

"My memory's good enough," said Don Camillo.

He was panting when he arrived at the top of the tower and it was only natural that he should fan himself with his big white handkerchief. And it was equally natural that when Peppone saw the handkerchief from the grandstand below he should be stricken with apprehension.

"He's up there again, just as he was the time before," the speaker from the city whispered into his ear. "I trust you've taken measures to prevent a repetition of the bell-ringing."

"Don't worry, Comrade," said Peppone. "Two husky boys are hiding on the next-to-last landing, just below the bells. If he tries to start anything, I don't think he'll get very far."

Everyone in the square was aware of Don Camillo's presence, and nervousness spread through the crowd. When it was time to begin, Peppone made a welcoming speech, but the proximity of Don Camillo caused him to stutter, and when he passed the microphone to his guest, he was swimming in perspiration.

"Comrades!" said the speaker. "This is the second time I have addressed you here, and once more I see the black buzzards of Reaction perched in their nests, ready to swoop down and cloud the blue sky with the beating of their lugubrious wings."

Peppone looked upward, but the black buzzard was perfectly quiet, and only his huge white handkerchief was stirring.

"Comrades!" went on the speaker, emboldened by the calm of his adversary, "today skies everywhere are darkened by black buzzards, and the dove of peace has a hard time surviving . . ."

The crowd looked upward, too, but neither buzzards nor doves were to be seen. Instead, an airplane flew over the scene, spiraling lower and lower and releasing tiny parachutes, which fluttered down among the crowd. The crowd became restless, because everyone wanted to grab one of them. And the restlessness grew when it was discovered that attached to every parachute were smoked sausages, tins of fruit and meat, cigarettes and chocolate bars. Except for the sausages and cigarettes, these things were all from America. The speaker proceeded at once to decry such provocatory and offensive propaganda, but he was interrupted by another visit from the airplane, whose second batch of parachutes met with even more acclaim than the first. A moment later the airplane came back a third time, but failed to calculate distances correctly, with the result that three quarters of the parachutes fell onto the street leading from the square into the country. People started to rush down this street, and on the fourth and fifth rounds (it turned out that two planes were involved), the parachutes were dropped even farther from the center of the village. Now it was plain that the purpose of the whole maneuver was to draw the crowd away from the meeting. And the maneuver was eminently successful, for at a certain point no one remained in the square except Peppone and the visiting speaker. The surrounding houses, too, were left empty, while their occupants joined the wild chase into the surrounding fields. Peppone was foaming at the mouth with rage; he shook his fist and when he was able to speak he shouted through the microphone at the placid Don Camillo:

"This is political banditry! Come on down, if you dare, you big black buzzard!"

Don Camillo came as fast as if he had flown rather than walked down the stairs and stood defiantly in front of the grandstand.

"Come down, yourself!" he shouted to Peppone.

But the visiting speaker tugged at Peppone's shoulder.

"Don't do it, Comrade. He's only trying to make trouble. I order you not to go down."

Peppone gritted his teeth.

"Come up here, if you're so brave!" he shouted, while the Party satrap tried to shut his mouth.

Don Camillo rolled up his sleeves and mounted the grandstand. By now, both men were beside themselves, and they leaped at one another, in spite of the efforts of the visitor, who was caught between them. Peppone got in the first blow, which landed on the left side of the speaker's head. And Don Camillo countered with a swat which hit it on the right. The poor man collapsed like a rag doll on the grandstand floor. Peppone and Don Camillo stared at one another. Then Don Camillo threw out his arms and said:

"There you are! Everytime this fellow comes out here from the city, he seems to suffer a ringing defeat!"

He walked slowly back to his base of operations and then tried to slip noiselessly by the main altar. But Christ called him back.

"Where are you going, Don Camillo?"

"Lord," Don Camillo replied, "I didn't have any lunch, and now I'm going to bed without any supper. That way, I shan't be able to sleep a wink, and I'll have plenty of time to think over my mistakes!"

HAMMERING IT IN

AFTER THE INCIDENT ON THE grandstand, the atmosphere grew increasingly heated. The political truce was over and the Reds were on the warpath again. But Don Camillo seemed serene.

Only when he read in the bulletin nailed to the wall of the People's Palace Peppone's comment on the Pope's last speech did he lose patience and set forth in plain terms from the pulpit exactly what he thought of Peppone and his irresponsible band.

He must have thought and said plenty, because as soon as Peppone was told of the contents of the sermon he marched upon the rectory with the avowed intent of "bumping off that cursed priest," so as to settle once and for all the question between them.

But he found no priest to be "bumped off" in the rectory, for the simple reason that Don Camillo was in the church, in fact standing in the pulpit from whence he had thundered at Peppone a short time before. He was equipped with a hammer and chisel and intent on boring a hole in the stone column which supported the pulpit. In the course of his vehement sermon he had heard the old wood of the pulpit creak ominously, and now he was making place for a solid iron rod which was to run from the supporting column to the upper edge of the pulpit and eliminate any chance of a collapse.

Peppone, having received no answer to his knock at the rectory door, was just about to return to his home base, when the sound of hammering from inside the church caused him to change his mind. The main door of the church was closed and so was the smaller one leading through the tower, but the window of the Chapel of Saint Anthony was open. Peppone made a small pile of bricks and stones below it and stood on top of this to look through. The pulpit was directly across the nave from where he was standing and at once he recognized the nocturnal worker. His anger redoubled in intensity.

"Father, are you pulling the church down?"

Don Camillo looked up with a start and in the light of the candle burning before the statue of Saint Anthony he saw the face of Peppone.

"Not I," he answered. "Other people make that their business, as well you know. But it's no use. The foundation is solid."

"I wouldn't be so sure of that," said Peppone. "Solid as it may be, it isn't strong enough to protect the deceivers who hide behind it in order to insult honest men."

"Quite right," Don Camillo replied. "There's no salvation for the deceivers who insult honest men. Only here there's no such deceiver."

"You're here, aren't you?" Peppone shouted. "And you're a hundred deceivers rolled into one."

Don Camillo clenched his teeth and kept his self-control. But once Peppone had started, there was no limit to what he would say.

"You're a coward and a liar!" he shouted.

Don Camillo could contain himself no longer, and hurled the hammer at the chapel window. His aim was terrifyingly exact, but God willed that a gust of wind should cause a hanging lamp to swing in such a way as to deflect the hammer from its course and send it into the wall, a foot from its destination. Peppone disappeared, leaving Don Camillo in the pulpit, with his nerves strained to the breaking-point. Finally he shook himself and went to confide in the crucified Christ over the main altar.

"Lord," he said breathlessly, "did You see that? He provoked and insulted me. It wasn't my fault."

Christ made no answer.

"Lord," Don Camillo continued. "He insulted me right here in the church."

Still Christ was silent.

Don Camillo got up and paced anxiously to and fro. Every now and then he turned around in discomfort, because he felt two eyes staring at him. He went to make sure that both doors to the church were locked fast; then he looked among the pillars and in the confessionals. No one was to be found, and yet Don Camillo felt sure that someone in the church was watching. He wiped the perspiration off his cheeks.

"Lord, help me," he murmured. "Someone's staring at me. I can't see him, but someone's here; I can feel his eyes . . ."

He wheeled around, because he thought he could feel the stranger breathing down his neck. There was nothing but empty semi-darkness around him, but he did not feel the least bit reassured. He opened the gate of the chancel and went beyond the rail to the steps of the altar.

"Lord!" he cried out. "I am afraid. Protect me!"

Then, turning his back on the altar, he looked slowly around. All at once he jumped.

"The eyes!"

The stranger's eyes lurked in the Chapel of Saint Anthony Abbot. It was from there that they were staring at him. Never in his life had he seen two eyes like these. The blood froze in his veins and then rushed hot and tumultuous through them again as he clenched his fists and swept forward. When he came to the chapel, his fists were thrust out ready to grab the intruder. He went one, two, three steps farther, and when he thought the stranger must be within his grasp he rushed at him. But his nails only scratched the walls, and the eyes were still staring.

Don Camillo took the lighted candle from the altar and held it near to the staring eyes. Really, there was nothing so mysterious about it. The hammer which Divine Providence had mercifully deflected against the wall had knocked down a big piece of plaster. And underneath this there was a fresco, which some priest of times gone by had covered over when he decided to pierce a window.

Don Camillo proceeded to scrape off more pieces of plaster and thus to enlarge his vision of the past. Finally he uncovered the brown face and mocking smile of a devil. Was it an ingenuous figure from Hell or a symbol of temptation? This was no time for research; Don Camillo was interested above all in the staring eyes. His foot brushed against an object on the floor, and stooping down he found at the devil's feet the ill-starred hammer. Just then the clock in the tower struck ten.

"It's late," Don Camillo reflected. And he added: "But it's never too soon for an act of humility."

He walked rapidly through the darkness. Most of the village houses had gone to sleep but there was still a light in the workshop of Peppone. Don Camillo groped for the catch of the iron grille. The shutters were open and he could hear Peppone breathe heavily as he hammered out a red-hot iron bar.

"I'm sorry," said Don Camillo.

Peppone stared, but quickly took hold of himself and continued to hammer without lifting his head.

"You took me by surprise," Don Camillo went on. "I was nervous . . . When I realized what I had done, the hammer was already out of my hands."

"You must be slow-witted, Father, if you don't wake up to your misdeeds until after you've committed them."

"There's some merit in admitting a mistake," said Don Camillo cautiously. "That's the sign of an honest man. When a man won't admit that he was wrong, then he's dishonest."

Peppone was still angry and went on pounding the iron, which had by now lost its red glow.

"Are we going to begin all over?" he roared.

"No," said Don Camillo. "I came to put an end to it. That's why I began by asking you to excuse the unforgivable gesture I made against you."

"You're still a coward and a liar. And I'll put all those hypocritical excuses of yours right here!" And Peppone slapped the base of his spine.

"Quite right!" said Don Camillo. "That's where stupid fellows like you keep everything sacred."

Peppone couldn't stomach it, and the hammer flew out of his hand. It was aimed with diabolical accuracy at Don Camillo's head, but God willed that it strike one of the narrow bars of the grille. The bar was bent, and the hammer fell onto the workshop floor. Don Camillo stared in amazement at the bent bar and as soon as he could move, he set off at full speed for home and arrived, all choked up, at the foot of the altar.

"Lord," he said, kneeling before the crucified Christ, "now we're even; a hammer for a hammer."

"One stupidity plus another stupidity makes two stupidities," Christ answered.

But this simple addition was too much for Don Camillo, who by now had a raging fever.

"Lord," he stammered, "I'm just a poor, lone priest, and I can't take it!"

After this, Don Camillo spent one of the worst nights of his life, pursued by a nightmare of hammers whistling out of his hand and then whistling back at him. The devil with the fearful eyes had emerged from the chapel wall, with a whole crowd of other devils in his train, and one of these rode astride the handle of every ricocheting hammer. He dodged them as well as he could, until weariness overcame him and they pounded his head with a monotonous "bang . . . bang . . . bang . . ." that finally sent him off to sleep.

Only at six o'clock in the morning did the banging cease, simply because at that hour Don Camillo woke up. His head was still so fuzzy that he hardly knew what he was doing and did not recover his self-possession until he stood saying Mass at the altar. The celebration of this Mass required truly epical courage, and God seemed to appreciate his effort, for he rewarded him by giving him the strength to stand on his two feet. When he had taken off his vestments, after Mass, Don Camillo went to look at the Chapel of Saint Anthony. The maleficent eyes were still there and the cursed hammer lay in a pile of plaster on the floor below.

"Aha!" said a voice behind him. "The criminal is drawn back to the scene of his crime!"

Don Camillo wheeled around and of course found himself looking into the eyes of Peppone.

"Are we beginning again?" asked the priest wearily.

Peppone shook his head and slumped onto a bench. His eyes were bleary and his hair glued to his forehead, and he was breathing heavily.

"I can't stand it any longer," he said. "Fix things whatever way you like."

Don Camillo suddenly realized that Peppone was laboriously handing him something wrapped up in a newspaper. When he took the object into his hands, it seemed to weigh a ton. He unwrapped it and discovered an elaborate wrought-iron frame which enclosed, instead of a commonplace picture, a copper sheet, and attached to it with brass wire an ordinary hammer. On the copper sheet were engraved the words:

To Saint Anthony for making me miss

: [243] :

"Lord," Don Camillo said the next day, when he was feeling stronger and more hopeful. "Thank You for Your Help."

"Thank Saint Anthony" Christ answered; "he's the protector of dumb animals."

Don Camillo looked up anxiously.

"Is that how You judge me, Lord, at this moment?" he asked.

"At this moment, no. But it was the unreasonable animal in you that threw the hammer. And Saint Anthony protected that animal."

Don Camillo bowed his head.

"But I wasn't the only one, Lord," he stammered. "Peppone . . ."

"That doesn't matter, Don Camillo. One horse plus one horse makes two horses."

Don Camillo checked the count with his fingers.

"Lord, that's not correct, because I'm a jackass."

And he said it so very earnestly that the Lord was moved to forgive him.

DON CAMILLO RETURNS

IN SPITE OF HELP FROM ST. Anthony, Don Camillo found himself increasingly provoked by the Reds as the pre-election campaigns got under way. Peppone managed to create a number of incidents in the center of which a certain party found himself with fists flying. These incidents were deemed "unfortunate" by the Bishop who sent Don Camillo (and it was not the first time) for a period to an isolated village in the mountains. There the air was cooler. Don Camillo's days were so monotonous that it was hardly worthwhile tearing the leaves off the calender, for they were perfect blanks, bare of any event worth recording.

"Lord," Don Camillo complained to the Crucified Christ from the altar, "this will drive me mad! Nothing ever happens!"

"I don't understand you, Don Camillo," Christ answered. "Every day the sun rises and sets, every night you see billions of stars wheeling their way overhead, and all the while grass grows and one season succeeds another. Aren't these the most important of all happenings?"

"Forgive my stupidity, Lord," said Don Camillo, hanging his head, "I'm only a poor priest from the plains."

But the next day he repeated the same complaint. There was an ache deep down inside him, which grew every day, and was indeed the only thing to impinge upon his attention. Meanwhile, down in the little world of the river valley, nothing very remarkable happened either. Except for a multitude of petty things, which would have distressed Don Camillo had he known anything about them.

The young priest sent to hold the fort during Don Camillo's political convalescence was a splendid fellow. In spite of his theoretical outlook and his polished big-city vocabulary, he did wonders in adapting himself to circumstances and made a mighty effort not to rub the villagers the wrong way. People of every political color responded to his courtesy and good-will and flocked to church in large numbers, but with this gesture they drew the line. No one, for instance, went to confession. "Don't worry, Father," they explained. "It's just that we're so used to Don Camillo. We'll catch up when he returns." And weddings were put off in the same way. It seemed as if even birth and death were engaged in a conspiracy, for since Don Camillo's departure no one had either come into the little world or gone out of it. Things went on like this for months, until finally a woman came to the rectory one day to say that old man Tirelli was dying. The young priest mounted his bicycle and hastened to the bedside.

Old Tirelli had lived so many years that even a bank teller would have tired of counting them and he himself had lost track of them long ago. He had always been hale and hearty, that is until the atomic blast upset climatic conditions and a mammoth attack of pneumonia laid him low. Before entering his bedroom, the young priest questioned the doctor, who was just coming away.

"Is it serious?" he asked.

"Technically speaking he should be dead. It's an affront to medical science that he should still be breathing."

The priest went in, sat down by the bed and began to pray. Just then the old man opened his eyes and gave him a long stare.

"Thanks," he sighed, "but I'll wait."

The priest felt perspiration break out on his forehead.

"While God gives you time, you'd better put your conscience in order," he advised.

"I know," said the old man, "but I'll wait for his return."

The priest couldn't bear to argue with a dying man, so he went to talk to the members of his family, in the next room. They knew the seriousness of his condition and how miraculous it was that he should still be alive. It was up to them to persuade him to make his confession. They went to the bedside and informed the old man of the doctor's verdict, but although he respected the doctor and was in full possession of his usual common sense, he only answered:

"Yes, I know it's a serious matter. There's not a moment to be lost. Go call Don Camillo, because I want to leave this world with my conscience clear."

They told him that, first of all, Don Camillo could not abandon his new parish in order to give one sick man his blessing, and second, it would be a matter of hours to fetch him from so far away. And this was a question of minutes. The old man saw the point of these objections.

"Quite right," he said: "we must cut down the time. Put me in a car and take me to him."

"Look here, Tirelli," said the doctor, who had overheard the parley from the next room, "if you hold my opinion in any esteem, listen to me. This is utter madness. You wouldn't last more than a mile. And surely you don't want to die like a dog, on the road. Stay in your bed and take advantage of this borrowed time to set your conscience at rest. God is the same down here in the plains as up there in the mountains and this young man is just as much of a priest as Don Camillo."

"I know," murmured Tirelli, "but I can't be unfair to Don Camillo. Surely the young priest understands. Let him come along, and if I give way during the trip, I'll make my confession to him. Let's hurry."

The old man was still alive and hence in his own house he was the master. They called an ambulance and loaded him into it, with the priest at his side. His son and the youngest of his grandchildren followed after on a motorcycle. The ambulance went speedily as the power of its four cylinders would allow, and every now and then the old man exclaimed:

"Faster! Faster! I'm racing against time."

When the car reached the mule track leading up to Monterana, the old man was still alive. His son and grandson pulled out the stretcher and proceeded to carry it up the mountain. The old man was only a sack of bones, some nerve and an inordinate amount of obstinacy, and so the weight was not too much for their shoulders. The priest followed after, and in this way they walked for two hours, until the village and its church were no more than two hundred yards away. The old man's eyes were shut, but he saw them just the same.

"Thank you, Father," he whispered to his escort. "You'll receive some compensation for all the trouble I've caused you."

The young priest blushed, and leaped like a goat back down the mountain.

Don Camillo sat smoking his usual cigar butt in front of the hut which bore the name of rectory. At the sight of the stretcher borne on the two Tirellis' shoulders, his mouth dropped open.

"He insisted that we bring him here," explained the son, "in order that you might hear his confession."

Don Camillo lifted up the old man and all his covers, carried him into the house and laid him gently on the bed.

"What shall we do?" asked the old man's son, peering through the window. Don Camillo motioned to him to go away and then sat down beside his father. The old man seemed to be in a stupor, but he was aroused by Don Camillo's prayers.

"I couldn't be unfair to you," he murmured.

"Now you're being unfair to God," Don Camillo protested. "Priests are ministers of God, not shopkeepers. The confession is what matters, not the confessor; that's why the priest stays behind a grating which serves to hide his face. When you make your confession you don't tell your life-story to one priest or another; you speak to God . . . What if you had died on the way?"

"I had your substitute along with me," murmured old Tirelli, "and I shouldn't really have minded unburdening my conscience to him. When a man's spent his life at hard labor, he hasn't much time left for sin. . . . The fact is that I wanted to tell you goodbye and ask you to accompany my body to the grave, wherever you may be. When you have a send-off from Don Camillo, you're sure of a safe arrival."

After this, he confessed his sins, and as might have been expected they were so trivial that he received an immediate absolution and blessing.

"Don Camillo," the old man said at the end, "do you mind if I don't die right away." And he was quite serious about it.

"Suit yourself," said Don Camillo, "if you live two thousand years longer, you won't disturb me."

"Thank you," the old man sighed.

It was a fine day, with a warm sun and a blue, blue sky. Don Camillo threw open the window and went out, leaving the old man asleep with a smile on his face.

"Lord," Don Camillo said to Christ, "something happened today that I can't understand."

"Don't torment yourself about it," Christ answered. "There

are things which don't require understanding. And don't go forgetting that old man. He may need you."

"He needs You rather than me!" exclaimed Don Camillo.

"Aren't you content with the fact that he came so far in safety?"

"I'm always content with what God gives me. If He holds out His finger, I don't grab His hand . . . And yet often I wish I could."

Don Camillo remembered that the old man's son and grandson were waiting outside and went to speak to them.

"He's made his peace with God and is sleeping," he explained. "Do whatever you think best."

"The miracle's done now," said the grandson; "there's no use expecting another. I'll go down the mountain and tell the ambulance to wait. We'll carry him back and bury him at home." Before Don Camillo could say that the old man had expressed a wish to be buried in this his new parish, the boy's father put in:

"Go down, if you like, but tell the ambulance to go away. I'll come after you and we'll go home together."

The grandson ran off, and the son turned to Don Camillo:

"We'll leave everything up to you," he said.

Don Camillo spent the night near old Tirelli. When he had to go say Mass the next morning he called the old woman that took care of the house to replace him. After Mass he rested for a while and then, having assured himself that the old man was still alive, he went to a house near the public fountain, where he had to take something to a boy that had broken his leg. On the way back he heard someone calling him from a second-story window. Looking up he saw a face which he was so unwilling to see that at first he actually didn't recognize it. But finally he called up to its smiling owner:

"What on earth are you doing here?"

Beside the girl's face popped up that of a sullen youth.

"We're here for a holiday," he said. "Must we have your permission?"

"Watch your tongue, young man," said Don Camillo. "If you've come here to spread propaganda, I'm warning you that the place isn't healthy."

The young man cursed and withdrew his head, but the girl went on smiling.

"We'll be coming to see you," she said.

"All right, but don't come without an invitation," said Don Camillo as he went on. And he added, under his breath· "What can those two savages be up to? Who knows what trouble they're in now?"

The trouble was a sizable one, and the direct consequence of an episode in which this same pair—Mariolino della Bruciata and Gina Filotti—had already involved Don Camillo. Their courtship had been a stormy one, their families disagreed violently on political matters and it had taken all Don Camillo's persuasiveness to get them to agree to the wedding. After some months of marriage it was Gina and Mariolino who disagreed violently.

"In my opinion it's going to be a boy, and I'm glad of it, because I know you want a girl," said Gina.

"I'm positive it will be a girl, in spite of the fact that you and that family of yours all want a boy," he retorted.

"Of course. Girls take after their fathers and boys after their mothers," she exclaimed, "and I'd hate to see a girl with a character like that of the men of your family You Bolshevik criminal! I'm going home to my mother!"

"Then goodbye for good; I'm going back to my father. Living with a reactionary's daughter is too much for me."

The logical corollary to these violent propositions was that, in the absence of both of them, their baby would be left quite alone. And they made up over this discovery.

A few weeks later they were faced by another grave problem.

"We've got to think of a name," Gina declared. "Boy or girl, we must have a name ready."

The names suggested by Mariolino were all tendentious because they started with Lenina and ended with La Pasionaria. While Gina's choice ranged from Pius to Alcide. Finally they came together on Alberto and Albertina.

"And how's it to be baptized?" groaned Gina.

"It's not to be baptized at all," answered Mariolino. "But if it is, the way to do it is to take it to church and get it over with."

"To church? But Don Camillo's not there any longer!"

"That's like saying you'd rather be eaten by a lion called Leo than a lion called Cleo," Mariolino said sarcastically. "One priest's as bad as another!"

Gina started to take up the cudgels in behalf of the clergy, but all of a sudden she grew pale and sank into a chair.

"Take it easy, Gina," said her husband gently. "You keep calm and so will I."

"When I think that I married a godless individual like yourself, it's almost more than I can bear. Poor little baby boy, I'll defend you from your father's intemperance!"

"Poor baby girl!" sighed Mariolino. "If I weren't here to save you from your mother's clutches . . ."

They went on this way until late that night, when Gina interposed:

"After all that Don Camillo's done for us, we can't let anyone else baptize our baby. But babies have to be baptized immediately after they're born. We can't wait six or seven months for Don Camillo's return."

"That's easy enough to solve," said Mariolino. "We'll register the baby's birth at the Town Hall, because, after all, Peppone did just as much for us as Don Camillo, and then we'll take it up in the mountains to that one and only priest!"

"Impossible," said Gina. "Babies have to be baptized in the parish where they're born. And the time's getting short. I'm going to pack a suitcase tomorrow."

Six days went by without anything happening. Old Tirelli hung between life and death and Don Camillo stayed home partly in order to look after him and partly because the girl he hadn't wanted to recognize had called out: "We'll be coming to see you." Early in the afternoon of the seventh day, his housekeeper came excitedly into the room:

"Come quickly, Father. There's something very unusual downstairs."

Don Camillo hurried down and saw an extraordinary sight: Mariolino and Gina, with the village midwife between them, bearing a beribboned baby in her arms.

"Well, what's this?" asked Don Camillo.

"The lady came here for a holiday, and proceeded to bear this very fine baby," the midwife announced.

Don Camillo wrinkled up his nose.

"Did you come all this way for that reason?" he asked the young couple.

"I'd never have come," said Mariolino, "but she insisted that you baptize the baby. As if all priests didn't come out of the same pudding . . . Well, if you don't want to baptize him, so much the better."

Don Camillo pondered the complications of the matter and made an indistinct noise. He went into the church, but the young couple did not immediately follow. Apparently, they were waiting for something. And indeed, while Don Camillo was preparing the baptismal fount two groups of strangers invaded the village. One came from the mule track and was composed of members of the land-owning Filotti family; the other came up a parallel path and was, naturally enough, the Red band of della Bruciata. From opposite sides of the square they converged upon the church door, and the young parents led them in.

"Who is the godfather?" asked Don Camillo.

Old Filotti and old della Bruciata both stepped forward, gritting their teeth and reaching out for the lacy robe of their reactionary-revolutionary descendant.

"Hands off!" said Don Camillo threateningly. And he signaled to a newcomer at the church door.

"Step forward, godfather!" he commanded.

And Peppone—for it was he—obeyed, although it was plain that the honor had been forced upon him. When the ceremony was over Don Camillo was called away by his housekeeper,

"The old man is asking for you," she panted.

Don Camillo burst impetuously into the dying man's room.

"No, Tirelli," he said, most uncharitably; "you simply can't throw cold water over the celebration by choosing this moment to die!"

"Father, I called you to say that I've decided to go on living. This mountain air has healed me. Send word to my daughter to come and move me into other quarters."

Don Camillo was breathless over the succession of events. When he went downstairs he found waiting for him the young substitute priest and Peppone.

"I'm here merely as the driver of a public conveyance," Peppone told him. "The priest asked me to bring him here, and after I'd left the car at the bottom of the mule track I came to see how things were going along. Unfortunately I find you bursting with good health!"

The priest, in his turn, gave Don Camillo an envelope.

"It's a letter from the Bishop," he explained. "I've come to announce a change of the guard. You can go back in Peppone's car."

"I contracted only for a one-way trip," Peppone objected. "I have no wish to take certain people back with me."

"I'll pay extra," said Don Camillo.

"It's a question of principle, not of money," Peppone replied. "The later you come back the better. Don't get big ideas from the visit of a soft-headed old man and two young rascals. We're getting on famously without you."

"All the more reason for me to hurry back!" said Don Camillo.

Two hours later, Don Camillo emerged from the church with the crucifix over his shoulder.

"Driver, take my suitcase!" he called out to Peppone.

He proceeded down the mule track, and this time the cross was as light as a feather. At the end of the trail stood the jeep which Peppone called a taxi. Don Camillo climbed in, holding the crucifix before him like a banner.

The della Bruciata band had come in a truck, and now they started off after Peppone. Nearby stood the two big, shiny cars of the Filotti family, and in the first of these sat Gina with the baby in her arms and Mariolino at the wheel. Mariolino skillfully steered his car in between the jeep and the truck, while the second one, with his father-in-law driving, brought up the rear.

At this point Smilzo rode up like a demon on his motorcycle, having been worried over his chief's delay. When he saw the little procession, he turned around and rode ahead of it, in order to clear the way. When they were within two miles of their destination he responded to a nod from Peppone by stepping on the gas and leaving the others behind him.

So it was that at the entrance to the village Don Camillo found the local band ready to greet him. And the Crucified Christ came home to the strains of the "International."

"Under the rope and to victory!" rejoiced Peppone, bringing the jeep to an abrupt stop in front of the church door.